DEDICATION

Matty,

Without your support, love, and encouragement, none of this would be possible. Can you imagine that? What kind of sad, sad world would it be if no one had the opportunity to read a book about Clam Jamming? Depressing thought, I know.

I'd also like to channel my inner Mya and let you know that your "love is like whoa".

P.S. I still love you more.

A,

Sure, you give me more gray hairs than in all my years of teaching but I wouldn't change anything for the world. You bring me and your father more joy than we ever thought possible. I love your kind heart, your constant cheerfulness, and the way you love so freely. Never change. You're my favorite girl in the whole, wide world. Always.

With that said, you're still on lockdown until you're forty. #ChastityBelt

To anyone who's ever been clam jammed or cock blocked, this book is for you. May you be un-jammed and un-blocked from here on out.

PROLOGUE

My name is Maggie Finegan, and I'm the continuous victim of a "clam jam."

To answer your questions:

No, I'm not Irish—I was adopted.

And, yes, clam jamming is a thing.

I'll wait until that one sinks in. *Taps toe of shoe quietly.*

Okay, ready? I'll go on. It's a pretty crazy story. It all started one dark, stormy night—wait, don't roll your eyes at me, people. Fine. So it *might* have been more of a typical Upstate New York overcast kind of day. I had left work early since my boss, whom I fondly referred to as Sybil, left work at lunchtime for a meeting in the city. I took advantage of him skipping out early, knowing that I could hurry home and clean up the apartment I shared with my fiancé, Shane, and set the mood to get lucky. Things had been a little off lately, with both of our work schedules usually residing in the "heinously hectic" realm, and I wanted to remedy this.

Sliding my key in the lock of our apartment door, I stepped one heel over the threshold, and my favorite pair of Jimmy Choos slipped, sending me off balance. I barely caught myself as one hand flew out to brace against the entryway wall to steady myself. Prepared to take offense with whatever object had made me nearly land on my butt, the next moment happened in slow motion.

You know what I'm talking about. Slooooow mooooooootion. Where a moment in your life is too freaking weird, crazy, or just all-around effed up, and your brain does some weird thing with the synapses, immediately slowing everything down. Like an out-of-body experience. That's what I had going on. Because the offensive object that had me nearly falling on my butt was a pair of woman's panties.

Fact: *Those panties weren't mine.*

You know. In case you were wondering.

My slow motion continued as I bent down to make sure my eyes weren't playing tricks on me because, yeah, that was my initial thought. They *might* be my panties. Because no way would my fiancé be getting "jiggy"—thank you, Will Smith, for that term—with someone else, right?

Go ahead. Say it. Say exactly what you're thinking. *Maggie, what the hell is wrong with you? Stop being delusional!*

I kicked those panties to the side, slid my briefcase's straps off my shoulder, and set it in the corner of the entryway. Walking down the hallway, I could hear my heels clicking along the hardwood floors. And do you know what I thought the entire walk to the bedroom—to *our* bedroom? I thought, *Wow, these floors are gorgeous. And those oversized windows looking out onto downtown Saratoga Springs have a gorgeous view. I'm so glad I chose this apartment.*

Weird, right? I think I had an idea of what I'd find in that bedroom, and my mind had officially gone into fullblown protective mode.

The noises were the worst. Let's be real here. I get that, in the heat of the moment, you're probably going to have harsh breathing and some moans, but what I heard as I approached that bedroom was something you'd likely find on the Discovery Channel. Elephants mating, perhaps? Something large scale. Maybe if wooly mammoths still existed, that would be the closest thing to what I heard coming from that bedroom.

That's right. I know you're cringing right now. It was absolutely *mammaliciously* awful. Yes, I made up that word, but you have to understand that mammals everywhere were shaking their heads in disgust at that moment.

I'm going to fast-forward a bit now because I'm pretty sure you know how what I call "the discovery" went. They both shrieked, he pulled out of her—out of her *mouth*, by the way—and claimed it wasn't what it looked like.

Because, you know, his penis inside of a woman's mouth was one of those blind taste tests or something. Like back in the day when they were all like, *"This is Coke? Wow! I can't believe it. I've drunk Pepsi my whole life."*

First of all, you should not be that amazed and mystified by a freaking beverage. That's just lame.

Let's move on.

I kicked them both out. Luckily, his name was not on the lease since he'd moved in with me. Not so lucky was the fact that this place was on the pricey side of things, so I'd have to watch my spending on happy hours, takeout, and dinner nights out.

Here's the quick rundown:

1. I left all of Shane's belongings outside the door. ALL of them.
2. Okay, so I *might* have tossed some of his things in the trash. My bad.
3. Luckily, our lead building attendant, Mr. Charlie, has adored me from day one and once I informed him of what went down, he told

me not to worry about anyone reporting the overabundance of crap piled up near the trash chute.

4. I Craigslisted the *hell* out of that mattress. Because God only knows what had gone down—pun intended—on that thing when I hadn't been home.

5. I did the whole bawling my eyes out to my best friend, Sarah, between bouts of inherent desire to maim Shane. Because, let's be honest, that's what women do. After too much Pad Thai—wait, I'm kidding; *no one* can have too much Pad Thai—at my pity party, I made some new decisions about my life.

   a. I was not going to date for a while. Now, I'm not saying I refused to ever date again because, really. It's not like I have my sights set on being *that* woman with seventy-two cats or anything. Plus, I'm allergic, so that's a no-go.

   b. If I were going to be single, footloose, and fancy-free—thank you, Auntie Patsy, for that phrase that I hope never spills from my lips again—I'd need to get a roommate because I'd need the extra money. You see, I'm not a fan of women who expect guys to buy them drinks. We all know those drinks often come with expectations. The single's world is flooded with douche bags, you know. Then again, so is the attached world, as my situation served as a prime example.

c. My roommate could in no way be a straight man. It couldn't be a woman, either, because I've never been able to cohabitate with another female. I know it's weird. But it is what it is.

d. I couldn't exactly put out an ad for a "gay roommate" because, uh, discrimination? Who doesn't want to get slapped with a lawsuit and has two thumbs up? *This* girl.

This is the point where the story really begins. Get comfy. Well, as comfy as you possibly can when preparing to read about a year of my life being clam jammed.

Shall we begin?

CHAPTER ONE

Maggie

One year ago-ish
October
Saratoga Springs, New York

Holy shadoobie. This guy is hot.

No, scratch that. He's the kind of hot teenage girls spell out as H-A-W-T. He's *that* kind of hot. And he's applying to be my roommate, which means only one thing.

I have to send him packing.

There's no way in h-e-double hockey sticks I'll be able to maintain any self-control around a guy like this. I mean come on, people. It's like the moment you decide to diet, and you catch a whiff of pizza or walk past a bakery when they're putting new pastries in the display case.

Temtorture at its finest. I know, I know. I made that word up—a mix of the word temptation and torture. It's accurate, though, isn't it? You know you shouldn't have it because it's so bad for you, but you know once it touches your tongue, it will be *so gooooood*.

Wow. That sounded more sexual than I expected. Because I wasn't exactly thinking of having this guy's anything touching my tongue. But now, the seed has been planted, so …

"I appreciate you taking the time to meet with me."

Ryland's voice brings me back from my not-so-G-rated thoughts. I am a terrible, horrible, no-good person, just like that Alexander kid in those children's books they turned into a movie. I nod, trying my best not to let his lips mesmerize me because, whoa, they're so nice and full and soft looking. And his hair makes me want to run my fingers through the short, light brownish-blond strands.

Sigh. Long, long sigh. There I go again.

"I admit"—he leans in, and I find the sparkle in his eyes captivating—"I was grateful you chose to meet in this spot since my company's offices are right above here. I had a few things to take care of this morning. And the fact that your apartment building is within walking distance is another plus."

Flattening my palms against the small table as we sit across from one another in Starbucks, I let out a slow exhale. Because it has to be said.

"I have to be honest with you, Ryland. You have great references." I gesture to his résumé and list of references, both work and personal, he submitted to me when he'd contacted me about the room for rent a few days ago.

After printing off a sheet with some key information about the room for rent as well as photos of the spare bedroom, I'd posted it on the corkboard located in the lobbies of a few of the large, well-known office buildings—both mine and a few others I was familiar with nearby. I had hoped that would decrease my chances of ending up with some college kid who would end up being a slob and skip out on rent. I had a few decent applicants, but Ryland James had stuck out amidst the others.

He's not only educated but also quite successful, as was clear from both his résumé and company's website. He'd explained he had been renting a room, but the guy had recently gotten married, and he didn't want to cramp the newlyweds' style, so he'd been temporarily staying with another friend. Ryland wasn't interested in buying anything—house or condo—at this point as he wasn't entirely sure his job would keep him local and didn't want the hassle of trying to sell a property or rent it out if he relocated.

Everything had checked out with him. Everything. He seemed like he had his act together. And his photo from the Eastern Sports company website didn't disappoint. Which was why I had been planning to nix him altogether. He was exactly what I *didn't* need right now. So why am I here, meeting with him face to face?

Sarah. She'd coerced me to meet with him. She went over each applicant's information with me, and she kept coming back to Ryland's. She'd hassled me about giving him a shot.

Inhaling deeply, I continue, "But I have to be honest with you. I've recently broken up with my dirtbag fiancé"—I break off with what I hope is a lighthearted laugh, but I swear it comes out sounding strained and a touch maniacal—"and I'm not interested in having a roommate who's a guy and—"

"I'm gay."

I jerk, startled by his interrupting admission. And if I didn't know better, I'd swear I detected a little hint of surprise in his eyes.

My eyebrows arch. "Really?" Shoot. That's rude because even *I* hear the tinge of disbelieving doubt in my voice.

"Yes." He nods, clasping his hands together and leaning forward to rest his forearms on the table. "Jack and I have been together for years now." One of his hands reaches up to tug on his earlobe. "We still have a bit of an"—he pauses, lips pressing thin as though he's trying to word it correctly—"open relationship, and I feel it's best … to have a separate place and not be continuously underfoot."

Huhhhhh. I'm still processing this information when he continues.

"So"—he flashes a smile that makes my insides all gooey—"you wouldn't have anything to worry about with me."

"Okay," I say slowly, "but what about guests and sleepovers? Because I'm not a huge fan of having to listen to moaning and—"

"Not a problem." He waves a hand dismissively. "I can totally stay at Jack's place. He doesn't have a roommate. It's no big deal." He flashes me another smile, and I feel my ovaries weep his name.

It's a good thing he's gay. Otherwise, let's be real. I'd likely end up being that roommate who accidentally-on-purpose "sleepwalks" into his bedroom—naked—and has sex with him.

Holy crap. Did I really just think that? Bad, Maggie. *Baaaad*, Maggie.

Glancing over his paperwork, I say, "If you don't mind, I have a few other applicants to interview." Lies. I'm totally stalling. Raising my eyes, I find him watching me expectantly; that gaze centered on me in such a way that I feel like I'm the only person who exists right now. "But, tentatively, I'd like to offer you the room for rent."

If I thought Ryland's smile was ovary-lurch inducing before, this one trumps that. *Big* time. It's blindingly bright and infectious, and I can't help but return it. We sit there for a moment before he clears his throat, and I remember what else I have to tell him.

"So, as I mentioned earlier, the utilities normally run this much per month." I use my capped pen to point at the sheet I had printed, which includes all the pertinent financial information. "We'll split it fifty-fifty. Rent is due on the first of the month, and a late fee will be imposed if it isn't in by the fifth day." I recap a few other details and ask him if he'd like to look at the room.

He agrees, and when we stand, pushing in our chairs, he helps me slip into my coat once I pluck it from where I'd draped it over the back of my chair.

I repeat: **Ryland took it upon himself to help me put on my coat.**

I know, right? He has to be gay. Because no normal guy would take the initiative to do that for a woman. Especially not in this day and age.

Exiting the busy Starbucks, we fall in step along the crowded sidewalk full of the usual Saturday foot traffic as I lead him to my apartment building. He rushes up to beat me to the large, heavy doors to the building, reaching out to hold it open for me. Flashing him a smile, I thank him.

Such a gentleman, this one. Jack is one hell of a lucky guy.

"Hey, Mr. Charlie!" I smile, greeting our lead building attendant. He's become like an adopted father to both Sarah and me. He's sweet as pie and always watches out for us.

"Have to use your handcuffs on anyone recently, Chad?" I can't resist teasing our security guard since an older woman on the second floor flirts with him *shamelessly*. It wouldn't be as funny if she weren't pushing ninety. I never knew women that age could still be hoochie mamas.

I introduce Ryland to them, and Chad steps around the desk where he was chatting with Mr. Charlie and walks with us to the elevators. I had already asked him if he'd be willing to accompany us up to my apartment in case I chose to show it to Ryland.

Chad waits in the hallway while I show Ryland around. After a quick peek in the spare bathroom, I lead him to the spare bedroom.

"Obviously, I still have a few more things to move out of here since it's been used as storage more than an actual bedroom. But no worries, it'll be cleaned out and ready to roll." I gesture to a few small boxes I've yet to toss out—mainly mementos of my relationship with Shane—one, in particular, is a box of photographs of Shane and me from over the years. I've been putting off getting rid of it, which is dumb because it's over and I know it. But those photos of us—especially the ones from early in our relationship—show us so happy and in love. It's painful to think about throwing those away.

"Looks good." Ryland's deep voice behind me sends shivers down my spine.

"Well"—I turn, facing him—"that's it." I reach out a hand. "It was great meeting you, Ryland. I'll definitely be in touch."

When he slides his hand in mine, grasping it firmly but not too tight, I feel tingles. "Call me Ry," he offers with a soft smile.

"Ry," I repeat and inwardly wince when it comes out sounding a bit breathless. "It was great to meet you."

"Likewise, Maggie."

He turns to leave, exchanging a quick good-bye with Chad at the door before I quietly lock up behind them. Leaning my back against the door, I let my eyes fall closed.

God just gave me an olive branch of sorts. A way to ease my financial situation a bit and eliminate any possibility of being tempted by a guy—just like I'd planned. No fear of getting involved with my male roommate because he's not into women. I should be relieved.

I *am* relieved.

Maybe if I keep repeating that, I'll start believing it.

CHAPTER TWO

Ry

"Y**ou what?**"

Jack stares at me as we sit on his couch—the same couch doubling as my bed lately. Ever since Heath and Elle got hitched, that is.

I've had some trouble finding a place I'm interested in renting and don't want to buy anything at this stage. Not to mention, I like having someone to come home to. It's a hell of a lot less lonely that way. And Maggie's place is a top-notch, prime location with the biggest draw, of course, being Maggie herself.

"I told her I was gay." I take a swig of my beer and wait for a beat before I drop the real bomb. He just shakes his head at me, mumbling something under his breath that sounds an awful lot like, "Jackass," before he tips his beer bottle to his lips.

"And I told her you were my boyfriend."

Beer sprays everywhere. Droplets spatter the fancy glass coffee table. Jack lets out a curse and grabs his huge, manly remote control that has more buttons than either one of us knows how to work, wiping it with the bottom of his shirt. Because in a man's world—especially in Jack's world—a television remote is sacred. God forbid it be harmed in any way.

Rolling my eyes, I rise from the couch to grab some paper towels and glass cleaner for the cleanup. Walking into the kitchen, he calls out.

"You told a chick I was your fucking boyfriend? Who the hell's going to believe that shit?"

Returning to the living room, I wipe the mess up off the table. Jack's still sitting, staring at me as if I'm crazy.

I shrug. "She believed me, so obviously I'm convincing enough."

The weight of his gaze is heavy, and I know what's coming. Slumping back onto the couch, I meet his eyes with a tired sigh. "What?"

"You lied to a chick just to get her to rent the room to you. Because you …" He trails off expectantly.

Looking down at my lap, I mumble, "Because she's it."

"Excuse me? She's what?"

Rolling my eyes and letting out an exasperated sigh, I glare at him. "Because she's 'the one,' man. I can't explain it. I just know it, and no way in hell could I let her slip through my fingers."

I had spotted Maggie in the Starbucks around the corner from my office building, but she was always with a guy whom I assumed to be her fiancé. And something about her captivated me. I'd had one of those moments I'd always scoffed at. The moments you see portrayed in chick flicks all the time when one character sees another and instantly feels a *connection*.

Except it actually happened to me. The moment I saw Maggie, watched her talk animatedly and felt the warmth of her smile—even though I wasn't on the receiving end of the it—each time I saw her in the coffee shop, I felt it. That connection. I'd try to ensure that my stops for coffee would coincide with the times she'd be there just so I'd get to see her, to hear her captivating laughter, see her stunning smile, to imagine what it must be like to have her focused on me.

The more I saw her and watched her interactions, the stronger my yearnings were to be the one to make her laugh, the one to cause her lips to form that beautiful smile I'd come to know. Vivid images flickered through my mind of us hanging out at home on a lazy Saturday, watching eighties movies …

Shit. Yeah, right. No woman in their right mind would want to stick around the house instead of getting all dressed up and going bar hopping downtown.

Regardless, whenever I would see her, I couldn't ignore the feeling—like something deep inside me was yelling, "She's the one! You're going to marry this one!"

There was no way I could turn my back on that.

"But she doesn't want anything to do with men, Ry. What are you going to do? Just casually bring it up one morning that you're actually hetero?" He scoffs, shaking his head at me. "I see that going over *real* well."

"I haven't gotten that far but, this way, I can get to know her without all that shit getting in the way. The whole nervousness, the whole showing the other person your best at all times until you're really committed and then it all comes out."

"And you're going to do this by being dishonest from the get-go."

Running my hands down my face, I let out a frustrated groan. "What was my other option? To let her go, to never have an opportunity to get to know her—to never get to be her friend, at the very least—without her feeling like I have any ulterior motives—"

"Which you do."

"—and be faced with the possibility of me being too late and another guy getting to her when she decides she's ready to start dating again?"

"I'd like to go on record and say that you've been watching too many damn chick flicks."

"Whatever."

He's silent for a moment, staring at me before his lips twitch, slowly forming a smirk. "So how long have we been together, love muffin?"

The breath I've been holding in comes out in a slow exhale. "For a while." Holding up a finger, I add, "But we have an 'open' relationship."

His eyebrows arch at that. "Why, you little player, you. Won't commit to being monogamous, huh?" He tips his beer to his lips, takes a swig, and grins. "I bet I can convince you to be mine within a few months tops, pookie bear."

I make a face, scoffing, "Not likely."

He waves a hand dismissively. "You'll be putting out before long. Mark my words."

"You're not right." I laugh, shaking my head at him.

"You're the one who's pretending to be gay."

"Point taken."

We both take a swig of beer and fall silent for a moment before Jack finally speaks.

"Can't say that I've ever pretended to be someone's gay lover before." His face stretches into a wide, toothy grin.

And, just like that, my best friend is officially involved in my game plan. All for the sake of a woman I'm convinced is "the one."

CHAPTER THREE

Maggie

It's move-in day for Ry. And it's confirmed—he's still as handsome as when we first met at Starbucks.

What I didn't expect was just how handsome Ry's boyfriend would be. Sarah wanted to be here to meet Ry, and I have to nudge her out of her trance when Ry introduces Jack.

"Hi, Jack. It's great to meet you." I reach out a hand to shake, but he opens his arms wide, a mischievous grin on his face, blue eyes dancing merrily.

"I come from a family of huggers, Maggie. Now, get over here, you beautiful blossom."

He gives me no warning, just tugs me into his embrace, and I'm folded against what appears to be well over six feet of rock-solid man. He smells delicious, which doesn't surprise me in the least. His dark hair is as perfect as everything else about his outward appearance. Once he releases me, his eyes take on an odd look as he appears to inspect Sarah, petite with straight blond hair and blue eyes. She's pretty much every guys' wet dream come true—typical hot blonde. If she weren't my best friend, I'd feel compelled to dislike her because of that alone.

"Now, who is this gorgeous being? Get over here and

give Uncle Jack a hug."

"Oof!" That's all Sarah can respond when he pulls her to him. If I didn't know any better, I'd swear that he hugged her for longer than is appropriate, but hey, I'm not exactly fluent in the whole protocol for gay men's hugs or whatnot.

"Break it up, you two," Ry warns, a sharpness in his eyes. *Ooh, jealousy.*

Sarah steps away, and Jack's arms drop from around her, clasping his hands together. "Well, let's get my love muffin moved in, shall we?" Turning, he picks up the large box he'd set down in the entryway, his muscles flexing in his short-sleeved shirt, and follows Ry's path leading to the bedroom.

"Holy shit," Sarah breathes out. Both of us stand rooted in the same spot, staring down the empty hallway.

"Yeah," I whisper back. "So unfair that they're gay, right? What a waste of two incredibly hot guys."

Her head whips around, staring at me with an odd look.

"What?" I hiss.

Her lips part and she tips her head to the side, studying me intently before whispering, "If he weren't gay, would you go for Ry?"

Furrowing my brows, I don't answer immediately. Just when I'm about to respond, the guys come down the hall.

"We only have a few more boxes to go, ladies, and then we'll have pookie bear all moved in." Jack winks at us before getting an affectionate shove in the shoulder from Ry. These two are just too cute together.

After they exit the apartment, I lean against the wall, pondering Sarah's question.

Wondering how my silent answer could be so immediate over a man I'd only recently met.

Yes.

* * *

"So there he was, standing on the sidewalk outside my place with a raincoat on the ground, stereo blaring Peter Gabriel's 'In Your Eyes,' begging me to go on a date with him."

We're all sitting around eating takeout sushi, and Jack's been entertaining us with stories about him and Ry and their early years of dating.

"Funny how I don't quite recall that happening." Ry flashes Jack a sharp look.

Jack waves him off with an easy smile, focusing back on Sarah and me. "He likes to pretend he's this gruff alpha male when, in reality, he's this sweet, soft"—he reaches a hand to the side of Ry's face and lays it across his cheek—"marshmallow."

"That's really sweet." My eyes dart back and forth between the two men before resting on Ry. "And the fact that you used a part from the movie *Say Anything* is a huge plus in my book."

"Isn't it, though?" Jack remarks with a wispy sigh. "Ry's so romantic."

Ry rolls his eyes before clearing his throat, gesturing back and forth between Sarah and me with his chopsticks. "How did you two become friends?"

Sarah and I look at one another, instantly giggling, before she turns back to Ry. "We met on an online dating website."

The two men glance at one another curiously before fixing their attention on us. I go on to explain the story.

"This was probably, what?" I look at her in question. "Over six years ago now, I think." She nods, and I turn back to explain to the guys. "So I made a profile online for shits and giggles at the time, not thinking I'd get anything out of it. Then one day, I get a message." My smile stretches across my face at the memory. "From a fifty-seven-year-old woman in Connecticut."

Sarah takes over this part. "My Aunt Sharon had a profile because she'd decided to start dating again after her divorce, and she let me log onto her profile when I was visiting her. I had just moved back here to Saratoga after being away at college and pretty much all of my friends had relocated far away. So I searched women in my age range, out of curiosity, in the area. And I found Maggie. So I emailed her."

I laugh. "She wrote, 'Hey! I'm Sarah, and I'm using my aunt's profile on here. I recently moved back to the area, and I am looking for friends. Don't worry—I like boys, too. Promise!'"

We laugh before Sarah chimes back in. "We exchanged a few emails and decided to meet up at the coffee shop down the road a few weeks later. And the rest, as they say, is history. We've been best friends ever since."

"That's a pretty cool story," Jack remarks. "Like you two were destined to become friends."

"Exactly."

Letting out a long sigh, he pats his stomach. "I'm stuffed. Thanks, ladies, for being such incredible dinner companions. Unfortunately, I have to head home." Turning to Ry, he winks. "Walk me out, love bug?"

"Certainly." Ry's words are flat, and I get the feeling that he's not comfortable with us witnessing him and Jack being affectionate in any way. I hope that will ease soon because I want him to feel comfortable in his own place.

The two men toss their empty sushi takeout containers

and chopsticks in the trash before placing their water glasses in the dishwasher. This alone makes me even more of a fan.

We exchange good-byes with Jack, of course, who hugs us before he walks to the door with Ry. I hear them talking softly and turn to place my leftover sushi in the refrigerator, tossing my chopsticks in the trash.

Sarah places her glass in the dishwasher before leaning close and whispering, "I think I'm in love."

Darting a surprised glance at her, I tip my head to the side. "With?"

"Jack," she says with a sigh.

I make a face. "I hear you. They're just too handsome for their own good, right?" *Too bad they're not straight.*

Feeling the weight of her eyes on me as I wipe the counter, I turn, noticing her looking at me with a thoughtful expression. "What?"

She merely offers me a smile, and I feel like I'm missing something. "I'm just—"

"Ladies," Ry interrupts, approaching us, "what can I help with?"

"Nothing at all, thanks." I hang the wrung-out dishcloth over the sink. "All done. Which means"—I wrinkle my nose—"I have to go and check my Outlook calendar to see if my boss has added any surprise meetings or tasks to it."

"Sounds like you could use a glass of wine while you do that," Ry offers, pulling one hand from behind his back and holding a bottle of wine out to me. "This is a sort of reverse housewarming gift, if you will. A thank-you."

Stepping closer to him, I accept the wine and look down at the label with pleasant surprise.

"It's a Chardonnay. I hope that's okay since I noticed

you had a little wine cooler there with some in it." He gestures to the cooler I'd splurged on when it was on sale a few Black Fridays ago.

"Thanks, Ry." I smile up at him, noticing the way the corners of his eyes crinkle when he smiles down at me. "That's really sweet."

"I'm going to head out." Sarah draws our attention, and I realize I'd forgotten she was there.

Stop being mesmerized by the hot gay guy, Maggie. Stop it.

When Sarah steps out the door to leave, she turns with a mischievous grin and whispers at the last minute, "If there's anyone who can turn him straight, it's you." With a quick wink, she skips off to the elevator.

Locking the door, I lean against it for a moment, baffled by her silly words. Because that's exactly what they are: silly. I know that and so does she. She's just harassing me.

But the idea—the thought—that he could be straight and be with me? It's far more intriguing than I care to admit.

CHAPTER FOUR

Ry

November

There's a knock on my bedroom door while I'm pulling on some clothes. I've just gotten home from work and wanted to change and chill for the night after a hellish day at the office.

"Hold on a sec," I say through the soft, worn cotton T-shirt I'm pulling over my head. Tugging it down quickly, I pad over to my door, opening it to see Maggie standing there, looking a bit nervous.

"Hey." She flashes me a shy grin as her eyes gloss over me, my hair likely ruffled from carelessly getting dressed. Running a hand through my short hair, I notice a quick flash of something across her face, but it's gone before I can decipher it.

"Hey, Mags," I say, returning her smile. Don't ask me why, but I just feel like she's a *Mags,* and she clearly doesn't object to me calling her that nickname. "What's up?"

"I wanted to see if you were interested in going to a hockey game with me tomorrow night?" Her head tips to the side, her long, brown hair shifting, and one thick lock drifts near the outer corner of her eye. Without thinking, I reach out and brush it aside.

The moment my fingertips graze her soft skin, I feel it. I feel that tingle—the intense awareness. The widening of her blue eyes tells me that she feels it too.

"I'd love to." My voice comes out huskier than normal.

Clearing her throat, she discreetly shifts out of my reach, making me realize I haven't moved my hand from her face. "I already have tickets. I won tickets to the Albany Devils game through a raffle at work. Sarah was supposed to go with me, but she has to work, so …"

"So I'm second best, huh?" I tease.

She playfully shoves at my chest. "Stop it."

"I'd love to. What time should I be ready to go?"

"Four o'clock. If it's okay with you, I'd like to check out a new place nearby afterward that's supposed to have pretty decent food *and*,"—she draws out that last word with a flourish—"some seriously awesome microbrews on tap."

"You had me at microbrews," I offer, grinning.

* * *

Today marks three weeks since I've moved in with Maggie, and if I weren't already convinced that she's the one for me, I would be by now. Case in point—she asked me to go see a hockey game down in Albany. *Hockey.*

We've nearly made ourselves hoarse from yelling along with other fans, at the refs, and at the opposing team's players who started fights and are presently digging in to our food at Rutherfords. After trying the sampler of six beers first before choosing what we wanted to drink with our dinner, Maggie orders fish and chips while I decide to go with the bison burger.

When Maggie falls quiet, I follow her line of sight

and see that it's resting on a couple sitting a few feet away. There's a wistfulness in her gaze that can't be missed.

"You miss him?" I ask quietly. It pains me to pose this question, but I want to—need to—know her answer.

Jerking her gaze to mine, appearing startled, she hesitates, "I …" before flashing a sad smile, "no, actually."

"But you miss having someone around."

I get it—I understand where she's coming from. It's hard to separate yourself from someone after being together—regardless of the circumstances—because you get used to having them around. You tend to miss their physical presence.

She wrinkles her nose. "It's stupid, isn't it?"

"Not at all."

Maggie lets out a tiny sigh, pushing her nearly empty plate aside before leaning toward the table. "He actually told me that one of the reasons he did what he did was because I let him see me without makeup."

"*What the*—" My voice is loud, and upon noticing glances from nearby patrons, I lower it, leaning forward, "hell, Mags? That's bullshit." I want to wrap my hands around this moron's throat so badly right now.

Shrugging, she looks down, running her index finger over the cool moisture on the outside of her beer glass. "I just want a guy who will love me even when I have no makeup on and still tell me—and believe—that I'm beautiful." Her eyes meet mine, lips twisting in a sad smile. "Is that so wrong?"

God, she looks so beautiful yet vulnerable right now. That doubt in her eyes is killing me because Mags is gorgeous, inside and out. She's one of those women you can meet and chat with for five minutes and just *know* in your gut that she's a genuine person. She's real; nothing about her is fake or pretentious.

Her hair is wrapped up in a clip, tousled and sexy looking atop her head. Her jeans mold her curves perfectly—and when she bent in her seat earlier, her jersey shifted, and I caught sight of a G-string.

A fucking G-string. She's trying to kill me.

Shaking off my errant thoughts, I hold her gaze. "Get out a pen, please."

She stares at me in confusion. "Um, o-kay," she answers slowly, rummaging through her small purse. Finding a pen, she holds it up. "Now, what?" The corners of her lips curve upward slightly as if she's amused.

Reaching across to the plastic bin holding the small, square napkins, I pluck one from the top. Sliding it across the table to her, I tap my index finger on it.

"Write that down."

"What?"

"Write that down. What you just said." When she doesn't make a move, I raise my eyebrows. "Didn't you ever hear that saying, 'If it is written, so it shall be'?"

Shaking her head slowly, her lips curve up as her eyes dance with amusement. "Never."

"Well, it's true. So," I tap the napkin again, "write it down."

Her head cocks to the side. "Only if you do it with me."

"Deal."

She writes exactly what she told me.

I want a guy who will love me even when I have no makeup on and still tell me—and believe—that I'm beautiful.

She slides the napkin my way, holding out the pen for

me. When I accept it from her, I feel that same tingle of awareness when my fingers graze hers.

Looking down at the napkin for a brief moment, I decide what I'm going to write and choose to be completely honest.

I want someone who will be cool with hanging out and watching movies we've seen a million times. Just to be with me.

Capping the pen, I hand it back to her before bellowing dramatically, my voice booming throughout the bar, "If it is written, so it shall be!"

Maggie laughs and reaches out to slide the napkin around so she can read what I wrote.

"Hey," her eyes light up, lifting to mine, "I do that with you. Even though I know I don't count." She winks at me, her smile bright—real—and I can clearly see that she's happier than she was moments earlier.

And it takes all of me to resist telling her that she counts.

That she's really the only one who does.

CHAPTER FIVE

Maggie

I never realized it could be so easy and ... *fun* living with a guy. It feels like Ry and I have been friends forever. It's like the big guy upstairs knew I needed someone in my life to get me through this really rough patch of everything pertaining to Shane. And, man, did he deliver.

"Stop hogging all of the damn popcorn," Ry grumbles good-naturedly when I snag an enormous handful from the large bowl he's holding and drop a few in his lap.

"Oops." I shovel it into my mouth before reaching over to grab the strays I dropped on him. As soon as my hand hovers over his lap, he snags my wrist, drawing me to a halt. When my eyes meet his, my breath hitches. Because I swear, there's heat in the depths of those hazel eyes ...

But just as quickly, it's gone, and he's flashing me an easy grin. "Don't you be going *downtown*, now, or Jack'll get jealous."

"Sorry." I smile, my cheeks heating up. Pulling my hand back, I direct my attention back to the movie we're watching. It's one of our favorites: *Pretty in Pink*.

"I really think she should've ended up with Duckie," I murmur, tossing a few more kernels of popcorn in my mouth.

There's a pause before Ry responds quietly. "Really?"

I nod, still watching the movie. "He's her best friend, right? Totally had her back the entire time. *And* goes to prom with her when she gets crapped on by Blane."

"But she still chooses Blane in the end."

Something in Ry's voice—almost like a hint of sadness—makes me turn and face him. His eyes are on the television, and there's a tiny crease between his brows. Without thinking, I reach out to smooth it with my index finger. His eyes dart to mine.

"There shall be no frowning, Mr. James," I say softly with a gentle smile, trying to draw him back from whatever troublesome thoughts he's having. "Not on my watch."

He holds my gaze for a brief moment before his face brightens, smiling down at me. Leaning my head against his shoulder, we resume watching the movie.

And I don't even register it when he wraps an arm around me, shifting my head to lean on his chest.

All I know is that today is one of the best lazy Saturdays I've had in a while.

* * *

"How much time do you think I'd get for stabbing him in the jugular?" I hiss quietly into my phone. My office door is closed, but I still don't want to risk "Sybil" overhearing me. No doubt about it, my boss is being moody as hell today and on the warpath. I overheard him complaining to one of the other partners about the fact they used a different colored highlighter on the paperwork.

"You wouldn't be able to make it, Mags. They don't let you binge watch eighties movies in prison. Not to mention, you'd likely become someone's bitch." Ry's voice is husky in my ear, and my eyes fall closed. God, his voice is so sexy. It just isn't fair.

"Oh! Better open your eyes and look like you're hard at work. Looks like you've got incoming in five, four, three, two, one, ze—"

There's a knock on my door and—literally—no wait time whatsoever before my boss pushes the door open abruptly.

"Finegan, where is that building inspection file for ..." He finally registers that I'm on the phone as I hold up a finger. Nodding my head and writing down ambiguous notes on my small pad of paper, I pretend the person on the other end of the line is informing me of something.

"All right, now if I can just confirm the building code for that site, please?" I ask, my tone completely business-like.

"It's coded for, *You're too sexy for that shirt*," Ry sings softly in my ear, to the tune of Right Said Fred's classic song "I'm Too Sexy." It takes every ounce of restraint not to grin like a fool.

"Thank you, again, sir. We'll be in touch." I hang up the phone, giving my boss my full attention. "Sir, I left the file on your desk—"

"I can't find it." God, his surly attitude is getting really old. If the pay and the perks weren't so great, I'd look for work elsewhere.

Rising from my desk, I walk around to the door, calling over my shoulder. "I'll show you where I set it."

Of course, the file is in the same exact place where I left it. Right on the left corner of his desk in the spot he'd requested I set it. Douche bag.

And do I get any apology? Of course, not. But I escape quickly, leaving him to pore over the thick file and returning to my office to finish my work.

My phone rings within a minute of my butt hitting the seat of my desk chair. I look at the caller ID display on the office phone. Turning to face my office windows overlooking Broadway, directly across from Ry's offices, I place the phone to my ear.

"Care to tell me how you knew my boss was about to enter my office, Mr. James? Suddenly psychic?"

"We got a brand-new pair of binoculars in the other day. Just testing them out since they're supposed to be the latest, most high-tech model."

I make a face. "Are you serious?"

"As serious as that little crease between your brows, young lady."

I laugh, and he instantly says, "Now, there's the smile I love." The way he says it makes warmth unfurl deep inside, and I wish—certainly not for the first time—that something was possible between us.

That we could actually be a "we" someday.

"How about happy hour after work at Max Londons?" His question draws me from my inner yearnings.

"Ah, Ry …" I smile, shaking my head with a little laugh. "It's only Wednesday."

"All the more reason to have a drink. Sybil would want you to," he teases before adding, "Well, one of the personalities would. I'm sure of it."

When I hesitate, he goes in for the kill. "The white sangria will be on me tonight."

This man already knows me too well.

"Fine." I smile, gazing out my window and wishing I could see him in his office. The glare of the sun is reflecting off the windows of his building, but he's likely sitting in his chair, watching me with those binoculars and a huge grin on his handsome face. "I'll meet you as soon as Sybil leaves the office at five."

"I'll wait for you in the lobby."

"See you then, handsome."

"Later, gorgeous." Hanging up the phone in the cradle on my desk, I can't help but smile at the way he calls me "gorgeous" and how his tone gets low and sounds huskier.

Sigh. I need to get a grip and quit lusting over my roommate.

CHAPTER SIX

Ry

These binoculars are the devil.

What the hell was I thinking, accepting a pair to test out from one of the other guys in the office who oversees product samples? And now, when I should be working on the expense budget, I'm watching Mags as she's talking to someone on speakerphone while she simultaneously types on her computer. Her hair is twisted up into a clip, a few tendrils loose around her face, with what appears to be no fewer than three pens stuck in her hair. It makes me chuckle, knowing she's likely forgotten they're there. And that concentrated expression of hers, the way she nibbles on her bottom lip just so …

I'm a goner. Not to mention, I'm veering into the realm of being a Peeping Tom. Damn it. But she's just so beautiful.

Dragging my eyes away, I swivel my chair back around to face my computer, setting the binoculars on the far left corner of my desk. I need to get my shit together and stop spying on my roommate.

Glancing at the time on the bottom right corner of my computer monitor, I mentally calculate how much time I have before Maggie and I meet for happy hour.

And it's depressing how long I have to wait.

* * *

One of our servers had something screwy going on, and I had to get my best people on it, trying to determine what the hell the deal was. Turns out, someone decided to try to hack into our data network, and it ended up being—*shocker*—a disgruntled employee. Needless to say, hacking into a company's data isn't exactly small peanuts. This former employee will now be dealing with a whole hell of a lot more than just being unemployed.

This is why I'm sprinting out of my building, willing the damn crosswalk to hurry the hell up and light the signal for pedestrians. As soon as that sucker lights up, I dart across Broadway, weaving in and around the slow, leisurely walkers to Maggie's building. Tugging the heavy door open, I heave myself inside, breathing heavily.

Letting out a sigh of relief when I don't see any sign of her, I pull my phone from my pocket, sliding onto the large bench inside the lobby. My phone says I'm barely a minute past five o'clock, but I hate being late. It's one of my pet peeves, like the other person's time isn't as valuable. Thankfully, Maggie and I share this viewpoint on tardiness.

Glancing down the hallway to where the two quiet elevators sit, I worry that maybe Sybil has piled some last-minute work on her. Maybe I should head up and see if I can't rescue her—

Ding!

One elevator opens, presenting Maggie, and the instant she sees me sitting, waiting for her, a wide, carefree smile forms. The same kind of smile that makes my chest tighten, makes it hard to breathe, and makes me not ever want a day to come when that same smile doesn't grace my presence.

I tsk with an expression of sham disapproval. "You're late."

Her heels click on the floor, echoing throughout the lobby, and my eyes can't resist slipping down to take in her legs and those heels of hers. She's wearing a fitted, pin-striped skirt and a matching jacket over a silky cream-colored blouse. With the entire picture she creates, I know I'll be thinking about her later. I'll imagine bending her over my desk, drawing her skirt up to see what kind of panties she's wearing beneath it.

"Ry?"

Shit. I've been staring. Attempting to shake off the cloud of horniness that's hanging over me, I offer her a smile and stand, gallantly offering my arm.

"Shall we, Ms. Finegan?"

"Oooh." Her eyes light up teasingly as she links her arm through mine. "All prim and proper now, are we?"

I wink at her. "Only for you, madam."

We push through the doors and head down the side-walk, still arm in arm. We make our way to Max Londons, slipping inside and managing to snag two seats at the bar. After I order a white sangria for her and a Saratoga Lager for myself, we both let out long sighs before turning to each other with a laugh.

"One of those days, huh?"

"Yep," I answer, nodding. "I'm so glad it's over."

I catch sight of us in the mirrored wall behind the bar, quickly locking that image of the way we both look in my memory—tired but happy to be in the other's company.

She takes a sip of her sangria, savoring the taste of her favorite cocktail before blowing out a long breath. It makes me instantly tense because I've gotten to know Maggie pretty well already, and I know by that long exhale that something's up. And it's likely not too pleasant.

She further confirms my suspicion when she falls silent, fiddling with the stem of her wine glass.

Leaning in, I nudge her lightly with my arm. "What's wrong, Mags?"

Turning her head, her eyes rest on me. "I got an email from Shane today."

My jaw clenches so tight it's a wonder I don't crack any molars. "What did that dipshit have to say?" I take a sip of my beer, trying to calm my rage at the asshole who hurt her. The asshole who discarded her so carelessly.

The asshole who's likely realized what he'd tossed aside; has likely realized how fucking incredible Maggie is.

Please don't fucking tell me you're going to get back together with him. Please. Don't. Say. That, I beg internally.

"He said he wanted to apologize for everything, but he didn't think I'd accept his calls or text messages. That he wanted to apologize in person and thought that maybe we could …" She trails off, waiting for me to meet her eyes before finishing with, "… get together sometime."

Oh, *fuck* no.

Nodding, I attempt to school my features by inhaling a deep, calming breath.

Which doesn't really work well at calming me.

Studying her expression, I try to decipher what she's thinking but come up empty. "What are you going to do?"

She lets out another sigh, shaking her head and turning her attention back to her glass of sangria. "It's been five months, and he suddenly feels bad?" Pursing her lips, she looks back at me. "I think I'm finally over it—over what he did—because I really didn't feel anything when I read that email. I just felt …" Tipping her head to the side, as if trying to find the words, she finally says, "… bored. Irritated, maybe. But good because I know exactly what I want now—more than ever."

My shoulders sag in relief at her words. "You deserve better, Mags."

She gives me one of those sweet smiles. "Thanks, Ry." Knocking her shoulder against mine playfully, her smile widens. "You know what we need to do, right?"

Grinning, I reach over to snag a fresh bar napkin just as she pulls a pen from her purse. Sliding the napkin over to her, she writes on it:

I want to be with someone who is not only the love of my life but my best friend, too.

When she offers it to me, I mull over my response for a moment before deciding to be simple and to the point.

I want the same. Always.

CHAPTER SEVEN

Maggie

"**R**yland James!" I bang on his bathroom door, hollering loudly. "Did you eat the last—"

The door swings open, drawing my speech to a sudden halt because … ooooh, sweet, dripping wet abs.

My eyes are riveted.

He's got a towel wrapped around his waist, and I don't even realize I'm moving until Ry releases a sharp hiss at my touch. Because my finger is tracing over the slight indentations in his abdominal muscles.

"Um …" He clears his throat, his voice husky and deep. "Mags?"

"Uh-huh," I murmur absently, my fingertip stopping one of the trickling droplets of water on his skin, tracing it down over his belly button, and—

His fingers grasp my wrist, drawing my hand to a halt, and my eyes dart up to his in alarm because *crap*. That was like an out-of-body experience.

"Oh, crap. I'm sorry. I just really, um … *crap*." That's all I can utter. Nonsense. No one would believe I have my graduate degree if they heard me right now.

If my tongue had a voice of its own, it would probably say something like, "Just the tip. That's all I want." The tip of my tongue tracing over Ry's abs, that is. You know, just to prove someone Photoshopped him. Or not.

Because I'll take one for the team. I'm a giver like that. People might even think of canonizing me as a saint after all this. Really.

Oh, and then … Abracadabra! *Poof!* He'd no longer be gay, profess his undying love for me, and wouldn't ever leave me for another guy.

Or woman.

Wow. That scenario even sounds crazy in my head.

Shaking off my thoughts, I take one more glance down at his abs—just one more glance—and that's when I see it.

"Oh, boy," I breathe out. Ry is hard, tenting the towel, and I really want it to drop. Accidentally, of course. Like an "oops" moment. Totally harmless and innocent.

Oh. My. God. I'm a horrible person. I'm thinking of my roommate's penis! My roommate who has quickly become one of my best friends.

Oh, the *shame!*

Where did this inner slut come from? It's like she's been lying in wait—for him, apparently.

But, really. I can take a *little* peek, right?

"No, you can't." My head jerks up to see Ry looking down at me, his expression a mixture of what looks to be amusement and pain.

Crap. I just said that out loud—that bit about taking a peek. Crap, crap, crap, *craaaaap.*

"Did you actually need something, Mags?" His voice sounds strained, and he's still holding my wrist captive. Which is likely a smart move on his part. *Ah-ah*, but I still have another one.

"Don't make me grab that one, too, Finegan."

He's on to me. Dang it.

34

Letting out a sad, defeated sigh, I pout. "Your abs are inhuman, Ry. It's like someone carved you or something." I shake my head, gazing adoringly at said abs once again. "Or Photoshopped the hell out of you."

His husky laugh washes over me. "You finished lusting over me, now, Mags?"

Sighing, I meet his eyes. "I guess." Then a thought hits me. "Wait a minute. You just got arous—"

"I ate your leftover sushi." His words are rushed, hurried, throwing me off track.

Glaring, I tug my wrist from his hold, hands going to my hips in a huff. "How could you? You knew that I was loving that kamikaze roll! Ugh!" Turning and stomping down the hall, I toss over my shoulder, "Just for that, I get to choose the movie for tonight, buddy."

"Can't," he calls out. "I'm going out with Jack tonight."

I stop dead in my tracks before darting over to the dry erase calendar we have on the kitchen wall. Sure enough, it's marked there: **Jack, 7pm.**

I don't want to admit how depressing that sight is, having nearly forgotten that Jack is actually Ry's boyfriend. He'd been out of town a lot lately for his job, and I guess I've gotten a bit spoiled by having Ry to myself. Aside from the times Sarah came over, of course. Just last week, the three of us ordered pizza, and when Sarah and I applied mud masks to our faces, Ry complained that he felt left out. The night ended with the three of us sitting there on the couch, mud masks in place, watching *The Princess Bride* and quoting the entire movie aloud.

That definitely went down as one of my favorite Saturdays to date. Not to mention, the surprise in Ry's tone when he ran his hands over his face after rinsing off that mask, remarking at how smooth and soft his skin felt.

"Mags?" Ry calls out from the bathroom as I hear him moving around, likely prepping for his date night with Jack.

"Yes, I just forgot. Sorry." I attempt to make my tone light. Sarah's working a crazy long shift at the hospital tonight, so I guess it's just me, myself, and I. I'll likely catch up on some episodes of *Kimmy Schmidt* and gorge on some popcorn.

Wild and crazy, that's me. Just living the dream, people. Living the dream.

Ry finds me standing in the kitchen, still staring at the calendar. Sidling up to me, he smells so freaking awesome that I literally want to grab him by his shirt, press my face to his chest, and breathe him in.

If that doesn't flash, "Weirdo Alert," I don't know what will. Good God, I need to get a grip.

"You want me to cancel?"

Turning to face him, I give him an incredulous look, shaking my head. "No. Absolutely not."

"You sure?" His head tips to the side, a tiny lock of hair shifting over his forehead.

Reaching up, I brush it back, offering what I hope is an easy smile. "Not a chance. You're all dolled up and need to have some one-on-one time with your man."

He huffs out a laugh that sounds … *off*, but then he pulls me in for a hug, wrapping his arms around me, and I get the chance to smell him again. *God*, does he smell good.

"I know it's pathetic, but I'm going to miss you," I mumble softly against his chest.

"I always miss my Mags when she's not around." His voice is soft, hushed, his words washing over me as his large hand rubs my back affectionately.

Smiling against his button-down shirt, I tease, "Do you always refer to me in the third person, too?"

He doesn't respond for a moment, but once he does, it's not at all what I'm expecting. "If you want me to stay in, I can cancel," he murmurs, his lips pressed against the top of my head.

With a sigh, I pull from his embrace and force a bright smile. "No. Don't you dare cancel your date." I pat his chest. "Jack's been gone for work, and I know you've missed him. Go." I tip my head toward the hallway leading to the front door. "Have fun, okay?"

His eyes study me for a moment before finally leaning in to press a soft kiss to my forehead. "Call me if you need anything."

"Will do."

He turns, and as I watch him, my eyes drift over him, observing how great he looks in those jeans that fit him in all the right places. His ass looks incredible; the black button-down shirt he tucked in emphasizing his trim waist.

And not for the first time—and likely, not the last, either—I curse the fact that I'm not his type.

CHAPTER EIGHT

Ry

"I've been thinking," Maggie starts out as we're sitting down eating dinner after work. We've both had a seriously hectic day and are too exhausted to care that we're eating an unbalanced meal of macaroni and cheese with wine.

"I'm ready to try dating again."

My fork clangs noisily against my bowl as my head whips up to stare at her. "What?"

She jerks back slightly at my sharp tone, giving me an odd look. "I'm ready to try dating again."

No. This isn't how it's supposed to go, damn it! Not that I knew how it was really supposed to go, but this ... definitely isn't it. She's supposed to say something like, *"Oh, I think I'm in love with you, Ry."* And then I'll say something back like, *"I love you, too. And also, I'm not really gay."* Then she'll say, *"That's a relief!"* And we'd commence living happily ever after.

Okay, so that isn't suave in any way, shape, or form but give me a break. I'm a dude. We're not exactly known for being flawless orators.

But the idea of her going out and meeting guys, *dating* ... It rips my fucking heart out. Because I want to be the one who gets to go out with her, to date her. I mean I kind of already do, but not in the same capacity. I don't get to kiss her, hold her hand, or touch her like *that*.

Fuck. I have to get my shit together. This can't happen.

"You look like you … disapprove?" Maggie remarks slowly, eyeing me carefully.

Trying to school my expression, I shake my head, tugging on my earlobe as I attempt to find the right words. "I just want you to be careful, that's all. I don't want you to get hurt again."

She lays her hand on my arm, giving me a sweet smile. "Thanks, Ry. I appreciate that." When she pulls back, I instantly register the absence of her touch. "I just feel like I've been relying too heavily on you lately. Kind of using you as a crutch, you know?" She forks a bit of the cheesy pasta into her mouth, chewing with a thoughtful expression on her face.

She swallows and takes a sip of her wine. "It's time to get back in the swing of things."

"Yeah." I fork some macaroni and cheese into my mouth, not tasting it. I barely register anything else she says as she plans her first, official night out on the town to "get back in the saddle."

I'm too damn busy trying to figure out what in the hell I'm going to do to thwart her plans.

* * *

"You sure about this, Mags?"

"Yep. It has to be done." She has an expression of stern concentration as she gazes down at the engagement ring in the small, black velvet box.

After dinner, she asked me if I'd help her figure out how

to sell the three-stone engagement ring Shane had given her.

Of course, I agreed, but now ... shit. Selfishly, it's like someone's taken an ice pick to my chest at the mere sight of another man's ring—someone she once loved and was prepared to spend the rest of her life with.

Look, I know she loves me, but she doesn't *love me-love me*.

Congratulations to me for sounding like a twelve-year-old chick just now.

"Ry," her voice is thick with emotion, "do you think he ever really ..." She trails off, staring down at the ring, and the moment I see a lone tear drop, trickling over one of the stones, I tug her into my arms.

Enfolding her in my embrace, I press my lips to her hair, breathing her in. "Mags, there's not a doubt in my mind that he loved you." Closing my eyes, I breathe in her intoxicating scent combined with the slightly fruity scent of her shampoo. "Sometimes, people are just not meant to be ... forever. There's no rhyme or reason to it."

It's brisk tonight, especially in downtown Saratoga Springs, and this street always manages to be more like a wind tunnel. Tugging Maggie's collar up on her fleece, I run my hand down her back.

As we stand there, a few steps away from the jeweler Jack had suggested we see, Maggie sniffles quietly against my chest. My heart aches, yet at the same time, I'm pissed off at the asshole. He clearly didn't deserve her in the first place, totally discarding her as if she wasn't the most incredible woman around.

I pray to God I can pull this off. Because if I can't have Maggie—have Maggie's love—then I'll have absolutely nothing. Which confirms that it's time.

Time to bring out my A-game.

* * *

"Hey, you two! Fancy meeting you here." I sling an arm around Maggie's shoulders, pulling her into a quick hug before releasing her to step toward the guy she's talking to. She had told me she'd meet me at Irish Times pub after work. Clearly, it hadn't taken long before she'd snagged someone's attention.

Holding out a hand, I introduce myself. "Ry James, nice to meet you."

He falters, eyes darting back and forth between Mags and me; he's likely wondering exactly who the hell I am. She pipes up, "He's my roommate."

"Ah," is all he manages to say, shaking my hand, and it's a shitty ass handshake. I squeeze a little tighter than I normally do. Just because. And I have to work hard at hiding my satisfied grin when I see him wince.

"So tell me about yourself ..." I trail off expectantly, since he has yet to tell me his name.

"Connor," Maggie supplies.

"Conner," I say and repeat, "Tell me about yourself, buddy."

Just as his lips part to speak, Maggie lays a hand on my arm. "If you'll excuse me for a moment, I'm going to use the restroom." Flashing a smile at Conner, she adds, "I'll be right back."

Looking over at the guy, he's clearly feeling the full effect of her smile, and hell, I can't say that I blame him. Especially with that lipstick stuff she's wearing tonight. She was telling me all about it earlier, saying she was going to try it out. It's supposed to last hours and not leave a mark on wine glasses or anything else. I really can't get into that stuff, normally, but I was proven wrong when she exited her room after getting ready for tonight, and I saw her lips.

Holy fucking shit. Whatever that stuff was, she needed to use it all the damn time. But only for me. Because it made her lips look more plump, more lush, and the deep shade of pink … It was torture not to kiss her.

Turning back to Conner once Maggie's out of earshot, I sling an arm around his shoulders. "So Con—you don't mind me calling you that, do ya? Did Mags tell you about me?"

He's eyeing me warily, and I feel like a shark who's just detected blood in the water. "No, she didn't."

"Really?" I widen my eyes in faux surprise. "Well, she's such an absolute doll face, taking it upon herself to try and find a new man." I wait—to drop the real bomb—before adding, "For us to *share*." And the moment my words really sink in, it's priceless.

Fucking priceless.

Disengaging himself from the arm I've slung around his shoulders, he begins to stutter. "I, uh, I don't …" Abruptly pulling his cell phone from his back pocket, he checks it, saying with fake urgency, "I forgot about something I've got to do."

Backing away, he holds up a hand as if he fears that I'll jump him. "Great meeting you both!" He disappears in a flash, and I'm left standing there with a smug grin on my face.

Job well done, James. Job well done.

"Hey." Maggie returns, stepping up beside me and glancing around in question. "Where's Conner?"

"Oh, he said he forgot about something he had to do." I twist my lips in a slight pout. "Bummer, huh?"

"Yeah." She sighs. "I thought we were getting along pretty well."

Tapping her lightly beneath her chin, I wink. "Chin up, gorgeous. Want to see if we can snag some seats at the bar?"

Brightening, she nods. "Sure." As we turn, I hear her murmur, "We didn't even get to exchange numbers before he left either, dang it."

Patting her on the back, I offer her some sympathy. It's not genuine, but luckily, she doesn't notice. "Bummer, Mags. Major bummer."

As I follow her over to the bar, a happy smile stretches across my face as I look forward to having Mags all to myself, once again.

So far, my evil plan is working.

CHAPTER NINE

Maggie

My birthday is a big deal. Like a *really* big deal. To me.

Obviously.

I love birthdays. Always have, always will.

Some people hate birthdays, hate getting older, and hate the idea of moving closer to their expiration date on this earth. Not me, though. I love the excuse to have a celebration, getting my favorite people together, eating a little too much, possibly (likely) indulging in a few too many of the adult beverage variety, and getting presents.

Sarah always gives me the best presents. But here's the thing—she doesn't go all out with the most expensive thing. She does things I would never think of. One year, she gave me a bottle of wine that had my own label on it. It was "aged" from my date of birth and had my photo on it. Cool, right?

Also, I have to add that, being the stellar friend that she is, she chose a great photo of me for the label. One where I don't actually have those deer-in-the-headlights eyes because I'm trying so hard not to blink at the camera's flash.

Another year, she had a calendar made that had a bunch of photos of us throughout the years. I still have that stashed away because I couldn't bear to write on it and use it. It was just too awesome.

Anyway, you get what I'm saying. She rocks at unique birthday gifts. So you can understand my anticipation when she, Ry, Jack, and I all got together at Sushi Thai for my birthday.

After inhaling more Pad Thai than I thought was humanly possible and once the waiter cleared our dishes, Sarah pulls out a large, cylinder-shaped wrapped gift with an enormous grin on her face.

After she hands it to me, I waste no time tearing off the wrapping paper. It looks like it's a rolled up doormat of some sort. My eyes flicker to Sarah's in question, but she just smiles. Sliding the large rubber band from around the mat, I unroll it and see that it has the outline of the state of New York on it and says *Home is Where the Heart Is.* Beneath that is *The Finegan & James Family.*

See? Yet another year with another perfect, unique gift from her.

"This is the coolest thing ever!" I turn the mat toward the guys to show them before thanking Sarah.

Jack pulls out a thin envelope with an apologetic look on his face. "I'm shitty at gift giving, Maggie. Sorry in advance."

"Stop." I flash him an admonishing smile. "I'm sure it's perfect." Opening the envelope, I pull out a gift certificate for a massage at the Gideon Putnam resort, which is pretty expensive.

"Jack," I breathe out, my eyes flying to his smiling ones. "This is too much."

He makes a face. "Please." Tossing a thumb in Ry's direction, he adds, "My princess doesn't like massages, so it's all good."

"And that's my cue to present this." Ry hands me a large gift bag. "I was afraid it wouldn't be finished in time, but I lucked out at the last minute."

Digging excitedly through the mounds of tissue paper in the bag, my fingers touch on something extremely soft. Pulling it from the bag, I see that it's a large, fleece throw blanket.

But it's not just any throw blanket. It has photos of Sarah and me, Ry and me, and of the four of us together printed on the fleece material. Looking over the captured moments—the specific photographs he chose for the blanket—I feel tears begin to prick my eyes. Because I know, without a doubt, I would have chosen the same ones. These photos are my favorites; ones that display just how much affection there is between us.

Raising my eyes to meet Ry's, I find him watching me with an unnerving intensity, and I swear there's a hint of vulnerability in his features.

"Ry, I love it." Emotion is clogging my throat, and I feel as though I can barely get the words out.

"Really?" he asks softly.

"Without a doubt."

And that's when it happens. For the first time in my life, I experience a movie fade-out.

You know, a movie fade-out where one of the main characters—usually in a romantic movie—sees the object of their affection and the rest of the world fades away. The other person comes into sharp focus and all the music—there's usually music in the background, by the way—fades or becomes extremely faint, and the two of them have a moment. And you're like, *Awwwww, so sweet!*

That's happening to me right now. The only problem is that I'm having that particular kind of moment with my roommate.

My gay roommate. While his boyfriend is sitting right beside him.

This is the point where you want to slap some sense into me, isn't it?

Tearing my eyes away from Ry, I catch sight of the look Sarah's giving me, and it appears as though she'd also like to get in on that little slap-some-sense-into-Maggie thing.

Get in line, sister. Because right now, I feel like I need to slap some sense into myself.

CHAPTER TEN

Ry

"Thanks again for everything, Ry."

Wrapping my arms around Maggie, I press my lips to the top of her head, her silky soft hair brushing against them.

"You're welcome, Mags. I hope you had a great birthday."

She leans back to look up at me, her eyes shining. "Are you kidding me? It was the best one yet."

Gazing down at her and the way she's looking at me with that easy, soft smile makes my breath hitch. When her eyes drift down to my lips, I see her own lips part, tongue darting out to wet her bottom lip, and I inhale sharply.

"Mags." My voice sounds hoarse, raspy even.

"Yes?" Her eyes remain focused on my lips.

"Happy birthday." I dip my head down, my lips dusting lightly over her own before I quickly relinquish my hold on her. "Good night." Slipping into my room, I close the door and lean against it with a sigh.

Running my hands over my face, I internally laugh because I know what I'll be doing to close out Maggie's birthday celebration tonight.

Glancing down at the slight tenting of my jeans, I thank

God she didn't notice the effect the sight of her tongue wetting her lips had on me. That wouldn't have gone over well.

Hearing the soft sound of Maggie's bedroom door close, my shoulders relax slightly, and I quickly unbutton my shirt, tossing it into my laundry bin in the far corner of my room, and my undershirt, jeans, socks, and boxer-briefs follow suit.

Pulling down the covers of my bed, I slide between the cool sheets. Closing my eyes, I wrap my hand around my cock and think of her. Of Maggie's lips, of how good it would feel if she were in here with me right now. If her lips were to trail a path down the center of my chest, down to the base of my cock.

My hand's moving in fluid strokes—not too fast but not too slow, either—and I feel myself harden further at the thought of Maggie's tongue on me. Licking and tasting me. The tip of that tongue darting out to taste the tip of my cock, to lick the pre-come from it.

"Fuck," I breathe out in the quiet of my room. "That's it. Taste me."

My thoughts take over as I imagine Maggie's tongue darting around the base of my cock again before pressing her lips to it and sucking gently.

My body arches at the thought of it, and another surge of arousal flows through me as moisture gathers at my tip.

Maggie's lips wrap around my cock before she begins sliding her mouth up and down my thick shaft. Her hair falls against my inner thighs, and my hands fist it as I guide her to stroke me with her mouth. I guide her in to take me as deep as she can, and her hot, wet mouth feels so fucking good. The way her mouth sucks my cock hard, my toes curl at the way she loves me with her mouth.

I throw my head back against my pillow as I feel the

tightening in my balls and know that I'm close. Thinking about Maggie's mouth, thinking about her swallowing my come, I imagine her eyes watching me. When I feel the tell-tale tingling, just before I find my release, I imagine looking down and seeing Maggie watching me as I come in her mouth.

"Fuck, yes," I expel on a whisper-groan, shooting my release all over my stomach. I lie there, allowing my breathing to even out.

I've just had a fucking hot-ass fantasy about my roommate. The one who's just begun to date again. The one I'm in love with. While I'm supposedly gay.

God, I'm fucked up.

Just as I reach over to grab some tissues from the nightstand beside my bed, I hear something—something that makes me immediately go still. Cocking my head to the side, I listen because if I didn't know any better, I'd think I heard Maggie through the bedroom wall. It sounded almost like a keening cry.

Waiting another moment, I don't hear anything more, so I shrug it off, going about my cleanup and then pulling on some pajama pants so I can head across the hall to shower.

In the back of my mind, though, I wonder what the hell that sound was that I just heard.

CHAPTER ELEVEN

Maggie

Ry's lips against mine. That's all I can think of as I return to my room, closing the door quietly behind me.

My brain goes off on a tangent, imagining Ry's soft lips brushing against mine, teasing me, before his tongue sweeps inside to taste me. Leaning my back against the door, I raise my fingertips to graze my lips.

Is it possible to have kisser's remorse? You know, like buyer's remorse except, in this case, you've kissed someone and are really regretting the fact that it's over? If so, I'm pretty sure I have a serious case of it.

It might be terminal.

Walking over to my dresser, I slide open my top drawer—the one I keep all of my underwear and bras in—and slip my hand to the back. When my fingers wrap around what I'm looking for, I get that tense feeling. Like the time Sister Margaret caught me throwing away my salami sandwich in the second grade. Dang woman had eyes in the back of her head, I tell you.

Shoving that nagging feeling to the back of my mind, I reach for the two batteries, quickly inserting them before snapping the lid shut and laying my vibrator on my bed while I undress. Once I'm naked, I slide beneath my covers and turn it on, praying the covers muffle the noise enough that Ry doesn't hear—doesn't realize what I'm doing.

Doesn't realize I'm thinking of him while I touch myself. Oooh, yes, that's right. Naughty Maggie has come out to play. My mind begins to run rampant with scenarios. One, in particular, takes hold …

Suddenly, my bedroom door opens, and Ry's silhouette is in my doorway.

"What do you think you're doing?"

"I … um," I stutter, knowing I've been caught red-handed.

He steps farther inside my bedroom, and I notice that he's wearing only a pair of boxer-briefs, the outline of his cock pressing against the fabric, and he's hard. *So* hard.

"Are you touching yourself, Mags?" His voice is raspy, like he's just as turned on as I am. And the fact that I turn him on is just all sorts of hot.

"Yes," I breathe.

He moves closer, standing beside my bed. "Show me."

Sliding the covers back, I allow him to see my naked body, watching me as I guide my bullet over my clit. The vibrations of the small toy mingling with my slightly staggered breathing are the only sounds in the quiet bedroom.

His gaze turns molten as he watches, and my eyes drift down to see him growing harder.

"You want to see me?" My eyes dart up to meet his; he obviously caught me staring at him. I can only nod in response. His thumbs tuck beneath the waistband of his briefs, tugging them down his legs before he kicks them off from around his ankles.

Standing there, beside the bed, my eyes are riveted to the sight of Ry's large fingers closing around his cock, sliding slowly from the base to the tip. His thumb circles the slit, gathering the moisture there before reaching out to lower his thumb to my mouth. I greedily open my lips, sucking the pre-come off his thumb. My tongue caresses his flesh as I watch his gaze grow heavy-lidded with lust.

"Mags," he groans as he watches me, scorching heat in his eyes. Withdrawing his thumb from my mouth, his hand returns to fist his cock, running his thumb across the top once more before giving me another taste. I grab his wrist, holding him steady as I suck his essence from his thumb, feeling myself grow even wetter.

When the bed dips with his weight as he slides beside me, he props his head in his hand while watching me. I can't resist reaching out to graze his hard flesh with one fingertip. When it jerks, my eyes fly to his.

He takes my hand in his, wrapping my fingers around his shaft, and guides me on how to stroke him, on what he likes. Watching our hands together, wrapped around his cock and moving in even strokes makes my breath hitch, and another flood of arousal flows through my body.

"Keep going." He nods toward where my other hand is running the vibrator over my clit. His voice is gravelly, hoarse with arousal. "I want to watch you come undone."

Dipping his head to my ear, while still guiding my hand in long strokes on his cock, he says, "I can't wait to hear you come." His lips brush against my ear, his teeth latching onto my earlobe and tugging gently. "Can't wait until you cry out my name." His tongue darts out to trace the outline of the shell of my ear.

My eyes are closed, my breathing becoming labored as I work my vibrator over my clit, feeling my entire body tighten in anticipation of my release. All the while, he continues to guide my hand, and I continue to feel his cock pulsing beneath my ministrations. His tongue and lips are wreaking havoc on me, trailing a path from my ear down along the column of my neck to nibble on my collarbone.

My movements become more frantic. I'm on the precipice of release, circling my clit before, finally, it hits me.

"Ry," my voice sounds faint, like a keening cry as I arch, my body pulsing with my orgasm as waves of bliss roll through me.

When I finally come down from the high, I realize that I'm fisting the covers in one hand. The same hand that I'd imagined was grasping Ry's cock.

"Oh, holy crap," I groan, throwing my head back against the pillow, wincing at what I've just done.

I've just molested my roommate. And came calling out his name.

Sister Margaret was right about me. I really am trouble.

* * *

"So you work at the firm on South Broadway?"

He's into me. Like, he's *really* into me. My inner dork is doing one of those happy-clap-bounce-up-and-down things. But I remain calm, cool, and collected.

On the outside.

"Yes, I've worked there ever since I graduated with my bachelor degree. It's stressful at times, but I enjoy it." Translate that to: *My boss is Satan reincarnated, but the pay is good, and I get a lot of perks with the job, so that's why I stay.*

But I don't need to unload all of that on him—on Stephen with a "*ph.*" Yeah, I asked because, you know. Guys like being asked questions about themselves.

Says the girl who's been celibate for the past year and

just read that in an issue of *Glamour* magazine. Listen to me. Who the heck am I kidding? I feel like a total fish out of water here. Like a kid whose parents just took off the training wheels—too early—even after the kid told them, repeatedly, that they *weren't freaking READY*!

Whoa. Clearly, I have some issues to work out. Sorry about that. Back to Stephen with a "*ph.*"

"So you work in marketing?"

Gah! What the hell? I'm going to start snoring at my own conversation questions. Just when I'm about to laugh it off and toss out my "deal breaker question" of *Breakfast Club* or *Pretty in Pink* (It's both, by the way. You can't actually choose between the two classic movies from the eighties, people.), someone interrupts.

My roommate, Ry.

Now, while I adore Ry more than anything in the world—well, not more than Max Londons' white sangria because I'm not getting *that* crazy, now—he's killing my game. Or something. I don't know if I can even claim that I have anything close to "game." Maybe a strategy? A faint idea?

"Hey, you two! I'm Ry James, Mags' roommate. Nice to meet you." He holds out a hand to Stephen, and I wait to see if he falters at the fact I have a male roommate. When he doesn't and instead shakes Ry's hand with a kind smile, my shoulders relax with relief. Until the next words leave his lips.

"Hey, don't you work for Eastern Sports?"

That right there? Not a good sign at all. It's the equivalent of "Are you Brad Pitt? Could I have your autograph?" here in Saratoga Springs.

Ry is the lead guy to oversee infrastructure for Eastern Sports and has one of those über cushy offices, too. My building is nice enough—we even have heated sidewalks that automatically melt the snow and ice during the winter—but it's older. Ry's office is a new addition on the top of an older, existing building across the street from mine, and if I time it right and look out my window when the sun's glare isn't reflecting off the office windows, I can sometimes see him in his office.

Not that I do that or anything. Because that would be creepy and weird. And he's not even remotely interested in women, so we'll toss in the adjective of *pathetic* while we're at it.

Cue my internal exasperated exhale. Because, yeah. I *have* looked over at his office window. And I *may* have seen him at his desk, talking on his phone, gesturing animatedly with his hands as he often does when a topic gets him all heated. I may have noticed him loosen his tie while he listened to whoever was on the other line as he stood at the window, absent-mindedly looking down at all the people walking along the sidewalks of the downtown area.

There's a teensy chance I may have wished that I had been the one to loosen that tie of his. Maybe push him up against that glass and—

Oh. *Oh, my.* Well, that's no way to start off a night with Stephen with a "*ph*," now, is it?

Tuning back to the conversation, I give Stephen my best smile and step an inch closer to him.

"Pardon me for interrupting, but I have to know the answer to this question." I ignore Ry's groan because he knows me well enough by now to know what my spiel is.

"*Breakfast Club* or *Pretty in Pink*? Go with your gut." My words spill out hurried because, for me, this is like one of those timed tests we had to take back in grade school. You know, the ones where you have, like, five minutes to answer fifty multiplication facts. Talk about pressure, right? I'm still scarred for life from that crap.

"Um ..." Stephen trails off before furrowing his brows in thought. "I've never actually watched either one ..."

My inner horrified gasps are so loud that I actually look around to see if anyone heard them. Ry's eyes dart to mine, his eyebrows raised as if to sarcastically say, *This is the one you chose, Mags?*

Giving him a brief, squinty-eyed glare, I turn my attention back to Stephen. "You really haven't—"

"Did you catch the latest *Avengers* movie? What'd you think of that one?" Ry interrupts me, and the two of them commence discussing the film and laughing about Thor's hammer. Stephen even goes so far as to swivel his barstool around to face Ry, fully engaging in the conversation.

Scintillating stuff. I mean don't get me wrong; I lust over Thor as much as any other hot-blooded woman, but my dating prospect has just chosen my gay roommate over me.

Me: Zero; **Ry**: Eight.

Or is it ten? Heck, I can't even keep track anymore. Either they end up liking Ry and "discovering their inner gay," as he's told me numerous times in explanation, they fall ill, or they recall something they forgot they were supposed to do and have to leave while I use the restroom, leaving Ry to relay the regretful message to me.

With a sigh, I turn my stool toward the bar, leaning my forearms on the lacquered wood, and sip my drink. I signal the bartender for another Dirty Shirley, my drink of choice. Mike knows not to make them too strong because—disclosure alert—I'm not exactly known for holding my liquor well.

Sliding a new napkin in front of me before placing my

fresh drink down on it, Mike removes my empty glass in a fluid motion. Thanking him with a smile, he winks at me in return. Then his eyes flit over to where Ry and Stephen are now in a discussion about weapons and yammering on about Tony Stark.

Leaning in close and lowering his voice, Mike curves the corners of his lips upward. "Another one bites the dust, huh?"

Letting out a long, dejected sigh, I nod. "Yep." Staring down at the ice cubes in my drink, I muse, "You'd think that the bulk of the men around here are all in the closet or something."

Mike chokes out a laugh. "Oh, I wouldn't be so—" When his words cut off abruptly, my eyes dart up, catching him looking over at the guys with an odd expression on his face. When I turn around, Ry offers me one of his smiles. The kind that makes me go weak-kneed and wish he were actually into women.

And when I say into women, I mean into *me*, specifically. But clearly, that's not going to happen.

That becomes more evident when I catch sight of Stephen typing Ry's number into his phone just as Ry tosses an arm around his shoulders, aiming his own cell toward them for a selfie.

Turning back to face the bar with a long sigh, a part of me wishes I had it in me to get sloppy drunk. Because the guy I'd wanted to ask for *my* number tonight, the guy I'd thought was into *me*, just chose my roommate instead.

I've just been clam jammed.

Again.

CHAPTER TWELVE

Ry

"Hey, snuggle muffin. I've missed you."

An arm settles around my shoulders as soon as I enter the men's locker room at the gym. Jack and I usually meet to play racquetball on Saturday mornings.

Shoving his arm off me, I shake my head. "Dude. It's too early for that shit."

His face is a mask of mock-hurt. "But … but it's never too early for love."

Tossing my bag and keys into the locker, I slam the door shut, ignoring him. "Ready?"

"Sure. You can fill me in on last night while we head over."

As we walk through the large, two-story gym, I fill him in on the latest guy I had to "woo" away from Maggie. He laughs when I get to the part about the dude asking for a selfie.

"No way," he chokes out in his laughing. "He treated you like you were some celebrity?"

It's not that funny to me anymore. It's actually more tiring than anything because while I'm a representative of the company, I hate when I come across people who think if they become your friend, it automatically means they'll get perks—like free or deeply discounted kayaks, skis, snowboards, free ski lift passes, or God only knows what else.

Living in this area with a bunch of large lakes and mountains, the population is pretty active and outdoorsy. I get that people get excited when they meet one of the directors for Eastern Sports, a company that has become the Mecca along the East Coast for all sports equipment and outerwear.

It doesn't mean that I want people to use me for my connection, however.

"Yeah, he asked me if I could 'do him a solid' so many times, it got to be painful," I mutter as we enter the racquetball court we reserved.

"I thought that selfie was pretty hot. You two make a cute couple." Jack smirks. "If you weren't already betrothed to me, of course."

My dark glare does nothing. In fact, I swear his smile gets even wider. "We're not betrothed, jackass."

He waves a hand dismissively. "Semantics."

"Just serve the ball, damn it."

Thankfully, Jack shuts up for a while. Until about halfway through the game when he says, "Maggie looked pretty hot in that dress she wore last night."

My serve goes out of bounds. "How do you know what she wore last night?"

He wiggles his eyebrows. "She posted a photo on her Facebook page, saying something like, 'I'm waiting on my roommate to finally finish beautifying so we can go out tonight.'"

"Ha-ha. You're hilarious."

"It said just as much. But she did look smokin' ho— *Hey!*" My serve whizzes right past his ear.

"My bad," I grit out the words. "Maybe you should keep your eyes off Maggie."

He just laughs, and we continue our game. Keeping the topic of conversation away from Maggie and whether or not she was smokin' hot in the dress she wore.

She had been. Which is why I ended up taking a selfie with Stephen last night, exchanging numbers and pseudo promising to let him know when Kastle came out with their newest, most upgraded premium graphite skis.

Maggie had gone home alone—again—and without exchanging numbers with a guy—again. This meant a job well done on my part.

As Jack and I exit the gym after we've both showered—separately, even though the douche bag gave me shit because it allegedly "broke his heart" that his own boyfriend didn't want to shower with him—we head down the sidewalk in the direction of my and Maggie's apartment. And he asks the same questions he asks me every time we're by ourselves.

"So when are you going to make an honest man out of me, James?" and then the more serious, "When are you going to come clean with Maggie?"

Two questions. And for only one of them do I have an honest-to-goodness answer.

* * *

"Hey, you two," Maggie calls out from the kitchen as Jack and I enter the apartment. There's a delicious aroma of waffles in the air, causing my stomach to growl loudly. Slipping off our shoes and dropping our gym bags by the door, we walk through the apartment, heading into the kitchen. Grabbing two bottles of water for us, I slip onto one of the high-top barstools at the counter of the small island. Jack sidles up beside Maggie as she's pouring batter into the Belgian waffle maker.

"Maggie May. Please say you'll marry me and make me waffles forever," he begs, leaning over and dramatically sniffing the stack of waffles plated on the counter beside her.

Laughing, her eyes light up as she shakes her head at him. "You know I can't do that to Ry. He loves you too much." She glances over at me, her eyes taking in the sight of my biceps in my old, worn sleeveless shirt, and my heart races at the appreciation I catch in her gaze before she wipes her expression clean.

"Pffft," Jack scoffs. "You know he's just biding his time before he manages to get you to fall for him. Then he'll leave me in the dust."

My entire body tenses, and if looks could kill, Jack would have his throat ripped out right now.

Thank God, Maggie thinks he's joking. She hip-checks him playfully, laughing it off. "Whatever. You two are perfect for one another, and you know it."

"He's actually the ugliest man I've ever been with," Jack says with faux sadness. *That's because you've never actually "been" with a man, dipshit.*

"I could say the same for you," I mutter, before narrowing my eyes, my tone full of insinuation. "Plus, you're kind of on the *small* side."

Jack's smile is wide and full of mischief. "I make up for it with this bangin' body." He gestures to himself.

"I came for waffles, not to lose my damn appetite," a female voice remarks from behind us.

Turning, we find Sarah standing there with a pointed look, hands on her hips. "If you two plan to continue this, you're going to have to take it somewhere else. I'm ready to get my waffle eating on." She slides onto one of the barstools beside me. Jack immediately slides onto the one beside Sarah, placing an arm casually on the back of her chair.

"So tell me, sweet Sarah. If I were to go straight, would you date me?"

I'm going to kill my best friend. It's confirmed.

She stares at him for a moment. "Nope."

He rears back in surprise. "Why not?"

"Because I want a guy with a big penis."

The drink of water I'd just taken sprays everywhere. Maggie spins arounds, gaping at her friend.

"Sarah!"

"What?" Sarah shrugs before tossing a thumb in my direction as I attempt to mop up the water. "He's the one who said Jack's on the small side." Another shrug. "I was only answering honestly."

Never one to let anything die, Jack leans in and says in a loud whisper, "What if I were to get one of those pump things—"

My eyes fly over to Maggie, and we both share a knowing smile because Jack and Sarah are always debating something off the wall and usually sexual in nature.

"Breakfast is ready!" she announces, sliding a plate stacked with waffles along with a platter of scrambled eggs and bacon onto the counter in front of us before handing over a stack of plates with silverware and a container of local maple syrup.

As we all dig in and I chew the first glorious bite of Maggie's homemade waffle, I turn, swallowing before I say, "Marry me, Mags. Marry me, love me forever, and make me waffles."

Maggie just laughs, like she always does when I say

something like this. Because she thinks I'm joking. As I hold her eyes, a part of me tries to silently convey that I'm serious. That I love her and wish she'd love me forever. Until I get interrupted by the "comedy duo" on the other side of me.

"Quit being a twat waffle," Jack mutters under his breath.

"Twat did he just say?" Sarah snickers at her own re-mark, and the two of them snort-laugh together.

Maggie and I roll our eyes with a smile at their juvenile humor. And just like that, the moment is gone. But I can't be too upset. Especially when Maggie pipes up with, "Hey, Ry. I like you a waffle lot."

Leaning closer, I say, "I like you, too, and that's no yoke."

And when she laughs at my silly joke, warmth runs through me along with a yearning to pull her close, kiss her laughing lips, and tell her how I really feel about her.

But I can't, so I resort to tucking the moment away in my memory bank, where dozens upon dozens more of Maggie memories will join it.

Someday, I silently vow. Someday, I won't be limited to just memories of "Maggie moments" but actually *make* some "Maggie and Ry moments" as memories.

Someday.

CHAPTER THIRTEEN

Maggie

"Oh, man, that's hilarious!" Clay slaps a hand on Ry's back, laughing, and I feel like the odd man out.

Again.

"*Super* hilarious," I mutter sarcastically beneath my breath before taking a sip of my drink and propping both elbows on the bar. As if that's not enough, I also slouch in my seat—things I was told never to do in Catholic school. Sister Margaret is likely rolling over in her grave right now because elbows, slouching, *and* drinking alcohol? I'm on a path headed straight for damnation.

"What was that, Mags?" Ry asks, eyes alit with amusement and clearly enjoying himself. Enjoying himself with *my* date. Or what should have been my date. Until Ry showed up, once again, and wooed the pants right off the guy.

Speaking of wooing the pants off men, now that I inspect Clay further—and from a different perspective—I feel like I should have noticed him wearing his pants a bit more snug than the average heterosexual male. Then again, Ry doesn't wear tight pants. He claims they cut off his circulation down below.

Yeah, I asked. And trust me, his explanation ended up getting one of those *I'm holding up my hand to stop you because you just said the words "balls" and "strangled" together in the same sentence, and I can't bear to hear any more* kind of response. Because let's be serious for a minute. No girl wants to hear about balls being strangled.

So. Gross.

"Ry's such a cool guy." "Ry's hilarious!" "Ry's got to be an awesome roommate, huh?" Or worse, I've heard, *"So is Ry single?"* That's all I ever hear anymore.

Wait. Did you catch that sound? It's the sound of me banging my head against the wall. In frustration. Because everything seems to turn into *Ry* this and *Ry* that.

Ry is freaking clam jamming the hell out of me. And it sucks. I'll never be able to find a guy—and manage to keep him—at this rate.

At least not within a five-mile radius of Ryland James.

"Man, I hate to run, but we definitely have to hang out again. You have my number now. Don't be a stranger."

Did you hear that? That wasn't directed toward me but toward Ry.

Shocker.

Turning my attention toward the two men, my fake smile firmly in place, I watch as Clay shakes Ry's hand enthusiastically. Finally noticing my attention—and possibly recalling, perhaps vaguely, that I'm still present—he offers me a polite smile.

"Nice to meet you, Margie." My smile dims, feeling brittle, and I raise my drink in salute. "Later, Clint," I mutter before swiveling around on my barstool.

What the hell just happened? I swear to you, Clay was the one who'd approached *me* when I was in the bank a few days ago. Only two tellers worked both the counter *and* the drive-through when half the population of Saratoga Springs decided they needed to do some banking. I'm not kidding—the line was nearly out the door.

I was trying to keep my cool even though the lady in front of me was talking on her phone—loudly—and about one of the many topics one should never discuss in public.

Yeast infections.

I had been—barely—managing to stifle my snickering when she began to detail how "unbelievably itchy" she was. That was the moment I heard a male voice from behind me utter, "Oh, Jesus."

When I turned, both of us flashed one another a knowing smile, and a few moments later, he struck up a conversation with me. I felt like he was really into me and had continued to feel that way during the few phone calls we had exchanged days later.

That all—*clearly*—fell apart tonight. Because I sure as heck don't have a penis.

Who knew that would end up being such a deal breaker?

* * *

"So he went home with Ry?" Sarah looks like she's trying not to laugh as I proceed to give her a quick recap of what's gone on since I've attempted to start dating again. She's been working crazy hours, and we haven't had a moment to catch up in person since our breakfast that one morning with the guys.

"Yes," I expel with a sigh before taking a sip of my hazelnut latte. We decided to meet up at the Starbucks a few blocks away from my apartment. Somehow, we managed to snag a small table right by the front windows, which is rare since this place is always hopping with customers.

"And the other one called you *Margie*?" She's losing the battle in restraining a smile. It's official.

"I'm so glad you find this amusing." My glare doesn't do any good.

A laugh bursts free, but she at least has the decency to cover her mouth with her hand. "I can't help it, Maggie. It's just"—she snickers again—"too funny." Managing to regain composure, she studies me for a moment. "You're pretty frustrated, huh?"

"You think?" I toss up a hand in exasperation, gesturing to encompass the bustling coffee shop. "I could meet a guy here, have a great conversation, actually click with him, and think maybe he has potential to be more if I get to know him. But if he meets Ry"—making a face, I shake my head—"it's all over. I swear—they end up liking him *way* more than me."

"Or they have to leave suddenly," Sarah adds, resting her chin on her palm, eyeing me curiously. "Don't you think that's a bit odd?"

I throw my hands up. "I don't know what to think anymore! I'm getting frustrated. I'm on the verge of trying to sneak out of the apartment without Ry knowing just so he doesn't end up snagging *my* date for the evening." Wrapping my hands around my coffee cup, I stare blindly into it, lost in thought. "Maybe I should talk to Jack about it."

"Talk to Jack about what?"

Sarah and I both jump, startled to see Jack step up to our table. Looking handsome as ever, his hair appears damp and darker, as if he just showered. He has on a pair of black, loose fitting shorts that show off his muscular, toned legs and a gray, sleeveless, cotton shirt displaying his strong, corded arms.

"Hey, stranger." I rise from my seat and give him a hug before Sarah follows suit.

"So what did you need to talk to me about?"

When I falter for a response, Sarah doesn't hesitate to help me out. "She's worried that Ry's cheating on you."

His eyebrows nearly hit his hairline. "Really?" I swear the corners of his lips twitch the slightest bit.

"And," Sarah pauses dramatically, and if I didn't know better, I'd swear she's enjoying this moment, "he's snagging all her potential dates."

Jack lets out a gasp. "*No.*" Shaking his head in dismay, he sets his iced coffee down on our table. "I just can't believe he'd do that to me." Focusing on me again, he asks, "Are you sure he was trying to steal these other guys away from you? You sure that he wasn't just his usual outgoing, friendly self?"

Spotting a free chair, Jack quickly commandeers it, bringing it over to join us at our small table. "Because let's be honest. Ry *is* pretty damn charismatic."

Giving him a look, I say, "He asked one of the guys what his sign was." I hold up a hand when both his and Sarah's mouth open to form protests, continuing with, "He also asked one of the guys what he thought of his pickup line, which was, and I quote, *'Are you a ninety-degree angle? Because, man, you are looking right.'*"

They both find this hilarious. Jack throws his head back in a loud laugh, gathering attention from quite a few people while Sarah's hiding her face in her hands, muffling her laughter as her shoulders shake.

I wait for them to collect themselves. The truth is, I know that I'd likely find it amusing, too—*if* it hadn't happened to me while I thought I was actually connecting with the guy.

"Or how about this one." I pause, waiting for their attention. "Hey, if my name were Microsoft, would you let me crash at your place tonight?"

Jack loses it on this one, head bowed as his shoulders rise and fall with his laughter. Finally, he points at me and says, "Now, that's Ry, for sure. The computer nerd in him would totally say that."

Sarah's lips press thin, and I know she's trying not to laugh. Narrowing my eyes on them, I shake my head as I take a sip of my coffee. "You both are overwhelmingly supportive."

Leaning back in my chair, I huff out a long breath. "What am I going to do? I'll never manage to find a guy if this continues."

"Maybe you're rushing things, and it's too soon to get back into the dating scene— *Ouch!*" Jack stares at Sarah, the two of them exchanging an odd look.

"Sorry," she says woodenly, still holding his stare. "My foot must've slipped." Their gazes are locked, and it gets to the point where it's getting awkward to watch.

"Um, guys?" I wave a hand between them as if to try to break whatever weird telepathic thing they have going on. Finally, they snap out of it, and Jack mutters under his breath about his shin having a bruise now and how "nurses are supposed to heal, not hurt."

"Things'll turn up, Maggie." Jack nods confidently. "I'm sure of it."

If only I felt as confident.

CHAPTER FOURTEEN

Ry

"You look like you just lost your puppy."

I look up to see Mike, the bartender, eyeing me as he's filling some glasses with beer on tap. "Just a rough week."

He glances around as if looking for someone. "Maggie head out with that guy tonight?"

"Yep." My curt response is punctuated with a slug of my beer. Self-disgust ricochets through me. Because I'd failed at clam jamming. And that leaves me here alone while Maggie's off.

With *him*.

Out of the corner of my eye, I see Mike hand off the beers to a server before returning to fill another order for cocktails, if the stainless steel shaker is any indication. Once he serves the two ladies at the end of the bar, he comes back and starts pouring a shot, sliding it in front of me.

Meeting his eyes, I shake my head, sliding it back toward him. "Thanks but no thanks, man. Not in the mood."

He slides it right back to me, tipping his head in the direction of the two women he's just served. "It's on them."

My eyes flit over to the women in surprise, forcing a smile as I raise the shot to toast them with a brief nod of thanks. They're attractive enough—one is a petite blonde with a wide, friendly smile and the other a redhead who's wearing a bit too much eye makeup for my liking. Not to mention, she has a sparkle in her eyes and not the kind of sparkle I'd welcome. It's one of those sparkles that says, *I like to tie up men and flog them until they call me Mama.* And I'm not into that kind of freaky shit. Even on a bad day when I'm feeling low.

Like today.

And yeah, they're clearly interested, but they're just not what I'm looking for. They're just not … Maggie.

Tossing back the shot, I welcome the burning path the alcohol leaves as it trickles down my throat, wishing it would either take away the burning ache in my chest at the thought of what might be going on right now between Maggie and Sean. Or wishing it would just burn enough to erase all thoughts of Maggie.

"Hey." My head turns to find one of the women—the blonde—at my side. She's standing a little too close, but a small part of me wishes I felt something—anything—right now. Enough to have a fraction of interest in her.

I've got nothing.

"Hi." Forcing a smile, I try to be cordial because the one thing they drummed into us when I joined the Eastern Sports family is that everyone could be a customer and to act accordingly.

Meaning: Don't be a shit show in public.

Right now, though, I'm considering giving myself a free pass.

"Thanks for the shot." I'm trying to channel the old Ry—the one who isn't head over heels for a woman who's been led to believe he's batting for the other team.

"I'm Serena." She holds out her hand for me to shake,

and as soon as I grasp it, I feel nothing but limpness. There's no firm handshake from this woman. Unlike Maggie, who has a great, firm business-like handshake.

"I'm Ry, nice to meet you." I barely restrain from wiping my palm on my pants after she relinquishes her hold. Barely.

"So what do you do?"

She smiles, and I notice her left front tooth is slightly crooked. Which means I'm fixated on it. Terrible but true.

"I work over at Fifty South Salon."

"Oh, cool."

That's all I've got. Because I don't have the faintest clue what working in a salon entails, aside from cutting and coloring hair. I go to the place down the road where an eighty-year-old man cuts my hair old-school barber style. And it costs like ten bucks. Mainly, I go because the old men who go there are the best gossips around. You want to know what's going down in Saratoga Springs then you need to head over to Marvin's on the corner of Broadway and Van Dam Street.

"You have really great hair, Ry." She reaches up to run her fingers through my hair, and I stiffen because who the hell runs their fingers through someone else's hair they've just met?

Apparently, women who work at salons. As I'm quickly finding out.

Trying to back away discreetly, I run a hand through my hair. "Thanks." My eyes dart around to locate Mike to see if I can quickly close out my tab. Catching his eye, I raise a hand to him, and he nods.

"You're leaving so soon?" Serena asks, giving me what I'm sure she thinks is a sexy pout.

It's not.

"I've had a rough week, and I'm exhausted. Sorry." Trying to appear apologetic and not as excited to make my getaway as I actually am, I thank her again for the shot. "You two ladies have fun tonight. It was nice meeting you." I pull out my credit card and quickly hand it over to Mike, who's just approached, hoping to expedite things.

"Oh." Her face falls, likely realizing I'm not going to ask her for her number. "You, too." Turning and walking back to where her friend waits, I shift to see Mike sliding a receipt and a pen across the bar for me. Quickly signing the slip, I pocket my card and thank him.

Exiting the bar, I'm overwhelmed at the intense melancholy that comes over me. The thought of being in that apartment by myself, waiting for Maggie to come back from her damn date with that Sean guy and wondering if he'll get lucky enough to kiss her.

And it's all my own damn fault. All of this. I've created this situation and trapped myself.

Heaving out a long sigh, I head up the sidewalk. Hands in my pockets, I idly walk past what seems like an overabundance of couples holding hands, enjoying one another's company on a Friday night.

Darting a glance in the direction of where Max Londons is, a part of me is dying to head over there to sit at the bar and spy on Maggie. But the more sane part of me realizes how pathetic that idea is, and I know I'd only regret it.

Instead, I head up in the elevator alone, entering the quiet apartment where photographs of a happy, smiling Maggie greet me. Stepping into my room, I kick off my shoes into the closet and reach up to grab the framed photo sitting on my dresser of Maggie and me from her last birthday.

Maggie had slid her chair over beside mine, asking

Sarah to take a photo of us after I'd given her the photo blanket. Her smile is wide, bright, and so beautiful that it makes my chest tighten. I'd slung my arm around her, and I'm smiling down at her while she grins up at me. It's one of those moments I wish I could rewind and revisit. It was that incredible.

Because, at that moment, when she looked up at me, I could see the possibility.

The possibility of Maggie loving me the way I love her.

CHAPTER FIFTEEN

Maggie

"Tell me the truth." Sean leans in from where he's sitting across from me at one of the tiny tables in Max Londons.

"How is it possible that you're single?" Eyes crinkling at the corners with his smile, his light blue eyes sparkle. His blond hair is short, parted to the side neatly, and while his nose is slightly crooked, it's endearing.

He's just so freaking nice and adorable. And sweet.

Wow, I think I've just managed to describe a Golden Retriever.

But really, he's fun to talk to, and he makes me laugh. Not to mention he's super cute. And he listens to me. Like, really listens. None of the nodding between glances at my boobs kind of thing.

The best part? He thinks I'm funny. Yep, Sean thinks I'm funny. Me, Maggie Finegan, dork of the universe. The same person who says in response to someone asking me to remind them of my name, *"Call me whatever you want, just don't call me late for dinner."*

Yeah, I told you. Dork of the universe, right here.

The odd thing about tonight is that for a split second, as Sean and I were walking down the sidewalk from Irish

Times to head here, I missed Ry. Which is crazy and ridiculous since he's been consistently clam jamming me. When I came back out from using the restroom and saw Sean standing alone, waiting for me with no sign of Ry around, I felt the tiniest tinge of disappointment.

Shaking off my thoughts, I force myself back to the present and smile at Sean. "I'm single because I've been having a hell of a time finding someone even remotely normal and, well," I shrug, "not interested in Ry instead."

He looks confused. "Interested in Ry?"

I nod. "Yes. It seems like so many of them end up channeling their inner gay or something." Shrugging again, I add, "Go figure."

Sean continues to stare at me oddly. "Are you saying that Ry's … gay?"

There's a beat of silence as I take in the fact that Sean didn't realize this. "Yes," I answer, drawing out the word slowly.

His head tips to the side. "Huh." There's a pause, his brows furrowing. "I wouldn't have guessed that in a million years."

Wanting to change the subject, I lean in, mimicking his pose. "So tell me. Why are *you* single?"

Smile softening, he glances away briefly before his eyes meet mine again. "I was in a relationship, but it didn't work out. We tried to do the long-distance thing, and it just kind of … fizzled."

"On whose end?" I'm curious to know, and the sangria has made me brazen enough to ask.

His lips twist a bit into a rueful expression. "Mainly hers. I had my suspicions that she had been interested in a new coworker at her new job. His name started to come up all the time, so …" He trails off.

"Well," I chime in, attempting to make him feel less awkward, "if it makes you feel any better, my ex decided to get it on with someone else." I wait for a beat. "In our bed."

Sean winces. "Ouch. Not cool."

"Nope, not at all."

"So what skeletons are you hiding, Miss Maggie?" His eyes flicker over my face. "Keep your toenail clippings in a jar on your nightstand? Have an odd obsession with Manga?"

Laughter bubbles out of me. "No, none of that. I'm just a girl, sitting in front of a boy, asking him to …" I tip my head to the side with a sly smile "… please be normal."

He throws his head back in laughter, and at that moment, I feel it.

The potential.

Things just might work out after all, I think to myself.

And I ignore that tiny part of me that's telling me I'm with the wrong guy.

* * *

"Well, this is my building."

We're standing on the sidewalk outside my apartment after Sean insisted on walking me home. We stayed at Max Londons until we were nearly kicked out at closing time. We talked the entire night, sharing a variety of appetizers and more than one pitcher of white sangria. Now, standing in the crisp evening air amidst the trees strung with white lights along Broadway Avenue, it's almost magical.

Sean gazes down at me. "I had an incredible time tonight, Maggie." Offering a self-deprecating grin, he adds, softly, "I'm glad I gave it a shot and approached you tonight."

"Me, too." I take a tentative step closer.

"I'd love to do this again." He takes a step toward me, closing the remaining distance.

Tipping my head back slightly to look up at him, I find my eyes tracking him as he leans in toward me, and our lips meet in a sweet, delicate kiss. One of his hands cups the nape of my neck as he brushes his lips across mine before placing one kiss at each corner of my lips, dusting one on the tip of my nose, and then leaning back slightly.

"Good night, Maggie." He presses one final kiss to my lips before backing away with a soft smile on his face. "I'll talk to you soon."

"Don't forget about the two-week wait time until you can start sexting me," I tease.

His lips twist into a fake pout. "That rule doesn't still apply for me, now, does it? Even after I fed you?"

I flash him a warning look, but my inability to restrain my smile lightens the severity of it. "Hey, buddy. I need more than food and sangria to get me to reconsider the two-week wait time."

"Bummer." He lets out a sigh, grinning wide. "I'll somehow have to make do for two weeks."

"Until next time." I wave before turning to head inside my building.

"Maggie?"

Turning, I find him standing a few feet away, hands in the pockets of his pants and wearing a sober expression on his face. "I really had a great time tonight."

"Me, too." With one final smile and wave, I enter my building and head to the elevator.

And the entire ride up to my floor, that smile is still on my face.

CHAPTER SIXTEEN

Ry

"You about ready, Mags?" I holler down the hall from where I've been prepping the living room, getting it ready for our usual Saturday movie night. Setting the large bowl of salted popcorn on the coffee table and pausing to straighten the stack of *Architectural Digests* upon it, I hear her bedroom door open and her footsteps approaching.

"Uh, Ry..." She trails off, and I don't need to turn around to know what she's about to say next.

Stiffening, I rise from straightening the magazines, heading into the kitchen to uncork a new bottle of wine.

God knows I'm going to need it. Because this pinching in my chest? The fact that she likely forgot about our usual Saturday night tradition?

It hurts. As though someone's driving a burning stake into my chest.

"Ry, I'm sorry. I didn't even think—" Her tone is apologetic, but it does nothing to soothe the hurt.

"Don't worry about it. I could use a night in by myself." Still not turning to face her, I concentrate on uncorking the wine.

"I can ask Sean if we can—" The knock on the door

interrupts her. "That's him now. Let me talk to him real quick, okay?"

Blowing out a long breath, I face her. "Mags. It's no biggie. Just go and have fun, okay?"

Her eyes search mine for a brief moment before turning and rushing down the hall to the door. Pouring my wine—a healthy amount—I try not to give in to the urge to strain to hear what they're whispering about by the door.

Just as I'm swirling the wine in my glass, musing about my pathetic existence, Maggie pops back into the kitchen. "So," she clasps her hands together with an overly energetic smile, "Sean and I decided to forgo our plans, and we can all stay in for movie night! Yay!"

My eyes flicker past Maggie to meet Sean's gaze, both of us parroting but with far less enthusiasm, "Yay."

* * *

If I wasn't already certain I'd made a mistake in not insisting Maggie and Sean keep their Saturday night plans earlier, I sure as hell am now. Because sitting through movie night with the two of them is much like what I imagine it must've been like for Guantanamo prisoners who underwent waterboarding.

Excruciating torture.

Instead of Maggie's legs draped over my thighs, she's sitting with her legs pulled up to the side and leaning into Sean. Sure, she's sitting between us, but it's not the same. Not by a long shot. To make matters worse, only Maggie and I are going back and forth, quoting *Weird Science*.

"*So what would you little maniacs like to do first?*" we both mutter at the same time, turning to each other and snickering.

The entire time, Sean's on his cell phone, texting like a madman with his brows furrowed in concentration. As if he's a neurosurgeon or something and people can't bear to be disconnected from him for the weekend.

"You okay over there, Sean?" There's a hint of a bite in my tone, and I attempt to disguise it with an earnest expression.

"Yep." *Tap, tap, tap.* Seriously. The dude has a low-level marketing job. Low. Level. Nothing where he'd be on call on the weekends.

"I'm going to get a refill." Rising from the couch, I look over at Maggie. "Need anything?" When she offers a quick, "No, thanks," reluctantly, my eyes fall on Sean. "How about you?"

Sean shakes his head dismissively, eyes still on his phone. Heading into the kitchen, I roll my eyes. While uncorking the wine and refilling my glass, I mutter beneath my breath. "Beautiful woman by my side and I can't be bothered to pay any atten—"

"Hey, man."

My hand jerks in surprise, some wine spilling onto the counter. "Shit." Hurriedly wiping up the spill, I look up at Sean. "Hey." When he doesn't elaborate on his reason for suddenly joining me in the kitchen, I lift the half-full bottle of wine. "You change your mind about a refill?"

His eyes don't leave mine as he casually leans against the refrigerator, hands sliding into his pockets. "I'm not going to pretend like I understand your game." His voice is low, making it evident he doesn't want to be overheard, but his gaze turns hard. "But Maggie is *not* going to be yours."

Casually taking a sip of wine before setting my glass back on the counter, I offer an easy shrug. "Don't know what you're talking about."

Our eyes war—neither of us looking away and neither of us wanting to break the stare. Like two juvenile boys.

"Hey, you two." Maggie slides up beside Sean, linking her arm through his, her eyes flickering back and forth between us curiously. "Everything okay?"

"Yep." Sean fixes a smile on her. "Ry was just saying how he wasn't really feeling well tonight and thought we should head out to give him some peace and quiet."

Maggie frowns at me. "Ry?" Her eyes dart to the counter beside me.

Stepping a few inches to my right to block the sight of my refilled wine glass on the counter behind me, I shrug. "Yeah. Tonight's been rough, so I'd better take it easy before the nausea gets to be too much for me to handle." My fingers give a brief tug on my left earlobe.

She steps forward, wrapping her arms around me in a hug. "Call me if you need anything, okay?" she whispers. "Love you."

Dipping my head down to press a soft kiss to the top of her head, whispering an, "*I love you,*" back, I don't break eye contact with Sean. Which means I don't miss the narrowing of his eyes.

He's on to me.

The gauntlet has officially been thrown.

CHAPTER SEVENTEEN

Maggie

My phone rings as soon as Sybil leaves my office in huff number five hundred and fifty-two. And it's only just now hit noon.

Glancing over at the caller ID lighting up on my desk phone, I heave a sigh of relief that it's actually someone I want to talk to.

"Ryland James," I draw out his name. "What are you up to on this glorious Monday?"

"Up to far more good than Little Miss Sunshine who just exited your office, that much is certain. How many times has he come in to bother you in the last four hours? Ten?"

"More like twel— Wait!" I swivel my chair around to peer out the window, but the sunlight is reflecting off the bank of windows on the building across from me, so I can't detect any sight of him. "Are you spying on me again?"

"Guilty as charged." Amusement laces his tone. "Does this mean you have to cuff me? Because if so, I'm on board. Especially with that prim and proper pinstriped duo you have going on right now."

Glancing down at my matching skirt and jacket, I snicker. "This is the most boring outfit I own." With a pause, I add, "Not to mention, you need to stop spying on me with those dang binoculars. It's creepy."

"It's not creepy."

"It's creepy."

"It's not. It means I'm dedicated to something. I know that this time, every day, you let out a long exhale, rub your temples after your boss leaves your office to head to lunch—where I'm convinced he goes to some dark, underground place where he feeds on the blood of pure virgins or something equally as disturbing—and you try to catch up on emails while eating your lunch at your desk."

"Like I said. Creepy."

"I prefer to say I'm just watching out for you."

"Mmm, still sounds creepy."

"No, it doesn't. If I said something about watching you when you adjust the strap of the black bra you sometimes wear and that it usually needs to be adjusted about a quarter of an inch, *that* would be creepy."

I hesitate, mulling over his words. *Do I do that? Do I have a black bra that—*

"Gotcha."

I laugh, shaking my head as I pull out my insulated lunch bag from one of my desk drawers. "You're not right." Opening my bag, I falter because inside is … not what I packed in a frenzied rush this morning after sleeping in due to getting back later than expected from dinner with Sean last night: a granola bar, some crackers, and a string cheese stick.

"Ry." His name is spoken on an exhale as I turn my eyes toward the windows again, wishing desperately that I could see him.

His response is husky. "Just a little surprise for my Mags. No biggie."

But he's so wrong. It *is* a biggie. As I pull out a container of sliced strawberries, reaching past a small cooler pack to withdraw another container with a mixed greens salad, I discover one of the individually wrapped Godiva chocolates Ry insists on keeping around the apartment for when he experiences his "time of the month."

My shoulders sag. "Ry. Thank you." I smile into the phone.

"Keep digging, Mags."

Curiously, I reach down to the very bottom to find a folded paper towel. Unfolding it, I read it.

I want the other person to be happy. Always.

Before I can ask him the meaning behind this, I hear another male voice in the background on his end. Hastily, he tells me he has to go.

"Enjoy your lunch, Mags. Love you." Then he hangs up.

"Thanks," I mumble, setting the phone back in the cradle in a daze. "Love you, too."

I eat the rest of my lunch in silence, staring at Ry's handwritten words.

* * *

"Maggie? A Ms. Sarah Eaton is here for you." I glance up from my desk to see Trevor, one of our interns, at my door.

"Thanks, Trevor. You can send her on in."

Glancing at the clock, I wince, realizing how much time has passed. I should be close to finishing for the day, yet I've been wrestling with one project in particular, and it's nearing five thirty in the evening.

"Hey, loser." Sarah walks in my office, slumping into one of the chairs in front of my desk. "Are you planning to live here now?"

"You're one to talk," I tease, referring to the long hours she puts in at the hospital. I take in her plain-clothes appearance, noting the absence of her scrubs. "Did you play hooky today?"

She leans her head back against the chair, closing her eyes. "Nope. I misread the schedule, so it turned out to be my day off."

"That's awesome." I honestly don't know how she does it, pulling all those long hours at the hospital while going to school. It doesn't leave time for much else, but she'll soon have P.A. beside her name—Physician Assistant—and that will open more doors and increase her paycheck, as well.

"Let me save everything and shut down my computer, and we can go ..." I trail off, raising my eyebrows.

Her head snaps up. "Eat. I want to eat dinner with my best friend. And not talk about work or about heart valves or episiotomies or anything else."

"Whoa. That was emphatically descriptive."

Sarah smiles. "Most emphatically descriptive."

I start clicking my mouse to save my files and am in the process of shutting down my computer when she clears her throat.

"Can we invite Ry along? I haven't seen him in a while, either."

It's not so much her question that draws my attention as it is the *way* she asks it. "I'll have to—"

My desk phone rings at that moment, and I know—without looking at it—who's going to be on the other end.

As soon as I put my phone to my ear, a husky male voice greets me. "Hey, baby. Whatcha wearin'?"

With a snort of laughter, I swivel my chair around to face the windows. "Are you spying on me again?"

He gasps. "What would make you say that?" There's a pause. "Tell Sarah I really like that color of blue on her, by the way."

"Ry says he likes that color of blue on you." I nod to her simple, sleeveless blue dress.

Her eyes immediately narrow as she glances toward the window, her lips quirking upward. "Tell him to lay off the Peeping Tom bit."

"She said—"

"I heard." He laughs. "You two beauties headed somewhere?"

"Actually," I move back to finish cleaning up my desk, "we were wondering if you'd like to join us for dinner."

There's a beat of silence. "Just the three of us?"

"Unless you want to invite J—"

"Nope. I'm good with it being the three of us," he offers quickly.

As we plan to meet across the street at Druthers, I can't help but wonder why Ry didn't want to include Jack in our plans.

And if part of the reason was because of me.

CHAPTER EIGHTEEN

Ry

"**S**o you're going out to eat without me? Oh, the betrayal! It tastes *so* bitter!"

Rolling my eyes at Jack's melodramatic response coming through the speakerphone, I clean up my office. "Pretty sure you'll get over it."

He sniffles. "I might not. But I guess I should try to get over your abandonment with someone new."

"You sound tore up about it."

"I really am." There's a brief pause. "And what do you know? I'm over it."

"That took long," I remark dryly.

"Getting over you is easier now that I've met someone."

"Ah, yet you're the one who spoke of betrayal earlier," I joke before sobering. "Who is she?"

"Someone I met in Boston while I was there last month. She actually seems … normal." The last word has a tinge of wonder to it. "Anyway, I'm considering heading up there over Easter weekend since I actually have some downtime."

"That's cool, man. I'm excited for you." Then, coming to a realization, I let out a small groan. "Easter. Can't say that I'm looking forward to that."

I had promised my mother I'd drive up for a visit. A

visit I'd been putting off for quite some time.

"Your dad's still trying to get you to follow in his footsteps, huh?"

"Yep."

My father has run his own construction company for years. His grand plan includes me taking over when he decides to retire. There's only one flaw in that plan.

I have zero interest—or desire—in doing so.

I swear that if you ask him what his son does all day at work, he'll say something about me playing video games or something. It's not as if I've never told the guy what kind of job I have—quite the opposite—but he just doesn't care to know what I do. It doesn't fit his particular mold.

And my poor mother has been in the crosshairs for years.

"Maybe you should bring Maggie home with you," Jack suggests. "She'd be a great buffer."

"Until she mentions something about you and me being together." I laugh quietly.

Jack falls silent for a moment. "It's just a thought."

After we hang up and I leave my office to head down to meet the ladies at the restaurant, I find myself mulling over Jack's thought.

* * *

"Seriously, Mags." Sarah is laughing so hard, her eyes are glistening with tears. "It's physically impossible for you to drink anything without your pinky sticking out."

Maggie, who's laughing nearly as hard, shrugs. "I can't help it. It's like maybe," she works one pinky finger up and down with a concentrated expression, "the tendons are too short or something?"

"No." Sarah immediately dismisses this theory.

Maggie offers another shrug. "I don't know what to tell you. It's just one of those things." She laughs. "Beer? Pinky out. Wine? Pinky out. Water? Pinky out. Tea? Pinky definitely out."

"What about a juice box?" I ask.

Maggie glances at Sarah before they both turn back to me and answer in unison, "Pinky out."

We all laugh, and just as it begins to fade, Sarah changes the subject. "So give us the scoop." Her eyebrows raise expectantly. "How are things with you and Sean? Have you slept with him yet?"

Of course, this would be the moment I'm chewing my loaded grilled cheese sandwich, and part of it gets lodged in my throat. Coughing violently, Sarah starts pounding on my back while Maggie looks on worriedly. Once I finally get myself under control by taking a sip of my water, I don't get much of a reprieve because Sarah starts right back up.

"Fill us in, Maggie."

With a sigh, Maggie leans in. "Things are going well. He mentioned something about bringing me home to meet his family the long weekend leading up to Eas—"

"That reminds me," I interrupt with what I hope is an easy smile. "Feel like putting on your superhero cape and rescuing me Easter weekend? I have to make a trip up to see my parents."

"Oh, Ry." Maggie's lips turn down. "You're really going?"

Lowering my gaze to the beer in front of me, I nod. "Yep."

"What's …" Sarah hesitates "…wrong with going home for a visit?"

"Oh, you know," I wave a hand dismissively, "just the fact that my father completely dismisses my job and the hard work it took to get where I am. He wants me to take over his construction business and stop," I use finger quotes, "'messing around with video games all day long.'"

Sarah draws back with a frown. "What? You don't even have anything to do with video games for your job."

I point at myself. "I know that." I point at Sarah. "You know that and," I point at Maggie, "she knows that, but somehow, he never got the memo."

"I'll go with you, Ry." My head jerks up in surprise at Maggie's quick response.

"But I thought you'd go with S—" Sarah starts.

Maggie holds up a hand. "There'll be plenty of time to meet his family. They live in Albany, not across the country. But," she gazes at me with kindness shining in her beautiful eyes, "Ry needs me more."

"I'll bet he does." Sarah's soft muttering gets my attention, and I turn to catch her eyeing me with a calculated look.

Shit. I knew it was only a matter of time. Although, never in a million years would I have expected to be upset about someone not believing I was gay. Clearly, I've sunk to new levels of low.

"Really, Ry." Maggie—thankfully oblivious to Sarah's muttering—pats my hand affectionately. "I'll go with you."

Relief pours through me. "Thanks, Mags. I can't tell you how much I appreciate it."

Standing from the table, she excuses herself to use the restroom, which isn't surprising since it's no secret that Maggie has the bladder of a field mouse.

As soon as she's far enough away from the table, Sarah leans in, eyes narrowed on me. And I know it's all over.

"Ryland James."

I feel my balls shrivel up hearing my full name spoken in that way—strict, no-nonsense, and stern-like.

"Ma'am."

Out comes the pointy index finger. In my direction, of course.

"You need to quit screwing around." She wags her finger at me. "You need to figure your shit out quick, or you're going to lose her forever."

Cautiously, I lean in closer. "Figure my shit out?"

Her eyes grow squinty. "You know what I mean."

We stare at one another for a long moment—with me refusing to budge. Finally, she casually leans back in her chair.

"So, tell me, Ry. How does it feel to take it up the ass?"

I choke on … air. That's how off-guard she catches me. Staring accusingly, I hiss, "What the hell, Sarah?"

Her expression is one of feigned innocence. "What? Is that not a normal question to ask?" Tipping her head to the side, she asks, "Specifically a man who has, allegedly, been in a sexual relationship with another man?"

I start to answer before my brain clicks, and it's like I mentally hear a *ding, ding, ding.* Because it trips over one word.

Allegedly.

My panic must be apparent because Sarah shakes her head with a little laugh. Not the kind of laugh that's easy, with humor behind it. No way. It's one of those laughs that have a bit of an edge to it. And then she says one word. One word that explains everything.

"Jack."

Fuck. Apparently, my lover had loose lips and threw me under the damn bus.

Taking it one step further, Sarah points two fingers at me before pointing them back toward her eyes. "I've got my eyes on you, buddy. Don't hurt her."

And so the charade of me pretending to be a gay man begins to crumble.

CHAPTER NINETEEN

Maggie

April

"It's so beautiful up here."

I'm looking out the window of Ry's car as we wind along the curving roads leading to Lake Placid, where his parents live.

"It's definitely beautiful when it snows." Tossing a quick glance my way before returning his attention to the road, Ry smiles over my childlike wonder at the scenery around us.

He looks unbelievably handsome in his khaki pants and simple, short-sleeved polo shirt, displaying his strong forearms. His hair is tousled, and I fight the urge to run my fingers through it; wondering how it would feel to tug on it when—

Stop it, Maggie. I feel like I need a swat from the wooden ruler on my knuckles from the nuns in Catholic school.

Repeat after me. Sean. I like Sean.

Once I chant this a few times, like a freaking mental patient, I feel like I have myself under control.

"Isn't the North Pole nearby?"

"Now, Mags. If you want to sit on a guy's lap and tell

him what a good girl you are, you don't have to go far."

"Ry." I laugh, swatting his shoulder playfully.

"To answer your question, yes. *Santa's Workshop* in the North Pole, New York, is only about twenty minutes away from my parents' place." He tosses me a look. "You want me to take you there?"

"Can we?" There's no mistaking the excitement in my voice.

"Of course. We can do whatever you want this weekend."

Anything to get away from his father. That's like the unspoken sentiment tacked on the end of his words.

As we get closer to Lake Placid, Ry makes a turn and parks the car along the street just past a sign for the LP Pub and Brewery. Turning off the ignition, he turns to me.

"You ready to have the best sandwich you've ever eaten?" The lightness in his eyes and his excited grin pulls me in.

"Absolutely."

As we exit the car and walk up to the door, he places his hand on my back, guiding me inside as we wait for a table. Once we're seated, he immediately orders a sampler of beers, and I take in the rustic inside of the restaurant.

"This has always been one of my favorite places." Ry slides one of the sample beers over to me, and he glances around while I take a sip.

"It's pretty cool."

"Just wait until you taste the Maple Melt." It appears as if he's going to elaborate but a female voice interrupts him.

"Ryland James? Is that really you?"

A tall redheaded woman is standing beside our table, hand now on Ry's forearm, and my first instinct is to swat at it. Pretty sure the only thing that stops me from doing that is when I take in Ry's expression. It's pale and almost panicked. *Odd.*

"Stacy ... hey." He rises from his seat to give her an awkward hug before he sits back down.

"Haven't seen your face in forever, stranger." Stacy smiles down at him before turning to me. "Sorry! My manners are usually better, but seeing this handsome hunk right here has thrown me off." She tosses a thumb in Ry's direction. "I'm Stacy."

"Nice to meet you, Stacy. I'm Maggie."

She smiles and then looks back and forth between us. "So are you two dating?"

"No, Mags is my best friend." Ry winks at me, and a heaviness settles in my chest at his denial.

I blame it on the elevation. We're up in the mountains so that could have something to do with it, right? Don't they call it elevation sickness? Thinner air can wreak havoc on ... people's train of thoughts and weird stuff like that. I think I read it somewhere.

Or I just pulled that out of my ass in pure desperation.

"Oh, well ..." Is it just me or did Stacy's smile get brighter? "Then maybe we can get together while you're visiting? It would be great to catch up with you."

Yep. Her smile is definitely brighter, and right hand to God, her eyes just ripped off his polo as if she were one of those dominatrix chicks in a snuff porn.

"I'll be showing Maggie around and getting some overdue time in with Mom, so I'll have to let you know."

That's a brush-off. One delivered kindly—with a sweet smile, no less—but it's a brush-off just the same. I know it, and Ry knows it.

Stacy, however, clearly doesn't catch on.

"I'll call your house and check on you in a day or so."

She gives his hand a quick squeeze. "It's so good to see you again." Turning to me, she offers a polite smile. "Great to meet you."

"You, too," I echo, watching her walk away before turning my eyes back to Ry. "Do you even realize how unfair it is that you seem to attract both men and women?"

Shaking his head with a funny look, he lets out a short laugh. "Believe me, Mags. I never realized that would even be a possibility."

"So are you going to,"—I tip my head in the direction where Stacy went—"take her up on her offer of catching up?"

He regards me carefully, not immediately answering, and my heart thuds painfully at the prospect of him saying yes.

Finally, he shakes his head slowly. "Mags, I'm here with you. There's no way I'm going to ditch you up here just to go and catch up with an old friend."

Yeah. Except for the fact that I'm pretty sure Stacy isn't just an "old friend." I'm certain she was one of the lucky ones who got to experience him before he realized he was gay. Or however that actually happened. Either way, it bums me out to think that she actually dated Ry and maybe even was his girlfriend.

Not that I want that. After all, I have Shane, right?

I mean Sean. Sean. I have *Sean*.

We've tasted the beers in the sampler, given our order choice to the waitress, and once she sets our glasses down with our food, Ry holds out his hand.

"Pen, please."

With a knowing look, I reach into my purse for a pen and hand it to him. He slides one of the fresh napkins closer.

"What's important when it comes to the special person in your life and road trips?" he muses, tapping the top of the pen to his lips in thought. Finally, he puts the pen to the napkin and writes as I peer across the table to try to see. Once he's finished writing, he slides it over to me, offering me the pen.

"Your turn."

When I read what he's written, I can't help but smile.

I want someone who wants to sit on an old man's lap.

I also want someone who loves road trips and actually enjoys being cooped up in a car with me, talking about everything and anything.

Thinking for a moment, I blush as I write:

I want the same thing but also someone who's willing to be naughty, too.

Looking up, I place the pen back in my purse and catch sight of Ry peering over at the napkin. His eyes dart up to mine, one eyebrow raised as he drags the napkin back across the table to read it.

"Ah, so someone wants a little sumpin' sumpin', do they?" His grin is wide. "You do realize that—*if* said man were in my position today—he would've likely driven off the side of the steep road and sent you both careening down the side of a mountain, crashing and burning."

"Wow. That's romantic."

Grin widening, he tosses up his hands. "What can I say? Someone's got to be the logical, level-headed one of the bunch."

"Meanwhile, I'll continue aboard the naughty train."

He laughs and raises his beer to toast me. "Toot, toot."

CHAPTER TWENTY

Ry

I t's hard to keep my eyes off Maggie. She looks incredible in a knee-length sundress the color of coral paired with a button-down cardigan sweater and some strappy sandals. Her hair is down in cascading waves, and I would give anything to slide my fingers through it.

As we walk up to my parents' home on Mirror Lake, her eyes get wider as she takes in the house I grew up in. It's pretty incredible, especially when you consider that my father and my uncle built it by hand back in the day. It's about seven thousand square feet and overlooks the lakefront. I always enjoyed sitting out on the deck and taking in the peacefulness of it.

Until my father decided I was going to be an exact replica of him. That was when this house became someplace I avoided. Like the black plague.

"Hey." Maggie reaches for my hand and gives it a squeeze. "It's going to be all right."

All I can muster is a pitiful excuse for a smile before reaching to slide my old house key in the door, only to have it swing open with my mother standing there before us. Her eyes are misty like I'm the prodigal son returning home after being gone for so long.

On second thought, it's actually pretty spot-on.

The moment she takes in the sight of Maggie's hand holding mine, her face brightens. Stepping toward us, she wraps her arms around me and squeezes me within an inch of my life. Releasing her hold, she leans back. Her hands frame the sides of my face, and she steers me down to press a kiss to my cheek.

"I've missed you, honey."

"I've missed you, too, Mom." And it's true. I have. It's been tough not visiting and only meeting her when she's down in Saratoga or passing through to meet her friends in Albany.

"Maggie," she gushes, reaching to enfold her in a hug. "I swear you get prettier every time I see you. It seems like forever since I was down in Saratoga and got to see you two."

Maggie blushes under the appraisal. "Thanks, Mrs. James."

"I've made some—"

"Is that my video gaming son at the door?" There's no way to restrain the jolt at the sound of my father's voice booming from inside.

Inhaling a deep, soothing breath, I press my lips thin. "Time to get this party started."

Maggie bumps her hip to mine and flashes me an encouraging smile. "Let's do this."

* * *

There isn't enough liquor in the world to make me numb enough to my father and his verbal digs at my career.

"You still insist on messing around with computers all day for a job?"

Jesus. He just won't quit. Mom thought it would be a good idea for us to have "guy time" out on the deck. I know she wants us to find some middle ground, but I'm convinced that it's impossible with this man.

Through clenched teeth, I explain for the millionth time, "I'm the director of infrastructure for Eastern Sports. I'm the *director*. I don't spend my time in the office playing video games. In case you're not aware"—I can't withhold the sneer in my tone—"Eastern Sports went public and is one of the highest rated, most valuable stocks out there."

He gives me nothing more than a dismissive wave. "You need to hurry up and get over your little childish tendencies and take over James Builders." With a firm nod, he says, "Now, that's a job to be proud of. Making something—building something from scratch—with raw materials. With your bare hands."

Never mind that my father oversees the business these days and hasn't laid a foundation in *years*.

Inhaling what I hope to be a deep, calming breath, I speak through clenched teeth—something that's a common occurrence when I'm around my father. "I've told you this numerous times. I'm not coming to work for you, Dad. I'm not taking over the business. I love my job."

My father makes a derisive sound. "You'll be singing a different tune when your company gets bought out, and everything goes down the drain. Then you'll be crawling back to me, begging me to have you run the company."

Jumping up from my seat, I explode. "I'm never going to work for you! I don't want to take over the company! Why can't you be proud of me? I graduated at the top of my class, got hired right out of college, and never asked you for anything! And not once—not *once*—have you ever had the decency to say, 'Hey, Ry, we're so proud of you' or 'Great job, son!' or 'Way to go in paying off your student loans, Ry.' Not one commendation. Noth—"

"You wouldn't have had to worry about student loans if you would've just come to work for me."

I feel like pulling my hair out. Like there's a distinct possibility I might. Scrubbing the heels of my palms against my eyes in aggravation before letting my hands drop, I stare at him.

"I get it." My tone is empty, devoid of emotion. "You're not happy with the choices I've made as an adult. You'll never be happy with them unless I make the choices you want me to make." Staring at him and wishing things were different, I finish, "I'm sorry, but it's obvious I'm never going to be what you want me to be, Dad."

As he sits there, staring back at me, I wait. Praying for something. An olive branch. Anything.

"Well, you're finally right about something," he spits out. "You're never going to be what I want you to be."

A stabbing pain radiates from my chest, making it hard for me to breathe, and I know I have to get away. Turning abruptly, I rush down the long set of steps leading down to the waterfront, needing to escape.

And with each step away from that deck of the house, the tightness in my chest eases even while I know a piece of my heart just broke.

CHAPTER TWENTY-ONE

Maggie

"I absolutely love your home," I can't help but gush to Ry's mother as I help her in the large kitchen. "It's beautiful."

She flashes me a kind smile. "Thank you, Maggie. My husband and his brother put a ton of work into it and made a beautiful home for us." Her head lowers as she stirs the freshly made potato salad. "We always thought we'd need a large house for the number of children we'd planned to have but …" Trailing off for a moment, her lips twist. "I had complications with Ryland, and the doctors had to do an emergency hysterectomy, so we never did get the handful of children like we'd planned. And my husband, in case you haven't noticed, is a stickler and didn't want to look into adoption."

With a wry smile, she looks up. "He put all of his hopes into Ryland, and while that's not exactly wrong, it doesn't make it right either. He wants him to follow in his footsteps."

I spoon the deviled egg mixture into each sliced half of hard-boiled egg. "Ry's really happy at his job. I can't imagine him ever wanting to leave it for the family business." Glancing up, I hastily add, "No offense," wincing at how it must have sounded.

Ry's mother smiles. "None taken, sweetie. I know exactly what you mean."

Wanting a subject change, I mention where Ry took us for lunch and running into Stacy. I know I'm digging, but I can't help it. I'm curious about Ry's earlier days.

"Ah, Stacy, yes. She owns a quaint little bakery in town. Makes such delicious things. The tourists—and locals, for that matter—go wild over her baked goods."

"So the two of them dated back in high school then?" I ask casually as I continue making the deviled eggs, and she bustles around checking the items on the stovetop and in the oven.

"Yes, they were quite the pair for a short time. But"—she peeks into the oven, lifting the glass lid of one of the large dishes before closing it, setting her pot holders down on the counter—"Stacy always had her sights on staying here and, well, Ry ..." She turns to face me, leaning back against the countertop. "Ry always wanted more—wanted something bigger. Heck, he was the one who raised money for an addition to their playground at school when he was in the fourth grade. Because he was certain the other kids needed more options, like a climbing wall, knotted rope climb, and some other things I can't recall." She looks off with a smile on her face, caught up in memories. "He asked me to help him set up a lemonade stand to raise money and even made sure to have a sugar-free lemonade option." She laughs.

"That's Ry. Ever the businessman." I smile, imagining the cute little boy wanting to do so much for others even at an early age. We stand there, each of us with large smiles on our faces until a timer goes off. She turns off one of the burners on the stove and carries a large pot to the sink, pouring it into a colander already placed there.

"Anyway, Stacy wanted Ry to stay here, and we all knew she wanted him to commit—to marry her—but it wasn't going to happen. The writing was on the wall. They parted ways—amicably, of course. Ry applied to colleges and universities away from here, holding out hope that he'd get into Boston University."

"And he did," I finish.

"Sure did." Mrs. James smiles with pride. "He got a full scholarship, and as soon as he finished his degree, he immediately enrolled in graduate school. And of course, as soon as he graduated with that degree, Eastern Sports hired him.

"Ryland would come back to visit periodically until a few years ago. He and his father got into a huge argument the day after Christmas, and something just snapped." Her expression fills with palpable remorse. "He started meeting with me when I would pass through Saratoga and would only drive up for a few hours on Christmas. Because inevitably"—her frown deepens—"his father would badger him."

Finished with the deviled eggs, I put the lid on the container, placing them in the refrigerator. "So then Ry must have changed his mind about dating Stacy and other women pretty late in the game," I muse, as if I'm not totally digging for information as to when it became clear that Ry preferred men to women.

Mrs. James looks at me oddly, so I decide to direct the conversation toward Jack. "So when did he and Jack meet? I don't think I've ever heard that story."

She laughs. "Ah, yes. Jack." Shaking her head with a smile, the corners of her eyes crinkle. "Ry met Jack at the university around the time when he was considering pledging a fraternity. Jack, although a year ahead of him, was the same age and looked completely different back then. Shaggy, unkempt hair, big glasses, baggy pants, and a beat-up T-shirt. He was the epitome of a nerd." She breaks off into laughter. "I remember when Ry brought him home for the first time. I think I stood at the door in shock, my jaw on the floor.

"He stayed with us for a long weekend, and Ry ultimately strong-armed his new friend into updating his wardrobe and getting a haircut. Basically, Ry didn't have room for much of his clothes in his dorm room, so they went to Jack as they were roughly the same size." She glances up at me. "You'd never guess it looking at him today, would you?"

Stunned, I shake my head slowly. "Not in a million."

She grins. "They both pledged the same fraternity and have been best friends—inseparable ever since."

Best friends, huh? Guess Mrs. James is in denial. Either that or she doesn't realize that Ry pledged more than a fraternity with Jack. Likely, he pledged a whole hell of a lot more.

Ahem, ahem. Wink, wink.

Suddenly, loud voices from outside interrupt us. Rushing over to the oversized windows in the kitchen, Mrs. James and I see Ry and his father arguing outside. Finally, Ry storms off and down the long set of stairs leading to the lakefront.

"Oh, dear." Mrs. James wrings her hands with worry.

"Should I …"

She grasps my hand. "Just give him a moment, Maggie. He likely needs to be alone down there. By the time dinner is ready, he'll be all right."

When dinnertime comes, the conversation is stilted, proving Mrs. James' prediction wrong.

So very wrong.

* * *

After everyone bids each other good night, I close the bedroom door softly with a click and rest my forehead against it. Releasing a part weary sigh, part huff of laughter, I let my eyes fall closed as an anxiousness settles over me.

I need to do it. I have to call Sean.

Slowly lowering myself to the bed, I swipe the keypad of my cell phone until my thumb rests over his name. After a millisecond of hesitation, I press the key, waiting to hear the dialing.

The moment he answers, I know I've made the right choice.

"Hey."

My brows instantly furrow because of the sound in the background. You know when you see a dog's ears perk at a certain sound? That's how I imagine mine are right now. Because in the background is a distinctive female voice. As if that's not enough, the owner of the voice is requesting that he "come back to bed."

Mmmmmkay. I'm done here.

"Yeah, so, I was just going to say that something's come up and I don't think I can see you again." After a beat, I hastily add, "But I'm pretty sure you're good with that, so I'm gonna go now. Bye."

I press the button to end the call before Sean can even respond. Because I know whatever he says won't be something I want to hear.

Throwing myself back on the bed with a huff of breath, I stare up at the ceiling.

I've done it. I've cut ties with Sean. That's not the worst part, though. My ego has taken more of a hit tonight than anything has. In the past few months we've been dating, I hadn't wanted to admit to the fact that something has been holding me back from taking our relationship to the next level.

And apparently, right along the lines of my creepy, internal foreboding, he'd had enough and began sticking it to some other woman. Talk about a blow to the ol' Magster's ego.

Great. As if things couldn't possibly get worse, I'm also referring to myself in the third person.

Brilliant.

CHAPTER TWENTY-TWO

Ry

A shower didn't help, regardless of my attempts at scrubbing away my father's words. Slipping on a pair of pajama pants but not bothering with a shirt, I glance toward my bed, knowing I'll only end up tossing and turning.

Everyone's in their bedrooms, fast asleep, and as I creep past the spare bedroom Maggie is staying in, I fight the urge to knock. It would be selfish of me to wake her just for a damn hug.

Not to mention, pathetic as hell.

Slipping outside, I step onto the darkened deck lit only by dim lantern-style lights along the perimeter and stairs, and I welcome the faint chill of the night air upon my skin.

Descending the steps leading down to the waterfront and our dock, I barely notice the slight chill from the smooth, oversized paving stones beneath my bare feet. Once I arrive at the dock, I open the door to the large boathouse and pull one of the cushioned chairs out. Lowering myself into it, I face the water.

Gazing out onto the lake that's reflecting the light of the moon like glass, I recall just how many times this very spot has been my safe haven, of sorts. Far too many to count.

When will I get it through my damn head that my father will never accept me as I am? His love for me is conditional; in order to gain it, I have to give up everything I love and everything that ultimately makes me, me.

Letting out a frustrated grunt, I rise from the chair. Walking over to the railing of the dock, I lean my forearms on it. I'm unsure of how long I stand here, gazing sightlessly over the expanse of the lake before picking up on the sound of light footfalls behind me. Tensing, I pray it isn't my father because, at this rate, I think I'd likely drown myself in the lake just to get away from his badgering.

"Ry?"

Maggie's voice carries over to me, its soft, tentative quality easing a bit of the tension in my back. I feel terrible for inviting her up here and then subjecting her to my family drama.

"Hey."

I expect her to come up and stand beside me, so it's difficult to withhold my surprised jolt when she wraps her arms around me from behind, hugging me, her breasts pressed against my spine. We stand like this for a long moment before I quietly admit, "I'm really not the greatest company right now, Mags."

Her lips press against my back, and I swear I can feel the kiss go straight to my heart as she whispers, "You're incredible, Ry. Don't ever forget it."

With a brief, derisive snort, I shake my head. "My father would be the first to disagree with you on that."

"Screw him." Her warm breath washes against my bare skin with her mumbled response.

Bringing my hand up to cover one of hers over my chest, a ghost of a smile forms on my lips. "Thanks, Mags."

We stand in silence for an indeterminable amount of

time before I notice a shiver run through Maggie at the cool breeze, which has begun coming off the lake. Turning around, I scoop her up, snagging a throw blanket from inside the doorway of the boathouse before walking back over to the chair and settling her on my lap. As she curls up on my lap, her head on my chest, I tuck the blanket around her.

One of her hands is splayed flat against my chest as we sit there listening to the quiet night. I'm not sure how long we sit before I realize that—with Maggie in my arms—my tension and stress have eased. Having her here with me is a soothing balm after everything my father verbally inflicted upon me earlier. And the reason I feel calmer, the reason my pain has eased, is likely because I have the most import-ant person in my life in my arms.

Running a hand along her blanketed back, I dip my head to press a kiss to the top of her head. With my lips still pressed against her silky hair, my eyes fall closed.

"I love you, Mags."

My voice is hushed, and especially right now, I mean those words more than she could possibly imagine.

"Love you, too, Ry." Her whispered words wash over me, and not for the first time, do I wish with everything I have that she meant them. That she would feel the same way.

That she would love me the way that I love her.

* * *

Making our way back up to the house, Maggie slips her hand in mine as we ascend the steps, quietly entering the house and closing the door behind us. Climbing the stairs to head to our bedrooms, I stop at her door and drop her hand.

"Thanks, Mags. For everything tonight." My fingers twitch in my attempts at restraining from tugging her to me and sliding my arms around her because I'm not sure I could let go.

I sure as hell don't ever want to.

"Good night." Turning away, I make it the few feet across the hall to my room, as she murmurs softly, "Good night, Ry."

Softly closing my door, I slide into bed, lying on my back with my hands behind my head and find myself wishing my bedroom door would crack open. Wish that I didn't have to fall asleep alone tonight.

With a derisive sound, I scold myself as my eyes fall closed. *You're a grown man, Ry. So you've had a shitty day. Doesn't mean you can't fall asleep without your "security blanket." Man up, for God's sake.*

Inhaling deeply, I silently remind myself that I shouldn't be acting this pathetic.

At the sound of the doorknob turning, my eyes fly open, and I stare as the door slowly opens.

"Ry?" Maggie's tentative tone draws me from my surprised daze. Because, hell, it's almost like she magically showed up the moment I wished for her.

She's standing with the door cracked partially open, her head peeking around it, and even in the dark room, only lit by streams of moonlight, I can detect the uncertainty etched on her face.

Wordlessly flipping back the covers, I slide over to make more room for her. The door closes with a soft click, and within a moment, she takes two quick steps before vaulting herself onto the mattress, making it bounce.

Laughing softly, I tug her to me, gazing down into her

smiling face and smoothing some strands of hair back from her forehead that were displaced. "That was impressive. Form still needs work, though."

Her lips form a dramatic pout. "I thought that at least warranted an eight point nine, buddy."

"Nope. Definitely a five point four."

Her palm flies out to shove me playfully. Falling onto my back, I take her with me, both of us smiling at one another. Her hair falls loosely around her face, and the ends tickle my shoulders.

And just like out on the dock earlier, Maggie knows what I need most.

Her.

CHAPTER TWENTY-THREE

Maggie

Reaching up, Ry smooths my hair back from my face, cradling my face, expression sobering. "Mags ..." He trails off.

"I know."

Dipping my head to brush my lips softly against the corners of his, his eyes fall shut. As if, although it's in no way passionate, my kiss went straight to his heart. When I press my lips to the opposite corner, his eyes open.

My breath lodges in my throat at his expression, the way his eyes lock on my lips. It seems like everything happens in slow motion, my head descending to press my lips softly against his. Except this time, it's not playful or meant to be comforting. It's ... different.

It's *more*.

As though Ry's paralyzed, he still doesn't move a muscle.

Mumbling softly against my lips, he says one word. "Sean?"

My eyes hold his, and I whisper, "We're over." After a millisecond pause, I have to ask. "You really have an open relationship?" *With Jack?* I tack on silently.

Once he nods, my lips dust over his tentatively—once,

twice, three times—until suddenly, everything changes. Ry's fingers entwine in my hair, angling my head to press closer as his lips feverishly move against my own. The moment my tongue slides between his parted lips to taste him, I hear the low growl rumbling from deep within him before he flips us so that I'm trapped beneath him.

My tank top has ridden up from the movement, and the feel of my bare stomach against his is nearly my undoing. As my breasts press against his bare chest, there's no mistaking the hardening of my nipples. My thighs instantly part for him, and at the feel of his arousal through the thin fabric of his pajama pants, arousal floods through me.

And absolutely shamelessly, I arch my hips, rocking against him. The moment he hears my muted moan, it's like his hands have a mind of their own, slipping beneath the fabric of my tank top and sliding it up farther to bare my breasts. Breaking the kiss, Ry lifts up on his arms, gazing down at me. His eyes travel from my lips, which I'm certain are glossy from our kiss, down to my hardened nipples.

"Perfect."

That one word, uttered so tenderly, sends waves of ardent need flowing through me. Reaching up, I slide my palm against his cheek, now covered with light stubble; his eyes darken before turning his head to press a kiss to the center of my palm. The action makes my heart jump, and it's at that particular moment that I throw caution to the wind, tugging his head down to me for a devouring kiss.

The pad of his thumb grazes over the tip of one nipple, and I arch into his touch, wanting—needing—more. He swallows my moan, continuing to toy with my nipple before he breaks the kiss. Dipping his head, he latches his lips onto my hardened peak.

"Ry," I gasp.

His tongue and lips drive me mad with desire, and I can't stop rocking against his cock, the tip pressing right where I want it most. He seems to know what I need, his lips returning to mine as I arch against his firm body, against his prodding hardness. I don't even care that my shorts are damp from my own arousal. Ry gives short thrusts against me, his cock hitting my clit, and my fingers grasp at the flexing muscles in his arms as I gasp at the sensations rolling through me.

The instant my orgasm hits, my back arches, toes curling as my inner muscles clench and release, and Ry's mouth stifles my loud moan. He gives two hard thrusts against me, his body stiffening before he slumps against me. Our lips part and he drops a kiss against my neck, still bracing some of his weight on his forearms.

"Shit," he mumbles against my skin.

At his words, I tense because I realize just what we did. What I did. God. I'm the one who crept into Ry's room, catapulted myself into his bed, intent on offering him comfort. And what did I do? Oh, not too much.

Except for the fact that I just *freaking molested the hell out of him.*

And came in my shorts.

Lovely. Just, lovely.

How does one even begin to apologize for something like this? I mean, really. Not like I can just casually toss out, "Hey, um, about what just happened. The whole using your cock—which feels pretty magnificent, by the way—as my personal sex toy? Mmm, sorry about that."

Except that I'm not really sorry. At all. Because it was *hot.*

Oh, my gosh. I'm a terrible person. A terrible friend. I'm like pond scum. Or that annoying tree sap that gets on your car and takes just about everything short of turpentine to remove it. But you have to remove it because, otherwise, it'll ruin your car's paint job.

Wow. That was way too entailed. Clearly, I have issues with tree sap.

And also with coming all over my roommate and best friend.

There's likely a special place in hell for people like me. Like, maybe they have a little nook that's specifically designated for "Those decrepit, soulless individuals who orgasm all over people who mean the most to them and also have serious issues with tree sap."

With my eyes pinched shut, I force myself to speak in the quiet of the bedroom with nothing but the sound of our breathing slowly calming.

"Uh, Ry, I ..." *Crap.* Inhaling deeply, my speech is hurried, and my words run together. "I'm sorry. Forusingyourcockandcomingalloveryou."

My apology is met with silence, and it takes a moment before I realize Ry's shoulders are shaking. Raising his head, his eyes meet mine, crinkling with laughter, lips quirked in a grin.

"Mags."

Biting the edge of my bottom lip, I'm hesitant. "Ry?"

His grin widens. "You weren't alone." Resting his forehead against mine, he whispers, "I haven't had anyone make me come in my pants in years, Mags. *Years.*"

Whoa. I hadn't realized that. "I'm just that good, huh?"

Raising back up, he shakes his head at me. "Don't get cocky."

"But we could actually say that I just *got* cocky, though, can't we?"

He chuckles at my play on words, smiling down at me

for a moment before his expression sobers, and I know where he's heading with his thoughts even before he speaks.

"Are we okay, Mags?" His eyes search mine. "I don't want this to be weird. I mean"—he breaks off, looking away—"we got caught up in the moment." The way he says the last part, more mumbled, sounds reluctant. Like he's tossing out a reason that's not entirely true. Or heartfelt.

"We're okay," I answer softly, wishing he would look at me. I know we crossed a line, and while I can't deny the tinge of awkwardness present, I want to dismiss it. I need to ensure that our friendship doesn't change.

His head turns, eyes finding mine once again, and I'm taken aback by the intensity of his gaze. His lips part, and it looks as if he's going to speak but falters. Lips pressing thin, he offers a brief, tight smile.

"I have to get cleaned up." Winking playfully, he slides off me, walking to his adjoining bathroom. "Since someone decided to take advantage of me." Grabbing one of the bed pillows, I toss it at him, but it falls short, his laughter fading as he closes the bathroom door behind him.

Staring up at the ceiling, I barely register the sound of water running in the bathroom as thoughts race through my mind.

What the hell is happening to me?

What just happened crossed so many lines, yet ... I don't regret it.

What happened was unbelievably hot. And my reaction to Ry's kiss was so different from Sean's.

Sean. Not once did he cross my mind. Not. Once.

Maggie, Maggie, Maggie. You know what that means.

Then a dawning realization hits me. I turned Ry on—that much was evident. I mean he came in his pants, for crying out loud. But he's never once mentioned anything about being bisexual. All he's ever talked about has been Jack. I mean, sure, I get that he once dated girls in high school—specifically, Stacy—but it was likely before he truly "came out," right?

Fingertips massaging my temples, I'm suddenly facing the realization that I'm caught in a crazy situation. One I'm not even entirely sure I understand.

But the moment the bathroom door opens and a freshly showered Ry exits, a towel wrapped around his waist as he walks to his small bag to retrieve a pair of boxers, his body so finely muscled and toned, I'm faced with something I can no longer deny.

I'm developing those more-than-friends feelings for my gay roommate.

CHAPTER TWENTY-FOUR

Ry

The faint tapping at my bedroom door rouses me from sleep. Lifting my head, it takes me a moment to realize that an arm draped across my chest traps me, holding tight. Gazing down at a sleeping Maggie, I can't resist grazing my fingertips along her cheek, mesmerized by how peaceful she appears.

The tapping sounds again, and I gently ease from Maggie's grasp and head over to the door. Cracking it open, I see my mother standing on the other side.

"I just wanted to let you know that I'm about to start breakfast." Her voice is hushed, and she tips her head to the side. "I didn't get an answer when I tapped on Maggie's door."

Shit.

I search for the words. "She's, uh …" I tip my head, gesturing toward the bed. "She had trouble sleeping." My eyes close on a wince. That didn't sound the least bit legitimate.

Braving a look at my mother, she appears to be fighting back a grin. "Well, if you can tell her to be sure to bring her appetite to breakfast, that would be great."

"Will do, Mom." Kill me now.

She turns away as I shut the door quietly, leaning my

forehead against it. How is it that my mother can still manage to make me feel like a teenage boy?

"Morning." Maggie's husky greeting turns my attention her way, and my chest tightens as I take her in, rumpled with a case of bedhead and a sleepy smile on her face.

"Morning."

"Guess I should get cleaned up for breakfast." Swinging her legs over the side of the mattress, she slides off to stand. "Don't want her getting any more ideas."

Maggie slips around me, a hand on the doorknob when I snag her wrist, tugging her close for a hug. Pressing a quick kiss to the top of her head, I whisper, "Thanks, Mags."

Leaning away, her eyes meet mine as she smiles up at me sweetly. "Anytime."

When the door closes behind her, I lean my back against it. Because I'm so screwed, not to mention, I'm also a dumbass.

I have to figure out a way to solve the fact that I've done something I never imagined was possible.

I've cock blocked myself.

* * *

"Look at them! They're amazing!"

Maggie's excited remarks make me smile as I watch her take in the sight of a few young girls who are figure skating in the indoor ice rink at the Olympic Center. They're not much older than eight years of age and have likely been training from the time they started walking. Watching them spin and jump on the ice is nothing short of impressive.

I've been showing Maggie some sights around Main Street. As we exit the Olympic Center after visiting the attached museum, I hold the door open for her.

123

Walking along the sidewalk, Maggie stops me in front of a small shop, which has a little wooden toboggan with the Olympic logo painted on the side for people to pose in for photos.

"Will you take a photo with me?" Her eyes sparkle with excitement, and there's no way I can deny her anything when she looks at me like this.

"Sure, Mags." I climb in, trying to slide my long legs out of the way so that she can situate herself between them. She pulls out her cell phone, changing the camera to selfie mode, and offers it to me. I know the drill since she's always telling me I have "longer arms" and, therefore, take better selfies.

She leans back into my chest, and we both smile as I press the button a few times to capture the pictures. Handing her phone back, I wait for her to glance through them and give them the okay. With her hand cupped around the screen to try to diminish some of the glare from the sun, she falters at the sight of one of the photos. Growing still, she draws my concern.

"What's wrong?"

The glare of the sun prevents me from deciphering anything on the screen of her phone.

Turning her head, her eyes meet mine. "I really like this one." She hands the phone to me.

Flashing her an odd look, I glance down at the photo and see our faces smiling wide, happy and, dare I say, looking like we're meant to be together? I stare at the photo so long that I have to swipe my thumb across it when the screen begins to time out, just to look a moment longer. Because we look like one of those happy couples.

No. That's not entirely true. We look like one of those happy couples, madly in love.

Raising my eyes to meet Maggie's, I say, "This is a total framer, Mags. I want one for my office at work."

"Yeah?" Her face lights up and her lips curve into a wide, happy smile.

"Definitely." My eyes drop to her lips, and when her tongue darts out to wet them, it takes everything I have to stifle my groan.

"Hey, you two!"

Maggie and I jump apart, interrupted by the energetic greeting. Turning, I see Stacy standing nearby, eyeing us curiously. Maggie scrambles to stand, exiting the tobog-gan as I try everything in my power—including thinking of such things as having to one day endure a colonoscopy, old, wrinkly, saggy women skinny dipping, and my parents having sex—to deflate my hard-on. Once I've succeeded, I rise, stepping out of the toboggan and onto the sidewalk beside Maggie.

"Hey, Stacy."

"You guys enjoying your day?" Stacy smiles, turning toward Maggie. It's not hard to miss the way her eyes take in Maggie's form, as if assessing her attire and finding her subpar.

"Absolutely!" Maggie nods enthusiastically. "Ry's been showing me around and this place," she waves her arm to encompass the downtown area, "is so cute. There's so much to see."

Stacy's eyes flicker to me. "You should stop in the shop. I'll be sure to have your favorite ready for you."

"Oh, that's right. Ry's mom mentioned you own a shop down here," Maggie says.

"Stacy owns Sweet Sensations bakery. She's had it for about," I turn a questioning gaze to Stacy, "how long now?"

"It's been opened for about eight years now." Stacy's

eyes fall on Maggie. "I make his favorite dessert."

"It doesn't happen to have chunks of peanut butter and chocolate in it, does it?" Maggie grins.

In a staged whisper, I pat my flat stomach. "As if I would eat that garbage."

Maggie knocks her shoulder into me, grinning. "Whatever. I've seen you dipping a chunk of dark chocolate into the peanut butter at home."

Aghast and with a mock indignation, I say, "I know not what you—"

"You live together?" Stacy interrupts.

With an easy smile, Maggie answers, "Ry and I have been living together for a while now."

It doesn't escape my attention that she doesn't specify that we're only roommates.

And that, in itself, makes the tiniest bit of hope unfurl in my chest.

CHAPTER TWENTY-FIVE

Maggie

D o you know those memes or GIFs where someone's quoted as saying, "Oh, no you di'int!"? Well,
that just happened.

In my mind. Like I totally finger snapped in a *Z* forma-
tion at Stacy. Twice. Once was for her little scan of my outfit
and clearly dismissing me as not good enough; the second
was the moment she discovered that Ry and I live together—have been living together. She did this little squinty
thing with her eyes, and her nose wrinkled the slightest bit
like she'd just tasted something bad.

She tasted me. Wait, no. That sounds weird. She tasted
more confirmation that Ry is *not* hers. He's mine.

Um, I mean … *Crap*. My mind is so convoluted right
now. The truth is I want Ry to be mine. Even though it's not
possible. Even though last night was a total odd, how-did-
that-happen, oh-we-just-got-carried-away kind of thing.

Doesn't mean I'm not channeling my inner mean girl
right now. Like in the movie, aptly named, *Mean Girls*, I'm
channeling my inner Regina George.

Minus about ninety-nine point nine percent of the
bitchiness, though. Which means that, basically, I'm lame.

"So you make desserts? That sounds so cool."

Confidently—and casually—I link my arm through Ry's, tipping my face up to his. "We should definitely stop in and check it out."

He's peering down at me with the slightest grin that seems to say, *I know what you're up to.* "Sure, Mags. If that's what you'd like to do."

Of course, that's what I want to do. Go and taste desserts at Ry's ex-girlfriend's shop. The same ex-girlfriend who clearly didn't get the memo—or shredded it, perhaps—that he's gay. And doesn't have any desire to move back here.

Sounds like a grand ol' time, right?

* * *

I take it back. All of it.

It was a *great* choice to come here. Brilliant, in fact.

"This. Is. So. Gooooood," I moan to Ry, who's sitting at the small round table across from me. He looks amused by my moan-speak.

"Glad you approve."

"You've got to taste this." Reaching out, I raise the strawberry covered in chocolate and peanut butter to his lips. "Seriously. It's like an orgasm in your mouth."

His eyes meet mine, and at that moment, I know he remembers what happened last night. Leaning in, gaze still locked with my own, he murmurs, "I *do* love an orgasm in my mouth," before wrapping his lips around the tip of the strawberry and taking a bite.

I'm sorry, but did my panties just go *poof*? Up in smoke? Because the look in his eyes made my hoo-ha feel like it was on fire.

Ummmm, not like *that* because that would mean something was seriously wrong. Like in the form of the clap or something. And just *ewww*, right?

But the moment his lips wrap around that strawberry—and he has nicer lips than any guy I've ever known—I feel it. That tingling arousal, down deep. Which makes my mind go where it has no business going.

To the gutter. We all know nothing good can come from going there. *Shame.* Oh, the *shaaaaame.*

"My eyes are up here, Mags." Ry's voice makes me aware that I've been, uh, staring at him. More importantly, at his crotch. My eyes fly up to meet his smiling ones, and I feel the rush of heat on my cheeks.

"I was totally zoning out. Sorry." *Lame excuse, Maggie. So lame.*

"Lost in thoughts about …" One eyebrow rises in question.

Shoving another peanut butter and chocolate covered strawberry at him, I give him my best squinty-eyed look. "Hush and take a bite."

Fingers encircling my wrist, he holds me captive while wrapping his lips around the strawberry, brushing against the tips of my fingers still holding it. The touch of his lips against my fingers combined with the look in his eyes makes me inhale sharply, recalling the way his mouth felt on my nipples.

Watching me while he chews slowly, the corners of his eyes crinkle, and his eyes flash with amusement. Then he leans back in. "Are you chilly?" His eyes drop to my breasts before rising to meet my eyes, again.

Slapping an arm across my chest, I fix a glare on him. "Yes."

"Mmmhmm." He sits back in his seat, lips stretching into a smug grin.

Pointing my fork at him as I anticipate digging into the

chocolate peanut butter cake, I threaten, "Don't even start or I won't share."

"As if you could deny me?" His eyes go wide with mock dismay.

Before I can answer, Stacy interrupts us.

"Are you enjoying everything?" Is it just me or is she standing a little too close to Ry? I mean, really. Any closer and she'd be in his lap, for God's sake. My grip on my fork gets tighter, and I realize that feeling I'm experiencing.

I'm feeling stabby. Literally. Like, in my mind, I imagine her hand reaching over to touch Ry's muscled arm just as my own arm shoots out, the tines of my fork meeting the flesh of her hand.

Whoa. That was pretty graphic. Sheesh. I'm starting to fear that I'll end up on that TV show *Snapped*.

Maybe I need more sugar, and this weird jealousy thing will subside. Forking a piece of the cake into my mouth, as soon as the flavors hit my tongue, there's absolutely no way I can refrain from moaning.

Bliss. Pure, unadulterated bliss.

And I make a decision right then and there that Stacy needs to live and needs her hands to continue making these deliciously decadent treats.

Dang it.

Back to the drawing board.

CHAPTER TWENTY-SIX

Ry

"I'm a heifer. It's confirmed."

Maggie's been groaning as we walk along the sidewalk after spending far too much time in Stacy's shop. She's been trudging along, hand over her stomach.

"You're not a heifer."

"I am. I'm enormous now. I can feel it. My thighs? They just melded together." She begins walking funny, and I roll my eyes.

"Mags"—I grab her hand—"you need to sit for a moment?"

We're walking through the park that faces part of the lakefront on our way back to my parents' house. A vacant bench has a bit of shade from the nearby tree.

"*Yessss*, please."

Walking over, Maggie immediately slumps onto the bench, hands on her stomach with a groan. "I have a food baby." She pushes out her stomach, rounding it before letting it deflate. "Nearly five months along, by the looks of it."

Rolling my eyes, I sling an arm around her shoulders as we sit, relaxing, with nothing but the sounds of bustling activity surrounding us. Shoppers, tourists, people enjoying the water, out kayaking on the lake. It's a gorgeous day and, luckily, stress-free since we've been away from the house and—more importantly—my father.

"I kind of don't want to go back."

Turning at Maggie's softly spoken words, I take in her profile as her eyes remain on the lakefront before us. Her long hair is pulled back in one of those loopy ponytail things, and she's a bit flushed from the warm weather. She looks happy, sated, and while much of that reason may be the indulging of sweets we just partook in, I'd like to think some of it is because she's here with me. God, I could stare at her forever.

Yeah, that was creepy as shit. But I don't care. When Maggie is happy, it makes *me* happy.

"Right now is just … perfect." She turns to me, the gentle breeze tousling some strands of my hair. "You know?"

Reaching out to tuck the stray strands behind her ear, I nod. "I know."

She leans her head against me, and we sit there, gazing out at the lake, not speaking but enjoying each other's presence.

It's just as Maggie said. Right now is perfect. Because I'm with the one I love.

Now if only I can get her to love me back.

* * *

I'm walking down the hallway toward the kitchen when I hear my mother and Maggie talking quietly. The hushed tone of Maggie's voice makes me slow, pausing at the edge of the doorway and eavesdropping like a little kid.

"Do you mind if I ask about Ry and his …" She trails off, and it's evident in her hesitation that she's unsure of how to ask her question. "About Ry and when he decided to come out?"

My entire body jolts in alarm. Like Sylvester the cat in those old cartoons where he gets electrocuted—every hair standing on end, entire body stiff as a board—during one of the many times he's chasing after Tweety Bird, the damn bird outsmarting him yet again. That's me right now. Frozen in horror and panic combined. Because I've been so worried about my father that I didn't take into account the chance that Maggie might ask my mother about my sexuality.

"I'm not sure what you mean, honey." My mother's confusion is clear in her voice.

"Oh, I'm sorry. I just thought you—"

"RYLAND!" My father's booming voice draws my eavesdropping to a screeching halt. Jerking around, I see him not but a few feet away in the entrance to the living room.

Stepping around, now in plain sight of Maggie and my mother in the kitchen, out of the corner of my eye, I notice them exchanging a worried look. Likely because my father looks pissed.

But there's nothing new there. If only I could make a living off that, I'd be a shoo-in for one of the top earners in *Forbes* magazine. Actually, now that I think of it, if being a world-class dick to your kid were something he could medal in in the Olympics, he'd be undefeated and bring home the gold.

Every. Four. Years.

"Yes." I don't phrase it as a question but as more of a resigned *Fuck my life* kind of way.

He gives me one of those head-nod gestures, telling me to follow him as he walks into the living room. With each step closer to him, my feet feel like they get heavier, more sluggish with dread. As if I'm trudging through wet cement.

Because the fact that my father wants to speak with me is never a good thing. Never. In fact, it would probably be better if we never spoke and, instead, just exchanged sign language.

Uh, yeah. Maybe not even that. Because the only sign language I see us utilizing would be flipping each other the bird.

Coming to a stop about two feet away from him, I do my best to maintain eye contact. You know, in all the books I've read, before graduating and while working for Eastern Sports, body language and displays of assertiveness and an air of authority are stressed. Yeah, I swear I forget every single damn thing I've learned and utilized over the years in the presence of this man.

Forcing myself to straighten my posture even more, I fold my arms across my chest and look him head-on. He stares at me, and I wait for him to start up with the usual: to badger me about my job and the overall path I've chosen for my life.

He glances past me quickly before his eyes return to rest on me, lowering his voice. "What the hell's the deal with Maggie?"

Brows furrowed, I frown in confusion because I have no clue what he's asking. "What do you mean?"

His expression turns hard. "I mean what the hell are you doing with that girl?"

Still confused, I shake my head. "I'm not doing any-thing with her."

"Bullshit."

"Whatever." I don't need this shit. Turning away, he stops me in my tracks with his next words.

"She's in love with you."

I can only manage to stare at him dumbfounded. "What?"

"You heard me." He gestures in the direction of the kitchen. "You think I'm stupid because I don't have a fancy piece of paper saying I'm smart, but I know enough that you're up to something."

Throwing up a hand, I protest, "She doesn't think of me as more than a friend!"

Fuck. Just admitting aloud that Maggie doesn't love me in that way cuts deep.

Shaking my head, I feel my blood pressure rise, getting more pissed off at his words. "And you know very well I've never once said or implied you were stupid, Dad. I don't care that you didn't go to college. But you, apparently, have a huge issue with the fact that I did!"

"I just want what's best for you!"

"Well, it's not building shit with my bare hands!" I explode. "It's never been what I wanted to do with my life! But you refuse to see that!" Attempting to calm myself, I inhale deeply. "I loved working with you when I was younger because we actually did things together. That's what I enjoyed, Dad. I didn't actually enjoy the act itself—I enjoyed being with *you.*"

My words appear to deflate him, his shoulders sinking, his entire expression wiped clean. But I'm not finished.

"I'm good at what I do, Dad. And it's sure as hell not sitting in front of a monitor playing damn video games all day. I am the director of my department, and I love what I do; I love the technology I work with each day. I solve problems and refine procedures to make them even better. I use my"—I tap my index finger against my temple—"brain. Every. Single. Day."

Feeling as though I'm running out of steam, I shake my head, glancing away. "All I want is for you to be proud of me. I'm not in jail, not addicted to drugs, and not on the streets. I'm Ry, a good guy—a good son—who has worked hard to make something of himself. Someone you should be proud to call your son."

When he still says nothing, I run a hand wearily over my face. "Never mind," I mutter, turning to head toward the kitchen, in the direction of the two people I know actually *like* me.

"Wait."

I freeze at his quiet command. Not because he told me to wait but because of the way he just said it. There's something underlying there in his tone. Remorse?

Inwardly, I snort at that, instantly dismissing it. There's no way in hell my father—

"Ryland, I'm ..." He trails off, and it's only then that I turn to face him. "I'm sorry."

They always say that it takes a big man—or woman, for that matter—to admit fault. And it's true. My father's a proud man and this? This is huge. Which means I have to look around in fear for lightning to strike.

"Don't be a smartass." He glares at me, knowing what I'm doing, but I see the gleam in his eyes.

Nodding slowly, I'm almost afraid to break the moment. "Thanks."

We stare at one another for a beat, and just when it gets to the point of being uncomfortable, my father tosses his hands up. "Well, don't just stand there making googly eyes at me. Get two beers and join me on the deck so we can talk about which buyout of my business I should accept."

Stunned, it takes me a split second to realize what's going on. My father actually wants to ... talk with me.

Holy shit. Has something happened to my father that's somehow made him soften?

"Don't make me change my mind," he grunts, turning on his heel and heading for the deck.

Nope. Nix that last thought. No fear of this guy softening.

He pauses with his handle on the door leading to the deck. "Don't think I've forgotten about the other thing." There's a beat of silence. "With Maggie." He exits, closing the door behind him.

Blowing out a long breath, it whooshes out. Of course, he wouldn't forget about that little detail. Shit.

This means I'm going to have to come clean to my father. About my lies, which have snowballed. To the point where I don't know how to get out from under any of it.

And about being gay, yet *not* being gay.

Fuck. I've managed to confuse even myself with that one.

Doesn't mean that I don't have a much lighter step as I approach the kitchen to get the beers. Because something's happened, and I'm not going to look a gift horse in the mouth.

I might just get something out of this Easter weekend.

I might just get my dad back in my life—as the father I've always wished for.

A supporter.

CHAPTER TWENTY-SEVEN

Maggie

"You're awfully quiet over there." I peer curiously over at Ry as he concentrates on driving along the winding roads on our way back to Saratoga. He has that crease between his brows, lips pressed thin as if he's lost in thought.

And it doesn't appear as though they're happy thoughts.

"Just thinking about some things my dad said when we talked."

I wait, gazing at him, and wait some more. Until, finally, I realize that he doesn't plan to elaborate.

"*Aaaaand?*"

Ry glances toward me briefly. "And nothing. I'm just mulling things over right now." I allow my eyes to take in the deeper tan he got from when he took me kayaking and our many walks through downtown Lake Placid. The bridge of his nose is ever so slightly pink, and I have the strangest urge to press a light kiss to it.

Okay, so now I'm channeling my inner nursemaid? *Oooookay, Maggie.* Next, I'll be imagining myself in a sexy nurse's outfit with Ry bending me over an examination table and—

Whoa. *Whoooaaa.* Maybe it's this upper elevation

making me have these dirty thoughts about starring in my own cheesy porno or something.

Or maybe it's the hot guy sitting beside you in the car? Maybe that's it? Maybe he'd like it if my hand slid over to his lap and—

And, there she is, ladies and gentlemen. My inner dirty whore making a guest appearance.

Isn't that just splendid?

Shifting in my seat, I attempt to ease my arousal and the dampening of my panties but garner Ry's attention.

"You okay?"

"Yep." I turn my eyes to the window, away from the delicious temptation sitting beside me. Trees, so many trees. *Deciduous and coniferous, deciduous and coniferous,* I repeat silently, attempting to calm myself and my apparently raging hormones. It's ridiculous since it's not like I haven't had action. I mean, heck, just the other night, we—

Crap. *Deciduous, coniferous, deciduous, coniferous. Think trees, Maggie. Think tall trees. Some bear fruit, some seeds. Some are firm and thick, just like Ry's—*

"So my dad and I actually had a good talk."

Ry surprises me—not only with what he says but jarring me from my inner porno-licious brain. His tone is what draws my attention, though, because there's a softness to it that's not been present ever before when he's mentioned his father.

"What did you guys talk about?"

"About college, my job and then he … asked for my input on whose buyout he should consider accepting."

"Wow." I'm stunned because that's huge news.

"I think you're my lucky charm, Mags." He flashes me a smile before turning his attention back to the road. "Never had a breakthrough before like this." With a deprecating laugh, he adds, "Not for lack of trying. So ... thanks."

"Hey, that's what friends are for, right?"

As soon as the words spill from my lips, I feel it. The discomfort of the words. The unease that ripples through me.

The dishonesty in them.

Watching him closely, his eyes trained on the winding road ahead, I wonder why his jaw clenches tight. My eyes are drawn to his hands on the steering wheel, the knuckles nearly white in color at the force of his grip.

"Friends." His voice is a flat monotone, and my throat tightens at the way he utters that single word.

Turning to stare sightlessly out the passenger side window, I wonder why that word elicits such a visceral reaction. And not only from him. Because when I uttered that word—*friends*—it had felt like I was nine and had just been caught spouting off a curse word by my mother. Like I could practically taste the nastiness on my tongue. Back then, it left a bad taste in my mouth because I knew I had done wrong, knew that my mother was upset with me.

Now, however, that word—although assuredly not a curse word in any way—felt like one the moment it slipped from my lips.

Never before in my life had I been so torn, so disheartened to use that word.

Friends. It's somehow become a bad word in my mind. Because it means I'm in a box, restricted to only one category.

Regardless of how freaking much I wanted to cross over to a different one.

* * *

August

"My first thought when I saw you across the bar was *I'd tap that like a maple tree*," a deep, masculine voice drawls in my ear, causing me to choke on my sip of wine.

Managing to get myself under control with an eye roll, I turn as Ry slides onto the barstool I've been saving for him. His grin is infectious, and I feel my lips curve upward, mirroring it.

It's Friday, and we decided to meet for a quick drink after work at Chianti. They have the best selections for their "wines of the week" during happy hour.

"What can I get you?" the bartender asks as Ry peruses the leather-bound wine list.

"I got the Merlot." I tap my finger next to the listing.

Ry shakes his head with a deadpan expression. "Can't. Merlot makes me slutty."

The bartender throws his head back in a laugh while I roll my eyes. Ry ends up ordering a red blend.

"So," I lean in, "any reason you chose this place tonight?"

"Um, because we haven't been here in a while?" He appears thrown off by my question.

"Do you not recall what I said the last time we came here for happy hour?"

"Nope."

"That this is a place," I lean in closer, with a hushed tone, "where sweater vests go to die."

Ry's lips press thin, eyes dancing with amusement as he glances around at many of the other male patrons of the restaurant before coming back to rest on me. "I had forgotten about that."

Turning my attention back to my wine, I look in the

mirror on the wall of the bar. It's creepy, right? The fact that I like to watch people in that mirror? It's voyeuristic, yes, but most people don't notice, and I like creating stories in my head.

"Your smirk is creepy."

Instantly, my eyes fly to my own reflection, and I wipe it from my face, attempting to school my expression. Meeting Ry's eyes in the mirror, for a split second, I swear I see something—heat in his eyes—but it's gone in a flash. So quickly that I find myself wondering if it was just my imagination.

Ever since we had that "moment" Easter weekend at his parents' house four months ago, we both adopted the unspoken "we aren't going to bring up what happened" agreement. I'm grateful it didn't screw up our friendship. And even though a part of me assumes he's bisexual, I can't consider broaching the subject because I don't want to risk us getting pushed five steps back and result in me losing one of my best friends. Because that's far more important to me. Plus, I'm pretty certain he doesn't have those more-than-friends feelings for me, so it's safer this way.

But times like this, when I swear I catch his heated looks, I can't help but recall how hot it was to be with him.

Watching as he leans in, his shoulder brushing mine, our eyes remain locked on our reflections. "Want to play?" His mischievous grin tells me everything I need to know.

Smiling wide, I nod. "Absolutely."

Our "game" is where we pick people and make up a backstory for them and, sometimes, make up dialogue for them. The more ridiculous, the better.

"Okay, that couple down there at three o'clock."

My eyes flicker over, following Ry's instructions, and I find the man and woman. She looks like her breasts might explode from her top, and is pressing them against the guy's forearm—which he continues to shift away from to no avail—and the fact that the guy's eyes aren't permanently fixed on them says a lot. Plus, she looks way more into him while he continues to stir his drink even though it's practically empty.

With both of our forearms braced on the bar top and our shoulders touching, I keep my eyes on the couple's reflection while murmuring to Ry. "Their best friends—who are happily married or in a long-term relationship of some sort—set them up. She's been bugging them for a while and, likely, the married guy's friend bribed him somehow."

"Tickets to a hockey game."

"Or to the horse races. Maybe box seats or something?"

"Mmm, good one."

"She's saying something like"—I change my voice to sound ditzy and nasally—"'Ooooh, Brantley. I've, like, been waiting to, like, press my boobs against your arm like this for *yeeeaaaars*. It's like, all I've thought about.'"

Ry nudges me. "What about him? Eleven o'clock."

My eyes flick over in the direction before my stomach promptly drops.

"Him?" I hear the faint weakness in my voice, coming out as a near whisper.

"Shit. I'm sorry, Mags." He realizes who he's inadvertently picked out. And I see why he didn't initially recognize Shane, my ex, since he's apparently dyed his hair—or, rather, had it highlighted. Which looks hideous.

That aside, he's with the chick that I'd found him with. And they're all cozy and snuggling together like one of those nauseating couples in love. The ones you gag over when you're single and hating anyone or anything that represents a happy relationship and the ones who make you go, *Awwww!* when you're happy and in love.

I guess I should be more grateful for the fact that I haven't run into him before now. Thank goodness, we run in different circles.

Needless to say, it's taking every ounce of my restraint not to start flinging every single one of the garnishes at them. And those garnishes are right here—so frigging close to me right now—that my fingertips are tingling with the urge to do it. Tingling, people! Those little maraschino cherries? Those would be *so* fun to fling over there. The olives? Even better if I managed to ping one of them in the eye. And then the juice would sting their eyes, and I'd toss my head back in one of those maniacal cackles like—

When strong fingers grasp my wrist tightly, my eyes jerk up in question, only to receive a stern look from Ry in return.

"I saw it, Mags."

"Saw what?" I try to play off innocently. Why do I even bother? He knows me better than I know myself sometimes. Because he gives me one of *those* looks. The "Don't try to bullshit me because I've got your number" look.

"They're just fantasies," I hiss.

"As long as they *remain* fantasies, Mags." He eyes me sternly. "I know you'd regret it afterward and feel like an ass."

Dang it. He's so right. But, geez. Does he have to take the wind out of my sails like that?

Flagging the bartender's attention, Ry pulls out his card to pay for our drinks as I sit dazed, attempting to discreetly watch the sight of my ex and his new love in the bar mirror. Finally, Ry guides me off the stool, and we stand, preparing to make our escape.

"Maggie." I feel a jolt run through both Ry and myself

at the sound of Shane's voice. And the only response is a silent prayer.

Dear God, can you please stop hating on me? Sincerely, Maggie.

CHAPTER TWENTY-EIGHT

Ry

There's no way in hell I'm letting this asshole shit on Maggie again. Tugging her close to my side, I smile down at her before turning an overly curious look at Shane.

"Hey, man." I offer a hand. "Ryland James. And you are?"

He gives me the up-and-down perusal, as if I'm lacking in some way, before shaking my hand—weakly, I might add—and looks down his nose at me in the snootiest way. "Shane Douglas."

Let me say this. As a guy—whether I'm pretending to be gay or not—there's no chance in hell I'd put fucking highlights in my hair like this yahoo right here. Oh, and the best part is that he's one of the guys Mags had been talking about earlier.

Because he's wearing a sweater vest. A fucking sweater vest.

God, she dodged a damn bullet with this one.

"Great to meet you, Shawn."

"It's Sha—"

"My Mags and I were just heading home." With a sly wink at the dickhead, I add, "My girl gets frisky after a glass of wine."

Maggie makes a choked sound, and I press a kiss to her temple, whispering, "Smile. Look like you're in love, not being tortured."

"You two live together?" Shane's eyes narrow, almost accusingly. Like he even has a right.

"Mags and I have been living together for, what?" I look over at her in question. "Almost a year now?"

Finally snapping out of it, she bats her eyes up at me. "Nearly a year of pure bliss," she gushes. Reaching a hand to hook behind my head, she steers me closer, nuzzling our noses before pressing a light kiss to my lips.

"Ugh. Gross." Both of us turn at the sound of disdain dripping from the words spoken by the woman standing beside Shane.

As if either of us gives two shits about the opinion of someone who slept with a guy while he was still in a relationship with another woman? Let me think on that real quick.

Nope.

With a dismissive wave of my hand, I flash a fake smile. "Well, blondie, we can't all be home-wreckers with no morals, now can we?" Winking at Shane, I give him a slap on his shoulder.

Far harder than necessary.

"Thanks, man. Because of you, I managed to get the hottest, most gorgeous woman in Saratoga Springs."

Exiting Chianti with my arm around Mags, it's not until we're around the corner, on our way back to the apartment that she breaks away from me, stopping abruptly on the sidewalk.

"Did you see the look on his face? And on hers?" Maggie's entire face is lit up like Fourth of July fireworks, and it's at moments like these that I feel my breath catch in my throat at her beauty.

"That was priceless."

"It *was* absolutely priceless!" She throws her hands in the air, looking up at the sky. "I feel like I'm finally free." Dropping her arms, she steps closer to me, her expression softening. "I feel like he no longer has that tiny, nagging … hold on me anymore." Taking another step closer, her voice becomes more faint, lowering to almost a whisper. "Thanks to you."

Sliding my hands into my pockets because it's the only way to prevent myself from yanking her toward me and kissing her like a madman, I shrug. "You're welcome."

Our gazes remain locked for an indeterminate amount of time. It could be for a second or for a few minutes. Regardless, there's no way to deny where my mind goes.

I imagine pushing her back against the brick wall of the building behind her. Pressing my lips to hers in a kiss so passionate, it's almost bruising. A kiss that she'll be feeling on her lips for days afterward. And at the end of that kiss will come something I've longed for.

No, not *that*. Well, yes, that, but it's not entirely what I'm referring to. What I truly long for is for her to realize that I love her and she loves me back. Not just as friends but as man and woman.

And then we'd get to the other thing I long for. The stuff I long for all the damn time. The stuff that would take the strain off my wrist. I swear to God, I've jacked off more this past year than I ever did all through puberty.

"Ry," she breathes out, a lilt of a question in her tone. Her gaze drops to my lips as her own part, worrying the edge of her bottom lip with her teeth.

"Mags…" I blow out a harsh breath. "You've got to stop

looking at me like that or …" I try to tear my eyes off her lips.

And promptly fail.

"Or what?" She whispers her words so softly, they're barely audible. My fingers clench within the pockets of my pants, but the look in her eyes sets me into action. Because the look in her eyes is pure want.

Desire.

Heat.

Fingers flying from my pockets and landing on her hips, I walk her back against the hard, unforgiving brick building.

"Is this what you want, Mags?" Pressing my body against hers, her gasp is instantaneous the moment she feels my arousal.

"I … shouldn't." I can see the conflict in her eyes, in her voice.

"Do you want to celebrate tonight—to celebrate you being truly rid of that dickhead—with a kiss?"

What the fuck am I saying? I need to put a stop to this insanity. I need to just tell her—

I lose all train of thought the moment she suddenly pushes up on her toes and her lips press against mine, stealing my breath. And the ability to think ceases. I operate on feel.

The feel of her body pressed flush against mine.

The feel of her lips, so lush and soft as they work over mine in the sweetest, sexiest kiss.

The feel of her hands sifting through my hair, sending tingles through my entire body.

But the moment her tongue sweeps inside my mouth, everything changes.

Game. On.

My restraint flies away with the light breeze of the evening, my hands moving from where I had them braced on the rough brick wall beside her. Cupping her face, slanting my lips over hers, my tongue delves deeper to play with hers, to taste her as my lips love her own.

HONK!

We jerk apart at the loud, jarring car horn. Our combined breathing is ragged as we stand there staring at one another, our eyes darting from each other's lips to eyes, before being drawn back to the other's lips. Like we both want to go back to kissing, but we're afraid. Like that car horn somehow broke the spell.

Turning, we make the walk back to the apartment in silence; both of us lost in our own—likely conflicted—thoughts. And somewhere deep inside me, I'm wondering if that car horn was a sign. Like *Your time's up, Ry. Come clean, now.*

Except I don't know how to do it. Because every scenario I've worked out in my mind is the same.

It ends with her hating me.

CHAPTER TWENTY-NINE

Maggie

September twentieth is special yet bittersweet for me. It's always a day, if it falls during the workweek, when I'll immerse myself in my work, staying as late as possible so that I'm exhausted and my main thoughts are centered on collapsing into my bed.

This year, however, it falls on a Sunday, and the weather appears to mimic my emotions. According to the weather app on my phone, it's rainy and dreary with a slight chill in the air. I didn't sleep well, so as soon as dawn breaks and tiny shards of daylight peek through the Venetian blinds, I quickly shower and dress. I always try to wear my "Sunday best" when I go to see them.

Slipping on my favorite black and white polka dotted knee-length dress paired with some black tights and my Steve Madden knee-high, black boots, I decide to leave my hair down loose and apply light makeup.

Grabbing my umbrella and sliding into my jacket, I quietly slip out of the silent apartment, leaving Ry sleeping soundly in his room. As I walk along the sidewalk on South Broadway, heading in the direction of the one stop I have to make before arriving at my destination, my mind wanders.

I think back to my first year of college at Skidmore.

Originally, I'd wanted to take time off and stay home to take care of my parents. But they had vehemently insisted I carry on with my life as planned.

Stopping in front of the local florist, I push open the door, and Ms. Paisley, the owner, instantly greets me.

"Morning, Maggie." She offers me her trademark crooked smile, the only clue to her recent stroke. It certainly hasn't slowed the woman down, though.

Sliding a small bouquet across the top of the display case, she winks at me. "It's on me."

"Ms. Paisley," I protest, only receiving a wave of dismissal in return.

"Go on. You can pay me next year." She winks again, with that crooked smile, and shoos me out of her shop. And she and I both know she won't allow me to pay her next year, either, since she says that every year. It's like that movie *Groundhog Day*. Every year is the same. But I adore her and always ensure that our office places an order for a bunch of her floral arrangements whenever we need a fresh centerpiece for the waiting area or have a big meeting in one of our conference rooms.

Flowers in one hand and an umbrella in the other, I walk slowly down the sidewalk to Congress Street Cemetery. My steps slow as I get closer to approaching the large wrought iron gated area.

The heels of my boots sink into the soggy grass as I near the two gravestones. Coming to a stop in front of them, I set the flowers in front of where my mother lies beneath the ground before backing away, one hand smoothing over my hair.

I know it sounds stupid, me getting dressed up to visit my parents at the cemetery, but after Catholic school, it's hard to erase the idea that angels or whoever look down on you from above. I feel like if I showed up in some frumpy sweats, unwashed hair, and hadn't brushed my teeth, my parents would be *tsking* their butts off in heaven. Not to mention they'd be up in arms and likely saying, "Look! She's clearly incapable of taking care of herself! We failed her somehow!" And I just can't have that.

I know, I know. I'm a weirdo who thinks about stuff like that. Don't even get me started on the whole *I wonder if they watch me when I masturbate* thing. Eeek.

My parents adopted me when I was young—not a baby, which is when most kids are adopted. I was nearing my seventh birthday and pretty resigned to the fact that I'd never have a family of my own.

When my parents and I were introduced, it had been one of those unexplainable things. It was like kismet. Meant to be. We instantly clicked, and I felt safe. Wanted.

Loved.

Years later, when my father had been diagnosed with cancer—an aggressive form, which had rapidly spread to all of his main organs within two months of his diagnosis—to say that our family had been devastated is an understatement.

When my mother's diagnosis followed shortly thereafter, I wasn't sure how to react.

For years, while owning their roofing and flooring business, they had repeatedly been exposed to asbestos. It started out slowly, the signs, with the coughing and breathing difficulties. And then, with wicked momentum, their symptoms worsened.

When my parents fell ill, they were forced to sell their business because they were becoming so weak that they were unable to keep up with it. Although I was due to begin college, I offered to wait and stay home to take care of the two people who had given everything to me. But my mother had merely taken my hand in hers.

"Maggie." She'd given me a smile that still managed to light up her face amidst the pain I knew she was experiencing. "Love, you need to go on with your life. There's nothing for you here. We'll just be here, lying around, taking it easy."

We both knew she was playing it off, but neither she nor my father would hear of me staying around instead of going to college.

"You're wrong," I had protested. "There's *everything* here for me. You both are here."

Tears gather in my eyes at the memory of that conversation. Because even though years have passed, I still recall how helpless I felt at not being able to give back to the two individuals who had given me so much of themselves. Never once had they made me feel like I was "the adopted kid the Finegans brought home." When people would ask if I was adopted, they would always raise their chins proudly, tugging me closer before answering with, "She's our daughter, if that's what you're asking."

Once my father passed, I knew in my heart of hearts that my mother would shortly follow. She was weaker than ever, and hospice had taken over her care, as well. I had begged her to let me stay back from school. I wanted to be there for her, but she had requested that I not be present. She'd said that she didn't want me to remember her like that. She didn't want me to watch her die.

I still hate that I never got that final goodbye. Within two weeks of my father's passing, my mother joined him in heaven.

Today's a special day, though. It was my mother's—er, would have been her—sixtieth birthday. And she'd always claimed she'd wanted a huge birthday celebration to mark that milestone.

"Not much of a birthday bash, huh?" I speak through unshed tears, forcing words past the lump in my throat. "Sorry, I couldn't do better."

A miraculous thing happens at that moment. The rain decides to stop so abruptly, as if someone just flipped a switch.

Glancing around in wonder, I lower my umbrella to the grass beside me.

"Wow. If that's what you're up to up there in heaven, I'm impressed." Cocking my head to the side, I peer up at the sky. "Do you think you could maybe do that when I'm running late for work, and it's pouring? Because I would *totally* be on board with that."

Silence. That's all I get. Not like I was expecting some sort of divine echo or something, saying, *"Sure, Maggie."*

Okay, so maybe a tiny part of me was. Because, dude, that would be super cool, right?

"Well, I'm still a weirdo, so nothing new there," I announce to my parents. Like they didn't already know.

Blowing out a long breath, I settle on the stone bench across from them, grateful my raincoat hits mid-calf, so it protects my body from the cold, damp surface.

"All right. Let me fill you in on what's happened since the last time we chatted." I take a deep breath before beginning.

"So my roommate, Ry—the one who was dating Jack? Turns out, he's also dated women. Not sure what's going on there, but sometimes he looks at me, and I just … I don't know." Staring blankly down at the soggy grass beneath my feet, I let out a sigh before turning my gaze skyward. "I wish you could give me a sign, like some sort of heads-up that it's just fun flirting and not something … more."

Suddenly, I realize that I've begun squinting against the glare. Although it's still cloudy, there appears to be a bit more sunlight peeking out.

Using my hand to shield my eyes, I peer up at the sky, mumbling, "Well, heck. Now you're just showing off."

Not to mention, I'm left wondering if that "sign" from my parents meant it was fun flirting with Ry.

Or something more.

CHAPTER THIRTY

Ry

I heard Maggie moving around this morning—albeit quietly—but it seems I'm in tune with her nowadays. I know what day it is and the relevance.

She's always made it seem like she would rather be alone during this time. I know that Sarah mentioned going with her once, a while back, but now, she's on rotation and unable to call off work without getting into serious trouble.

It's Maggie's mother's sixtieth birthday today, and I know Maggie had mentioned something about her mother always wanting to have a big birthday bash. They'd discussed what they'd have at the party and all the desserts since her mother had a major sweet tooth.

I'd planned it because I knew what I had to do. I couldn't—wouldn't—let Maggie be alone today.

Following a few yards behind her on this bleak, rainy morning as she makes her way down the sidewalk of South Broadway, I carefully enter the small bakery a few doors down from the florist shop she enters.

"Morning, Ryland," greets Michelle, the owner of Sweets N Treats. Sliding a small pastry box across the counter with two plastic forks taped to the top, I hand her my card to pay for it. After signing the slip, I thank her and am off to head to the cemetery.

After exiting, I see Maggie's about to enter the cemetery gates. I slow my pace to allow her time alone with them, not wanting to fully intrude on the moment.

Taking my time, I stroll down the remainder of the sidewalk of South Broadway, approaching the intersection of Congress Street, and that's when the rain stops. It gives me pause as I look around before lowering my umbrella, the sky appearing to brighten ever so slightly. Carefully tucking the box under one arm, I secure the attached wrap around my umbrella to contain it and carefully take hold of the box in time for the pedestrian signal to light up, alerting me to go.

Entering the cemetery, I make my way through the burial plots until I see Maggie. She's sitting on the bench facing her parents' gravestones. Her lips are moving, so I assume she's speaking to them. She must hear the sound of my shoes squishing on the soggy grass because she turns in surprise at the sight of me.

"Ry?" Her eyes drift to the box in my hand before returning to me. "What are you doing here?"

"Well, I remembered something." I walk around the bench and sit beside her. Setting my umbrella off to the side, I reach into the pocket of my rain jacket and pull out a candle and a small box of matches. Handing her the candle, she accepts it, confusion lining her features.

Opening the box, I show her the small, four-inch round cake with "Happy Birthday" written on it. I look at her for a reaction, hoping that she's okay with this.

"Ry." My name sounds choked when she says it. Her eyes cloud with tears. "You did this for me—for my mom?"

"Of course." *I'd do anything for you, Mags. Anything.*

She slides the single candle into the cake, and I carefully

light it before pocketing the box of remaining matches. Then I start singing.

"Happy birthday to you. Happy birthday to you. Happy birthday, dear Mrs. Fin—" I break off with a look at Maggie, wondering what I should sing for her name.

With a wet smile, she chimes in softly, "Mom," and I pick right up singing, inserting "Mom," and end the song. We both blow out the lone candle, and I set the cake upon the bench on the other side of me. Sliding a hand into my other pocket, I pull out the other item I brought and show it to her.

"You think your dad would approve?"

Her gasp sends unease throughout me as her gaze settles on the small Matchbox car in my palm. A red Ferrari. Exactly the kind of car she had mentioned her father always deemed his dream car. Her fingers tentatively reach out to take it from me, eyes darting up to mine as tears begin rolling down her cheeks.

Throwing herself into my arms, she squeezes me so tight that I fear some of my ribs might end up bruised.

"Ry," she murmurs through her tears.

Smoothing down her hair, I press my lips against the silky softness. "I know, Mags. I know." Pressing another soft kiss to her hair, I whisper, "Sometimes, it's hard to express the words in your heart." *Trust me, Mags. I know this all too well.*

As I hold her tight, she eventually calms and releases me, rising to walk over to place the small toy car upon her father's gravestone. Returning to her seat beside me, she inhales deeply, wiping her cheeks before offering a bright smile.

"Ready to dig into that cake?"

"Ready."

Sitting there, eating the birthday cake individually before we get silly and began playfully feeding each other, I realize that today's a day where I can say I'm experiencing a first.

I'm attending a birthday party—for someone *in* a cemetery—with the woman I'm in love with.

Weird as shit, but I wouldn't change it for the world.

Except maybe the part where the woman knew I was in love with her, of course.

CHAPTER THIRTY-ONE

Maggie

"What are you doing here?" I hiss at Ry.

He just showed up at the small pub a few blocks away from our apartment. Sarah and I were supposed to meet up, but she'd been called into work at the last minute, and I'd already ordered a drink. Adam had approached me, and we talked for a bit before he'd asked me if I'd be interested in playing pool.

"I'm waiting for Jack to get here." He pauses. "But right now, I'm here to protect you." He states this like it's obvious.

"From what?"

"Dude was totally trying to cop a feelski."

I stare at him. "He was not trying to cop a feelski, Ry."

He gives me an exasperated look. "Mags. Any guy who offers to get behind you so that he can"—he breaks off to use finger quotes—"'help your form' is trying to cop a feelski."

My mouth opens only to snap shut a second later. Lips pressing thin, I glare at him. "You've tried to help me with my form before."

"I was sincerely concerned that you might not hit any of the correct balls that night." His lips quiver in an attempt to restrain a smile.

With a dismissive sound, I roll my eyes, trying to tamp

down my own grin threatening to break free.

"So what's so urgent with 'feelski boy' that he had to interrupt your pool game for a phone call at," Ry glances at his watch, "eight o'clock on a Saturday night?" He peers closer to where Adam stands a few feet away, leaning against the wall with the phone to his ear.

"Wait a minute." He wrinkles his nose in disgust. "*Please* tell me he does not have a flip phone." Turning his attention back to me, he pleads, "Tell me you're not considering having anything to do with a guy who carries a flip phone."

I swat at him. "Stop it." Glancing over at where Adam's still standing, I offer, "Maybe he's just … frugal."

"*Orrrr* maybe," Ry raises his eyebrows, "he's a cheapskate."

"He's not a cheapskate. He said he owns a condo above Chianti's." This is impressive considering the fact that those condos are known to sell for no less than a million dollars.

"Then he was sent back in time from the early nineteen nineties."

I can only manage to stare at Ry. "You need to stop watching so much TV."

"And you need to stop agreeing to pool games with men who are time travelers."

"Oh, my God!" I throw up my hands in exasperation. "I'm going to go back to enjoying his company." I back away. "Later, Ry."

"Have fun going rollerblading! Be sure to ask him about his Trapper Keeper!" he calls out to me.

And, thanks to Ry, now I'm half expecting the guy to either disappear, leaving a pool of clothing at my feet like in the movie *The Time Traveler's Wife*, or end up talking like Arnold Schwarzenegger from *The Terminator* movies.

Awesome.

"Everything okay?" I offer a smile as Adam ends his call, snapping his phone shut before sliding it back into his pocket.

"Sure."

That's it. No further elaboration on that. O-kay. Well, then.

"I'm actually going to head to the restroom real quick. Then maybe we can start a game of darts?"

"Sounds good, Maggie." He flashes me a warm smile, and I turn to head to the restroom.

After I finish washing my hands in the sink and fluffing my hair a bit in the mirror, I exit the restroom in time to see Adam practically sprinting out of the pub, as if a pack of rabid dogs was nipping at his heels.

The fact that I catch the not-so-discreet fist bump between Ry and Jack says a lot. They clearly had something to do with Adam's retreat.

"What did you do?" Resting a hand on my hip, my eyes volley between the two men accusingly.

"We actually saved you, Mags." Ry answers dramatically, placing a palm over his heart.

Jack follows suit. "Indeed, we did."

Sputtering in exasperation, I glare at them. "How do you figure?"

Jack gives me a sympathetic look. "The guy had a flip phone, Maggie."

"Oh, my God." I rub my temples wearily. "Not this again."

"We saved you from being exposed to his collection of Beanie Babies," Ry says with a dramatic sigh. "That would've been terrible."

"And from his VCR tapes of all the episodes of *The*

163

Power Rangers."

"Or his Tupperware collection."

"You think he really has one?" Jack's expression is one of utter seriousness.

"Totally looked like a Tupperware kinda guy."

"Stop! Please. Both of you."

They turn, faces a mask of innocence. Finally, Ry winks at me. "I should go and get us both a beer."

I offer him a reluctant nod because, apparently, he's my newly appointed evening companion.

"Well." Jack clasps his hands together. "As fun as this has been with you two crazy kids, I'm actually beat and think I'm going to have to head home." He and Ry exchange a quick hug-slap-on-the-back kind of thing before Ry heads off to get our beers.

That's when I take notice of the weariness in Jack's face. Concerned, I take a step closer, laying a hand on his arm, "Are you okay?"

Offering a tired smile, his head dips in a quick nod. "Just been a hell of a day on top of a hellacious week." He drops a quick kiss to my forehead. "Have fun."

I stop him just as he turns to leave. "Hey, Jack?"

When his eyes meet mine in question, I lose the nerve to voice my question. "Be careful going home." Crap. That wasn't at all what I meant to—wanted to—ask.

The smile he offers is different somehow, but I can't put my finger on it. "Be careful with our guy, Maggie."

With a wink, he says a soft good night, leaving me with his words swirling around in my mind and my eyes staring after him.

Be careful with our guy.

CHAPTER THIRTY-TWO

Ry

I'm about to pounce.

Like a pride of lions pounce on a weak, slow warthog. Except that I'm only one man acting alone, and my prey? It's a guy who—I'd be lying if I said otherwise—looks pretty sharp in his tailored suit vest, shirt, and pants, as he mingles with the rest of the after-work business crowd on a Friday.

Maggie's looking exceptionally hot in the dress she has on. Jesus, this morning when I was pouring coffee in my to-go mug, she came into the kitchen, heels hanging from her fingers, and I had to use the counter to hide my insta-boner. I felt like telling her to go back to her room and change because no way in hell did I like the idea of other men getting to see her throughout the day looking like that.

The dress itself isn't risqué in any way, but on Maggie, it molds to her curves. And not for the first time, I wanted to shove her against the kitchen counter and fuck her silly.

Shit. That's definitely not my inner gentleman coming out. But, hell. She just looks … fuckable. So in my fantasies, I'll fuck her silly first, and *then* I'll make love to her, the way I've imagined doing.

It's no surprise that, after my being held up at the office,

Maggie would attract someone. It just helps that, at the precise moment I enter the bar, I see her speak to the guy before making her way toward the restroom.

Time to pounce.

"Hey, man, I'm Ry, Maggie's roommate." I lean an arm against the wall beside him, inserting myself into his personal space and smiling wide.

And, in case you're wondering, yeah, I lay on the smolder.

Letting my eyes ever so slowly drift over him, my gaze lingers on his crotch area. Long enough to make him shift with unease, his eyes going wide.

Oh, yeah. He's picking up what I'm putting down.

"So I was thinking"—I drag one fingertip down his cheek, dropping to his shoulder, drawing swirly patterns on it—"maybe after you're done with Maggie, you could, you know"—I wink slowly—"have fun with me, too."

His entire body stiffens, rigid as a board, and I watch his Adam's apple bob as he swallows hard. "Uh, you know what? I just remembered—"

"You've got somewhere to be?" I chime in helpfully. Because that's what I am. A helper. Just good ol' Ry, helping old ladies cross the streets, rescuing cats from trees and …

Being a deterrent for Maggie's vagina.

"Yeah." And with that, suit guy is gone. Impressively fast. For a second there, I feel bad about not asking him who his tailor was because they did an impressive job.

Maggie's heels signify her approach, and when I hear the exacerbated firmness of the *click, click, click* of her favorite red-bottomed shoes, I know she's noticed the absence of suit guy.

"Ry."

My face is a mask of innocence. "Hey, Mags. Sorry, I'm

late." Leaning in, I press a perfunctory kiss on her cheek. I lean back, tucking my hands in my pockets.

"Where did he go?" Her stare is intense, and I suddenly feel like I'm back in time in the principal's office for using craft glue and gluing beads into Steph Wilder's hair in art class. Steph was a grade-A bitch even back in the sixth grade, and it wasn't my fault she fell asleep in class. I thought I did a pretty bang-up job on her hair.

She didn't agree.

Nor did the art teacher. Or the principal. *Or* my father.

Maggie waves a hand in my face. "Hey! You just spaced out on me." When she places her hands on her hips, I wince because it thrusts out her chest, and I'd give anything to palm them … just one—

"What happened to him?"

"What happened to who?" I attempt to shake off my thoughts.

She heaves an exasperated sigh. "Matt, that's who!"

"You mean the dude in the suit?"

An exasperated eye roll is what I get next. "Yes."

Tugging on my ear, I answer as nonchalantly as possible. "He forgot he had to be somewhere."

Her eyes narrow. Frantically, I know I have to come up with something. And fast.

"He had to go out and get some evening chocolate."

Oh, fuck. That's the best I can do? Jesus. I should just stand in front of the dartboard all night as penance for that poor response.

"No one else has"—she breaks off to use finger quotes—"'evening chocolate' but you."

"Ah-ah." I wag my finger at her. "Not true. A ton of people have evening chocolate just like I do."

She's referring to the stash of chocolate I keep in the

top cabinet in the kitchen. She'd discovered it recently and accused me of holding out on her. When I told her I didn't share my evening chocolate—which is specifically dark chocolate—she looked at me like I was crazy.

"As opposed to 'morning chocolate,' I suppose?"

Tapping a finger against my lips, I pretend to be deep in thought. "Hmm, I don't have morning chocolate, but I think you might be on to something."

"It's confirmed." She gives a short nod to punctuate her words. "You're weird."

"What? You're acting like no one else has special chocolate. Come on," I protest, "tell me the truth." Deepening my voice, I cock my head. "Do you have a special chocolate, Mags?"

For a split second, it's like she's mesmerized and under the spell of my voice, her eyes darkening with … lust?

But only for a split second. Because as fast as it happens, it's gone.

Smiling up at me sweetly, she leans toward me, placing her palm flat against my chest. "Wouldn't you like to know."

And just like that, this round goes to Maggie.

CHAPTER THIRTY-THREE

Maggie

"It's … not you, it's me. I just can't do this …"

I stare back at Tim oddly. "You can't … have drinks with a woman?" I pause for a beat. "In a bar?"

What. The. Heck? It's not like I'm asking him to watch dinosaur porn with me, for God's sake. Tim had been the one to ask *me* to meet up with him for a drink after work.

I repeat: He. Asked. Me.

He had been in our office, talking with another consultant, and when my coworker had introduced me in passing, I noticed the interest in his eyes. So it wasn't a surprise when he stopped by my office after their meeting, chatted a bit, and asked me out for a drink after work to celebrate the fact that it was Friday. When I had suggested we meet down the street at my favorite place that makes their own craft microbrews, he'd readily agreed.

Now, however, Tim's completely bugging out. And I can't even exchange one of those *What the heck is going on right now?* looks with Ry since he's currently in the men's room. I mean, seriously. What could have taken place in the brief time it took me to use the restroom? Ry had arrived a few minutes after I returned to my seat at the bar beside Tim.

"I just think it's too soon. Great meeting you, though." Tim slips off the barstool after tossing down money for our drinks at the bar. He grabs my hand to shake it so aggressively, I nearly feel a case of whiplash coming on. Then, in the blink of an eye, he's gone.

Dazed, I'm still staring after him when Ry returns, sliding into Tim's now vacant seat.

"He had to go somewhere?"

"Apparently so." My words are slow, drawn out. When I swivel my seat back toward the bar, I instantly catch sight of the money Tim had tossed onto the bar.

"Whoa." I reach out to finger the bill. It's a fifty.

My eyes fly to Ry, and he looks amused. "Well, I guess this TGIF celebration will be courtesy of Tim."

Propping my chin in my hand, I stare into my glass of beer. "He talked about us getting together for dinner. Or maybe even catching a hockey game."

"Please, Mags." He gives me a look. "You dodged a bullet with that one. Pretty sure he's about as exciting as a night in reading Homer's *Odyssey*."

I make a face. "Seriously?"

He shrugs. "Would you rather I talk about his hair? Because it sucked worse than an Amish virgin."

I throw up my hands. "Where do you even come up with this stuff?"

"It's a gift," he deadpans with a dramatic sigh. "God gifted me with wit, but it's honestly *so taxing* sometimes."

Eyes closed with a groan, I drop my chin to my chest. "Why me?"

He slings an arm around my shoulder. "You love me, you know. Would be lost without me."

I huff. "Is that so?"

"Yep. Now, come on." He reaches for a bar napkin, holding a palm out for me to provide a pen.

With a long sigh, I pull a pen from my small purse and slap it into his palm.

"Now." His eyes focus on writing on the napkin. "*I want someone who will stay and have a drink or two and not bug out,*" he says as he writes.

Peering over at him, I wait to see if he's going to crack a grin, but it appears that he's serious. "I want the same." Then, with a weary sigh, I add, "Obviously." When Ry hands me the pen and napkin, I quickly jot down my response.

I want a guy who will actually stick around long enough to finish a drink.

Huh. If only I were kidding. Seems like every guy so far has left their drink either half full or more.

Ry's arm nudges mine. "Hey, don't be so glum. We have drinks on us tonight, Mags."

"Yeah," I say without an ounce of enthusiasm. With a sigh, I turn to him. "Actually, I feel like just going home. It's been a crappy week, and I just want to go home and veg out."

Ry flags down the bartender we're familiar with, who's always super-efficient and friendly. Handing over the fifty-dollar bill, which covers our tab more than four times over, he wishes him a good night before helping me off the barstool and exiting the bar.

* * *

I'm in my frumpiest pair of sleep shorts—the kind that are loose when you're on your period and feel as appealing as that creature in the movie *The Predator*—and a tank top when I come out to the couch where Ry's lounging.

"Can I get your help?"

Turning his attention from the television to me, his curious gaze hits me, noticing the large box I'm holding.

"What do you need?"

"Can we …" I drop my gaze to the box, suddenly embarrassed. "Can we take this down to the patio's fire pit and burn all of it?" My voice is muted. When he doesn't respond, I raise my eyes.

Dropping his bare feet back down from where they're propped on the edge of the coffee table, he presses the remote control to turn off the TV. Rising from the couch, he takes a step closer, peering at the box before his eyes watch me intently.

"What's in the box, Mags?" His tone is subdued, a mixture of curiosity and tenderness. And understanding.

"Pictures." My eyes beg him not to make me elaborate. And, thank God, he gets it.

Briefly nodding, he steps closer, cups my face in his hands, pressing a quick kiss to my forehead. Stepping around me, he tosses over his shoulder, "I'll be right back."

When he emerges a moment later, he's tugged on a hooded sweatshirt, one hand holding another sweatshirt and a pair of sweatpants. Taking the box from my hands, he sets it on the coffee table. He tugs the hooded sweatshirt down over my head, helping me slide my arms through the large sleeves. When he carefully pulls my long hair out, my chest aches at the way he smooths it down. Makes it hard to breathe.

Handing me the sweatpants, he nods, gesturing to my bare legs. "You need to cover yourself, or you'll freeze outside."

Slipping on the pants over my shorts, I have to roll the

waistband a few times because they're so long. Once I'm sufficiently covered for the colder weather outside, I take a deep, fortifying breath.

"Let's do this." Reaching down, I grab the box and hold it tight to my chest.

I know it's long overdue to get rid of these reminders. I'd actually forgotten about this box in the back of my closet, but tonight, something made me think of it. And at that moment, I knew. Tonight was it.

It's time to rid myself of the last remaining tie.

CHAPTER THIRTY-FOUR

Ry

I'm not sure what brought this on, but I'm not about to second-guess the fact that Maggie wants to—that she's ready to—rid herself of the photos of her and Shane's relationship. The callous, caveman part of me wants to beat my chest with my fist and yell at this step forward while the other part of me knows this isn't exactly going to be a cakewalk for her.

This much is apparent in her silent demeanor and the crease between her eyebrows as we ride down the elevator.

I follow her out of the elevator as we exit through the side doors of the lobby leading to the patio. Luckily, no one is gathered at the fire.

Maggie takes a seat on one of the cushioned patio chairs, and I slide into one beside her.

"I know you think I'm crazy. Doing this. But it's just … Something just clicked tonight …" Her words trail off as she turns back to face the fire.

"I don't think you're crazy, Mags." I shake my head, my tone fierce. "Not even remotely." Reaching out, I gently turn her face to me. "I think you're the most incredible woman I've ever met. Kind, funny, sweet, and beautiful." I swallow past the emotion lodged in my throat at the heartfelt truth in my words. "You're the whole package."

You're everything I've ever wanted.

Her attention falls to the box, carefully pulling the cardboard flaps apart. With a weak smile, she asks, "Ready to help?"

"Always."

Grabbing a stack of photos, she hands them to me. It makes me smile because Maggie's one of the few people who still takes the time to have digital photos printed. Because she wants to keep the memories so vivid and on display. Our apartment is scattered with numerous framed photos of her and Sarah, of Maggie and me from various outings, along with some of the girls out with Jack and me. I love it because it shows that we're important to her.

Gazing down at the top photo on the stack she's given me, something pinches in my chest. It must have been taken when she and Shane had first started dating. They look like a couple so much in love.

Inhaling deeply, I have to say the words. As painful as they might be, I have to say it. "Mags, if you're not ready—"

"I am." Her voice is soft yet firm. When she jumps up from her seat, she sets the box down with one thick stack of photos in her hand. She gives them a hefty toss into the flames, and we watch as the fire rapidly eats away at them.

Destroying memories.

Damn, this is hard for *me*. God only knows how it must be for her right now.

"Mags—"

In an instant, she heaves another handful into the flames. Then another, repeating the process until the only remaining stack of photographs is the one in my hand.

Turning, she eyes me. "Are you going to toss them in?"

"I, uh, don't know that I should be the one doing this.

They're yours."

"Fine." She huffs out a breath, grabbing the photos from me and quickly tossing them in with the others. Or what might remain of the others, more aptly.

We stand side by side, watching the flames flicker, burning the memories until they're nothing but ashes that float away with the cool, night breeze.

I'm at a loss for words. Because I know she has to be hurting, regardless of the fact that she says she's over him.

Turning to her, I open my arms, and she steps into my embrace, wrapping her arms around me. Eyes falling closed, I run my hands up and down her back in what I hope is a soothing manner.

"Love you, Ry." Her words, spoke against my chest, are barely audible, so softly spoken.

"I love you, too." I press a kiss to her hair, resting my cheek against it.

More than you know.

* * *

I heave myself onto Jack's couch with a tired groan, slumping down onto the soft leather. "God, I'm exhausted."

Sitting in the oversized chair, he looks over at me, one eyebrow raised, tipping his beer to his lips. "I don't doubt it. I mean"—he takes a swig before gesturing to me with his beer—"what, with clam jamming poor Maggie all the time."

"The one dude actually tried to kiss me."

Jack chokes on the swig of beer he's just taken. Fist covering his mouth, he coughs into it before finally regaining composure. "You're serious."

Leaning my head back against the couch, my eyes fall

shut. "Dead serious."

"Did he get far?" There's a pause. "Did he get a little handsy?"

My eyes fly open to glare at him, and I see Jack grinning. "You think this is funny?"

"I think it's hilarious as shit." He tips his head to the side with a wide smirk on his face. "Tell me the truth. Did you play hard to get?" When I hurl a pillow at him, he swats it away without batting an eye, expression turning serious. "You know she's getting pretty fed up with you, right? Especially since some of the guys ended up leaving with *you* at the end of the night."

Abruptly standing, I start to pace the living room. "I know. Hell," I run a hand through my hair, "I'd get frustrated with me, too."

"Well, I've got to tell you. Her game plan is to try and thwart you from pulling any more of your stunts."

He has my attention now. "What are you talking about?"

Jack lifts his beer bottle to his lips and takes a leisurely swig, wearing a smug grin on his face. "What's it worth?"

Glaring, I clench my jaw. "Just spit it out."

"Jesus." He makes a face. "Surely, you don't get all growly and mean with your other lovers, do you?"

Grinding my palms into my eyes, I let out a groan of frustration. "Why do I put up with this shit?"

"Don't be like that, pookie bear," Jack admonishes with mock sternness. "That kind of attitude will make you lose the best damn thing to ever happen to you: me."

Some days. *Some days*, I really want to dropkick him.

Today would be definitely one of those days.

He holds my death glare for who the hell knows how long—seems like an eternity—before letting a long sigh loose. "She's thinking about maiming you or"—he holds up a finger to stop me when I'm about to protest—"*or* trying to be sneakier about when she goes out and not letting you know about it."

Something pinches in my chest. "So basically, she's planning on trying to avoid me. Great."

Jack's shoulder lifts in a half shrug. "Can't really blame her." When I flash him a dirty look, it doesn't faze him. "You know what that means, right?"

Eyeing him warily, I draw out the word, "What?"

"It means you need to upgrade things from the Basic Clam Jam package to the Deluxe one."

* * *

"Hey, Mags?" I call to the closed door of her bedroom, knocking softly. I know she's awake because I heard her shower running a few minutes earlier.

"What, Ry?" she calls out, not opening the door for me. Which isn't good. At all. Normally, she'd tell me to come in, and I'd sprawl on her bed, and we'd chat while she put her laundry away or while she was in her adjoining bathroom, applying her makeup. And if she was getting dressed, she'd tell me to wait a moment before telling me to enter.

"Mags, can I come in for a moment?" I pause. "Please?"

There's silence for so long that I think she's planning to ignore me. Until the handle of the door turns slowly, only opening a few inches. And I know I'm up shit creek by the way she's looking at me.

"Hey." She looks irritated and maybe a bit tired. Her boss has been riding her harder than usual about some big project, but the knowledge that I'm contributing to some of that irritation and possibly some stress, as well, doesn't sit well with me.

"I know it's Friday night, and you probably have plans but, on the off-chance that you don't, I brought home some salads from Putnam Market ..." I trail off, hoping she'll take my offer as what it is: an olive branch, of sorts.

She doesn't speak, her eyes drilling into me, the silence nearly deafening. Then I see it. That tiny flicker in her eyes.

"Which salads did you get?"

I can't help the relieved smile that spreads across my face at her question. "A pear, walnut, and goat cheese one for you, of course." With my hands bracing the doorframe, I lean in. "Your favorite salad to go along with your favorite ... guy?"

"Now, you're pushing it." She's trying hard not to smile; that sparkle in her eyes obvious now.

Pushing back off the doorframe, I wink as I turn to head to the kitchen. "Get your fine ass out here, so we can eat, drink, and be merry."

"Drink?" Maggie says this with a groan. "I really want to drink more than I should tonight, after this week, especially." Her footfalls behind me tell me she's following me to the kitchen.

"Well, lucky for you, I also stopped by Saratoga Winery and brought home some Bloodroot for dessert." Reaching into the refrigerator for our salads—mine, which is loaded down with grilled chicken, of course—I turn to see her pulling the bottle of wine from the bag on the counter. Bloodroot is one of her favorites, and it's an unusual wine, to say the least, since it's a Melomel wine made with honey and aged in a Kentucky bourbon barrel.

It's also fourteen percent alcohol, so it packs a hell of a punch.

It turns out that I had no idea just how much of a punch that Melomel would end up serving.

In more ways than one.

CHAPTER THIRTY-FIVE

Maggie

I've indulged in this particular wine before. However, let it be said that I haven't indulged as much as tonight. Between my boss driving me to drink—literally—and Ry snagging pretty much every guy I come into contact with, I'm feeling the urge to drown my problems in some Bloodroot.

And I do. *Ohhh*, do I ever.

You know the point when your words start slurring, and you notice it? So then you try harder to not slur your words but only end up talking slower and sounding even more intoxicated?

That's me right now. I'm one glass of Melomel past caring, though.

Ry and I are sprawled on the couch. I'm leaning against pillows with my legs draped over his thighs, his palm resting on my bare knee. I'm dressed in a pair of comfortable cotton sleep shorts, a tank top, and a zip-up hoodie over it. The worst part right now is, for some reason, the way Ry's hand feels on my bare skin makes me recall exactly how long it's been since I've been touched by a guy. You know, like *that*.

Way. Too. Long. Not to mention, the last guy to touch

me was *Ry*. And the memories of what happened between us in his parents' house …

Shifting my legs slightly, I turn my head to look at his profile as he watches the movie. His straight nose, strong jawline, and lips all mesmerize me. My fingers itch to trace his face, to touch him.

"Ry?" My voice comes out soft, tentative.

He turns his head to look at me, and I suddenly wish the lights were on instead of only having the television to illuminate his face; the other part of it shadowed in the dark living room.

"Mags?"

"Can I ask you something?"

"You can ask me anything." His response is immediate, and I can hear the sincerity in his tone, which makes me feel bad for being angry with him over everything.

"You've been with a girl, right? I mean, Stacy and you …"

Oh, crap. Drunk Maggie has officially taken over, people. Because that? That question. Uh-uh. *Noooo.* Sober Maggie would *not* go there.

He hesitates so long that I'm on the verge of blurting an apology when he surprises me.

"Yeah, I have."

And this, ladies and gentlemen, is what we refer to as opening Pandora's Box. Because no way in hell am I going to leave it at that.

"So … was it not good? Is that why you…" I trail off, unsure of how to ask him.

His chuckle is brief. "You're asking if it was terrible and if that's why I'm with Jack?"

"Yes."

Ry turns his attention back to the television. "No, it

wasn't terrible." There's a brief pause. "I always enjoyed it."

"What was your favorite part?" That's it. I'm cutting myself off. Except that the damage is already done, and I … *really* want to know his answer.

When he turns his attention back to me, the heavy weight of his gaze focuses on me, and if I didn't know better, I'd swear there was heat behind it, too.

"My favorite part?"

Does he realize that his hand has begun to graze my knee and lower thigh? That I have zero desire to stop him?

"My favorite part might be touching the woman's nipples and sucking on them, flicking them with my tongue until they're hard and she's arching into my touch."

Oh, sweet baby Jesus. My breathing stutters, my nipples hardening just listening to him say that. And not wearing a bra, I wonder if he can see them trying their best to poke through the thin material of my hoodie.

To make matters worse, he continues, his voice gravelly and deep. "Another favorite part would have to be sliding my finger inside her pussy, feeling how wet she is, feeling her clench around me. Or," he pauses, and I find myself holding my breath, waiting for him to continue, "tasting her for the first time, sliding my tongue inside her. Or sucking on her clit and making her come, riding my face."

Oh, God. I'm so turned on right now, just by him talking to me—telling me his favorite things to do to a woman. Mesmerized by his words, my eyes fall closed, and I don't realize that his fingers are grazing over the hem of my shorts, which have ridden up. I'm soaking wet right now, aching, my body yearning for release from something other than my vibrator.

"Or the moment when I'm fucking her with my tongue."

I try to stifle the moan his words elicit, but I can't be

sure I've succeeded. I'm too busy imagining that I can feel his fingers sliding beneath my shorts, drifting to where I'm bare beneath them, his fingertips grazing over my center.

"The moment I feel how wet she gets for me ... How fucking delicious she smells." It sounds like his breathing has become ragged, like my own, as if he knows how naughty my thoughts have become. I'm far too lost in my fantasy to pay much mind as I can almost feel his fingertips tease me, sliding over me and gathering my wetness, my legs falling apart farther.

"The moment I feel how hot and wet she is for me." Two of his thick fingers slide inside me, and I can't resist arching into his touch.

"Ry," I breathe out, feeling myself get wetter with the in and out motions of his fingers thrusting.

"You like that?" His voice is harsh, breathing ragged, as if he's exerting himself.

Gasping when he curves his fingers, hooking them inside me, I can barely form a breathless, "*Yes.*"

"But you want more, don't you?"

I can feel the tingling and know that I'm getting close, but not close enough. I need more. And it's as if he knows this when he whispers, "You want me to put my mouth on you, Maggie? For me to suck on your clit and make you come?"

"God, yes." I barely register the movement of my shorts, mindless to only ensuring the sinful torture continues, as they are pulled down my legs. Feeling the cooler air hit my bare center and hearing a muted curse from Ry, it startles me slightly. Just as I'm on the verge of opening my eyes, his mouth is on me, his tongue taking the place of his fingers, thrusting inside me and tasting me deeply. There's no way I can restrain from pushing against him, as if trying to get his tongue to slide deeper.

His fingers tweak my clit before his thumb presses down, circling it while his tongue darts in and out of me. When I feel myself get tighter, my entire body growing taut in anticipation of my impending orgasm, he whispers to me, "Come for me, Mags." His tongue and mouth devour me as his thumb increases its pressure, the pace of its circular motions becoming more rapid. My body arches as my inner muscles clench and release, rapid fire, and his tongue continues to drive me wild.

"Ry ... I'm coming," I gasp, brokenly, as I ride out my orgasm, tremors wracking my body. When the waves finally subside, my breathing beginning to calm, my haze starts to subside.

And that's when it hits me. When awareness sets in; some sort of alert that not all is what it seems—that not everything happened in my thoughts, alone.

My eyes fly open as if I'm daring myself to be wrong. Daring myself to believe that what just happened was a figment of my imagination.

The moment I focus on Ry's face, still barely inches away from where my legs are still spread on the couch ... The moment I focus on Ry's face—the one that's still between my spread legs—I know the truth.

"Oh, crap."

CHAPTER THIRTY-SIX

Ry

I'm a bastard.

I took advantage of my roommate and best friend while she was under the influence. It's so fucking wrong. Yet a part of me is undeniably pleased that I just managed to make her orgasm with my fingers and tongue.

That it was my name she cried out when she found her release.

But before I can say anything, her eyes open, and instead of the sated afterglow upon her beautiful face, all I see is horror.

And regret.

"Mags," I say calmly, slowly rising from my position between her legs. God, I can still taste her on my lips, on my tongue, and it wouldn't take much to have me coming in my shorts right now. Maybe one more taste of her. Never before have I been in fear of shooting my load in my damn shorts just by going down on—or even making out with—a woman.

Until Maggie.

"It's okay, Mags."

"Oh, my God, Ry," she cries out. "What the hell did I just do?"

Sliding up her body so that we're eye to eye, I brace myself on my forearms. I speak calmly, trying to soothe her before she gets too hysterical. "It's okay."

Her face twists, wearing a tormented expression. "How is it okay? How is what we just did okay?" Her hands cover her eyes, her head giving a brief, tiny shake. "I basically just used you to get off. *Again*. How is that okay?"

"Because you know me, and you know that I won't do anything to hurt you. That it's safe."

"But what about Jack," she whispers.

"Jack's been …" I hesitate, attempting to steer toward more truths than outright lies. "Out of town. A lot, lately." I let the insinuation hang there. And it's true; he has been out of town a whole hell of a lot lately. For work.

Her fingers part slightly, her eyes peeking through at me. "You think he's …?"

I give a small shrug as an answer, my hand reaching up, giving a brief tug at my left earlobe. "The thing is I haven't been with anyone else, Mags." *Because I'm in love with you.* "We can … help each other out."

"Ry, I don't know." But I hear it in her tone. She's considering it.

Which is why I play dirty. Because I'll do anything to have her. Because, while I realize she might not be ready just yet to hear me tell her how I feel, I certainly plan to show her how I feel.

"What are you unsure about?" I lower my head, pressing my lips to her earlobe before darting the tip of my tongue out to trace the shell of her ear. When she inhales sharply, I know I'm on the right track. "Did you not like my tongue inside you?" My teeth tug gently on her earlobe. "Did you not like coming all over my tongue?"

Her chest is rising and falling with heavy breaths now.

Shifting to slide a hand to her hoodie, I watch her while my fingers pull the zipper down slowly before parting the fabric, displaying her already puckered nipples poking through the fabric of her tank top. With my gaze still locked on hers, my thumb grazes over the top of one nipple, watching her eyelids grow heavy with lust as her body arches of its own accord into my touch.

When I dip my head to suck her nipple through the fabric, she gasps loudly, shamelessly pushing her breast into my mouth. Suddenly, her hands grip my shoulder, pushing me away.

"Wait." The urgency in her tone has me lifting up, concerned, and to be honest, more than crestfallen that she's stopping me.

"You have to tell him." I have no idea what she's talking about, and it must show on my face because she adds, "You have to tell Jack before we do this. I don't feel right about it otherwise."

"O-kay," I draw out the word before scrambling for my phone, uncaring that the old pair of athletic shorts I have on can't do shit to conceal my massive boner. Grabbing my cell phone off the coffee table, I hurriedly type out a text to Jack.

Hey. I'm about to sleep with Maggie. Just had to let you know.

Surprisingly, Jack's response comes back mere seconds later. He must be pulling another late work night and have his cell close by.

Jack: Sounds hot. Thanks for letting me know.

Instantly, I turn the phone to Maggie to let her read his response. Appearing slightly surprised by Jack's apparent nonchalance at receiving that text, she gapes at me.

"You're just telling him in a text?" There's a hint of

disbelief in her tone. Then, in a quiet, more thoughtful murmur, I hear, "I guess that's one of the many differences between men and women."

Turning to replace my phone on the coffee table, I'm more than ready to resume things, but before I set it down, the light blinks with another incoming text notification.

Jack: Since we're sharing, the only action I'll be getting here is with the shit ton of work I've got going on. Oh, and I guess I should mention that you suck for throwing me over for a chick? And your penis was WAY too small for me.

Yeah, he's a comedian.

Turning back to Maggie, I realize she's regarding me carefully. Reaching for the bottom of my cotton T-shirt, I pull it up and over my head and discard it on the arm of the couch. The moment her eyes take in the sight of me, I feel the heat upon my skin, nearly scorching me. Sliding over her in the position I was in mere minutes ago, I gently slide up her tank top, grazing her smooth skin, baring her full breasts, her nipples dark and puckered as if begging for my mouth again. Cupping their weight in my hands, I drag the pads of my thumbs over the top of her nipples, loving the way her body arches into my touch. It's like she's silently begging for more.

So, of course, I give her what she's asking for. Taking one of her nipples between my thumb and forefinger, I tweak it, reveling in her gasp before grazing the other with my teeth then sucking on it with just the right amount of pressure.

Her hands fly to my head, her fingers sifting through my hair, tightening as if trying to restrain me from moving away. As if there was a chance of that happening? Not in this lifetime.

Between sucking, licking, and flicking her nipples with tongue, I murmur, "Are you getting wet again for me?"

Her laugh is short. "Again?" She lets out a tiny moan, her tone breathless. "I'm still so wet."

Trailing kisses downward, over her stomach and across her hipbones, I realize that this location is going to pose more of a difficulty if we continue here. Abruptly making an executive decision, I shift off her, sliding my arms beneath her.

"What—" Her protest dies once she realizes where we're headed as I rush down the hall and into my bedroom.

Gently laying her back on my large bed, I realize the small lamp beside the bed is already lit, casting a glow upon her skin. Reaching to help rid her of her hoodie and tank top, I bask in the sight of her as soon as they're discarded, and I swear that I get harder just looking at her.

Hurriedly shoving down my shorts, my cock juts out, and the moment her eyes shift to it, I nearly blow my load then and there. The way her eyes darken, the tip of her tongue darting out to wet her bottom lip as she sits up, almost makes me come undone. When she shifts on her knees, coming closer to where I stand at the edge of the bed, I nearly swallow my tongue when she reaches out to wrap her hand around my cock.

Watching her hand grip the shaft, sliding up and down slowly, I'm transfixed by the sight. When her thumb swipes the moisture at the tip, my entire body jerks, and my fists clench to refrain from taking her right then and there, like a rough caveman.

"You'd better have a condom handy." Her voice is low, breathy as she strokes me, her eyes darting up to meet mine.

"Only one?" I can't resist teasing her, and when she lets out a husky laugh, I can't help but wonder if it will always be like this between us.

"Don't get cocky."

Moving swiftly, I reach out, sliding my hands into her hair. My fingers thread through it, tugging her face up to meet my kiss—and it's fucking perfect. Our lips move against one another, our tongues sliding inside, darting at each other, tasting deep. When she doesn't relinquish her hold on my cock during the kiss, I grow even harder.

Breaking the kiss, she drags her lips across my cheek to my jawline and whispers, "I need you, Ry."

Pausing, I have to ask the question nagging at me. My hands frame her face, gazing into her beautiful eyes. "Mags." My thumbs graze her cheekbones as I search her face. "Are you sure about this? You've been drinking."

When she leans into one palm before turning her head to press a kiss to the center, my heart feels like it's about to beat right out of my chest. Facing me again, her eyes meet mine. "I trust you, Ry. I want this."

How is it possible to feel gutted and exhilarated simultaneously? Because that's exactly how I feel right now. She trusts me. And I've been lying to her. But she wants me and—

The hand grasping my cock begins to work me again and draws me from my inner turmoil. "You'd better hurry up and find that condom." Releasing me, she settles back on the bed, and I watch as her hands glide over her body, slowly sliding over her hardened nipples before beginning their descent down over her stomach to—

"Ry." Her voice jerks me from my stupor, and I rummage through my nightstand for condoms, thanking Trojan that they make these suckers with a long expiration date since I haven't been with anyone in quite a while.

Anyone besides my hand, that is. But he doesn't count.

Ripping open the wrapper, I roll the condom over my length, glancing up to see Maggie's eyes focused on me. If I thought I couldn't get harder, I was wrong. I'm harder than I've ever been. More than that, though, I'm nervous as hell because so much is on the line.

I have to show Maggie that I care for her—and not just as my roommate or a best friend. I have to show her that I love her.

I have to show her that I'm the one who wants to be with her. Not just for tonight but … *always.*

CHAPTER THIRTY-SEVEN

Maggie

I'm pretty sure I'm having an out-of-body experience. But I don't want it to end because it's so addictively surreal to watch Ry—*my* Ry—naked and hard, with his hand gripping his hard cock, watching me with a look full of such intense emotions.

My hands are touching my own body, stoking the fire he started out there on the couch. His eyes darken, heavy-lidded with lust as he watches me; my fingers begin circling my clit, turning me on even more.

Easing himself over the top of me, I can't withhold a gasp the moment he lowers himself, his bare chest brushing against my breasts, his hard length prodding between my legs as I bring my knees up, my feet flat on the bed.

"Fuck, Mags," he breathes against my neck between kisses and tiny nips. "I'm trying to take this slow and make it good for you, but you're killing me."

There's no way to stifle my grin at his words because the knowledge that he's as turned on as I am sends gratification running through me. Gliding my hands down his back, I trace the curves and indentation of his muscles beneath my fingers, and when I reach his firm ass, I can't resist grabbing it and pulling him closer toward me. Feeling the tip of him prodding my entrance, I tug his ass closer.

"Trying to rush me, Mags?" he teases, his hot breath washing over my skin as he trails kisses along my collarbone.

"Yes." I have zero shame right now.

Propping up on his arms to look into my eyes, I feel like he's trying to tell me something; the softness in his eyes makes something in my chest tighten. His lips form a smile that's tender with a hint of playfulness, and when he dips his head to brush his lips against mine, the kiss sweet and soft, I can't resist sliding my tongue inside his mouth to deepen the kiss. The instant I do, his groan encourages me, and I tilt my head, sliding my tongue against his while my hands tug his ass toward me. The tip of his cock slides in only an infinitesimal amount, but it's enough to have us both gasping.

Rocking my hips, trying to encourage him, I break the kiss to toy with his lower lip, my teeth nipping at it before I suck at it, my tongue darting to it soothingly.

"Please, Ry," I whisper, my eyes locked with his. "Please."

He appears as though he's trying to resist giving in, warring with himself, until I rock my hips again and he fastens his mouth to mine in a feverish, passionate kiss while simultaneously pushing inside me. Gasping into his mouth, my fingers dig into the muscles of his glutes as I embrace the way his cock is stretching me, the way my body's working to adjust to his size.

He breaks the kiss, pausing his movements with a look of concern on his handsome face. "Am I hurting you?"

"No," I say in a ragged breath. "It's just been a long time." Reaching a hand up to his face, I whisper, "Don't stop."

When he pushes all the way inside me, my eyes fall closed, lips parting at the way he feels inside me. It's indescribable. But I know he's holding back. Opening my eyes to peer up at him, his jaw is clenched tight, his face a mask of concentrated restraint.

My hands move, placing my palms against his chest, my lips twisting in a slight grin. "It's my turn to be on top."

He stills, obviously faltering for a response before saying, "I don't think—"

"I didn't ask." My palms press against his firm pectorals. "I'm telling you."

Something shifts in his gaze, and in one fluid motion, he turns us over on the bed, with him beneath me. As soon as I shift my body, I feel it—feel him slide deeper inside me, feel the difference in this position. His hands move, one gripping my hips while the other tucks my hair back behind my ear. The tenderness in his gesture combined with the way he's watching me sends a shiver of awareness—and something else—through me.

Bracing my palms against his chest, I lean in closer, bringing my lips barely a hairsbreadth away from his to whisper, "What are we doing?"

It feels as though his eyes are staring right through me, so intense with emotion and heat. Just when I think he's going to answer, his hand cups the back of my head and his lips latch onto mine. Our mouths meld, tongues sparring. His other hand is gripping my hip as he gives a strong thrust upward into me, eliciting a loud gasp from me before I begin to work myself over him in a rocking motion, my clit rubbing against his pelvis.

An inner voice whispers in the back of my mind, "*What are we doing?*", while the other part of me is left to wonder about that intense emotion I saw in the depths of his gaze.

Ry's hand at the back of my head shifts, and his fingers tighten in my hair, slanting his lips over mine as he devours me. His taste is addictive, and I'm growing increasingly wet from both his kiss and his cock pushing me closer to another orgasm.

The moment his hand moves to grip my other hip is when everything changes. With his stronghold, he pulls me down on his cock while simultaneously giving a deep upward thrust into me. It nearly sends my eyes rolling back in my head; it feels so good, hitting *that* spot, sending shivers through my body.

"Ry," I breathe.

He does it again, his cock hitting deep, hard; his heavy-lidded gaze locked onto mine. "You're so beautiful, Mags."

The way he says it—in a low, husky whisper—makes it feel like the air just got sucked out of the room. Before I can react, he slides his thumb between our bodies to press against my clit. With just the right amount of pressure, his fingers begin to move in circles.

Arching, I ride his cock while he toys with my clit. The sight of his large hand transfixes my eyes; his thumb toys with me while I watch his thick cock disappear in and out of me. Giving myself over to the pleasure he's giving me, I let my eyes fall closed as I continue to work myself over him.

"That's it," he murmurs. "Feel how good we are together." He inhales sharply when I rock against him, shifting just so. "God, Mags. I'm so fucking close ... but I don't want to come without you."

Quickening my pace, nearly frantic now, his words spur me on as I slide up and down his cock, watching as his lips part, his breathing harsh and ragged. Bracing my palms more firmly on his chest, my eyes again draw to where our bodies are joined, at the sight of his thumb circling my clit.

"Looks so fucking hot," Ry groans, and when I glance

up, I see that his eyes are focused on the sight, too. As if knowing how close I am, his thumb and forefinger pluck at my clit, and that's all that it takes. My eyes fall closed as I clench around his cock, my body arching as I ride out my release. Ry's thrusts turn frantic, pushing deep and hard before letting out a low groan. When I finally collapse on him, my cheek against his heaving chest, we lie there in silence with nothing but the sound of our labored breathing.

I don't think I've ever come that hard before. Weird that Ry would be something of a clitoris guru, right? Especially since he's—

It hits me. Oh, no, no, *nooooo*. What did I just do?

I just had sex with my roommate, my best friend, my … Ry. And if that's not bad enough, there's more.

I *really* liked it.

CHAPTER THIRTY-EIGHT

Ry

Holy shit.

In all of my imaginings of what it would be like to be with Maggie, none of it could have come even close to this. And now that I know what it's like, there's no way in hell I can go back to one-on-one time with my palm.

Fuck no.

Which means I have to ensure that she'll be up for doing this again and again.

Wait. *Fuck!* What the hell? I have to get my shit together here. The whole point of this wasn't just to get into Maggie's panties—or lack thereof—tonight. Not that it wasn't hotter than the surface of the sun. It was. And the way she clenched so goddamn tight all around my cock when she came … *Fuck*.

The point is, though, that I'm trying to get her to see me as more. As the guy who loves her. As the guy who really hopes to hell that she'll be able to forgive me for not being gay.

Jesus. Just thinking that makes me sound like an idiot.

I swear there was a moment there when she could see it in my eyes—that she saw the love in my eyes. Maybe she's not quite ready for it, but I plan to remind her of it.

As our ragged breathing begins to slow, as my hand caresses the soft curve of her back, I feel it. The stiffening of her spine—the indication that her brain has kick started into panic mode. And that's exactly what I don't want.

"Hey." My tone is gentle, and I press a soft kiss to the top of her hair. "Talk to me."

She shakes her head against my chest. "I can't."

"You can talk to me about anyth—"

Abruptly, her head lifts off my chest, her eyes searching mine, worry lining her features. "Ry," she swallows hard, "I don't want to mess things up." Her gaze drops, focusing on my chest, as if embarrassed. "What does this mean?"

What does this mean? Everything, Mags. Everything.

Gently steering her chin up with my fingers, willing her eyes to meet mine, I offer her a small smile. "There's no way you're going to mess anything up."

Her eyes flicker over my face as if trying to gauge the truthfulness of my statement before whispering, "Promise?"

"I promise," I whisper back, my thumb grazing over her bottom lip. "I love you, Mags. Nothing could ever change that."

She's silent for a beat before her breath comes out in a whoosh. With a tiny but seemingly relieved smile, she lays her head back down on my chest. "I love you, too."

While those words are the ones I want desperately to hear her say, there's a problem. Because right now, she's saying them with "as a friend" silently tacked onto the end. And it's my job to ensure that changes. To ensure that someday—hopefully soon—she can say those words back to me and mean them the same way I do.

She spills over me to land on the bed in a sprawl with a long exhale while I turn to dispose of the condom in the nearby wastebasket. Rolling onto my back and turning my head to face her, I reach out to slide some stray hair back from her face. While Maggie isn't considered show-stoppingly gorgeous by society's standards, she is to me. Sure, her nose isn't perfectly narrow, and her hair can sometimes be a crazy mop of curls, but she's one of those people whose personality shines through like a blasting beam of light.

Maggie is the person who will see a homeless person on the side of the road and give them her lunch. If that doesn't make you melt, I'm not sure what would. She just has a freaking heart of gold.

She also smiles with her eyes. Sounds like I just grew an ovary saying that, but seriously, there's just something about it. When she really smiles, her eyes crinkle, and it's just … *God*, it's just gorgeous. And the way her entire face lights up when she's excited about something makes it impossible not to feel the same.

When she turns to face me, watching me with those beautiful eyes of hers, she flashes me a mischievous grin. Scooting over to place a palm on my chest, she props her chin atop it, eyeing me.

"You look like you're up to no good, Mags." I can't resist smiling back at her. She's just too damn cute.

"Well," her eyes flash, and her grin widens, "I was just thinking that now I know what your *O* face looks like."

"And?" I cock an eyebrow.

Her face twists in a look of faux disappointment, but her eyes give her away, still sparkling with humor. "It could use some work."

"Really?"

"Yep." She pops the *p* at the end.

"Huh. That's interesting." I pretend to mull over her words. "Because I recall someone—mere minutes ago—going on and on like"—I imitate her higher pitched voice—*"Oh, Ry, I'm coming! Oh, Ry, right there! Ryyyyyy—"* My words cut off when a pillow is shoved against my face.

"Ryland James! I do not sound like that!"

Tossing the pillow aside, I roll over on top of her. Our bodies press against one another, and my cock is already rising to the occasion. Gazing down at her, I dip my head to whisper against the column of her neck. "I bet I can prove you sound exactly like that."

Slipping down her body, I press my mouth against her core.

And, oh, I prove it. Over and over again.

CHAPTER THIRTY-NINE

Maggie

"**M**ags," Sarah winces with a concerned expression, "are you sure you know what you're doing?"

No. Not at all. "It's just ... nice, you know? To have someone I feel so comfortable with being the same person that I ..." I trail off, unsure of how to finish. I've been *beyond* nervous about coming clean to her about what Ry and I have been, uh, doing for the past few weeks.

Sarah glances around the coffee shop where we decided to meet for a long overdue girls-only coffee date Saturday morning. The same coffee date I was unusually late for—a whopping ten minutes—and I *hate* being late. Hate. It. But today, I didn't mind so much. Because, well, the reason I was late was ... because someone had insisted on making me come a fourth time.

Yep, when I had somehow blurted out that a guy had never brought me to orgasm more than three times in a row before, Ry took it as a challenge. A serious challenge. God, just thinking about him going down on me this morning, my fingers tugging on his short hair while I rode his face—

"Stop it right now." Sarah's sharp tone draws me from my thoughts, and I see her pointing a finger accusingly at me. "That's not permitted." Sipping her coffee, she mutters, "Especially not when I haven't gotten any action in far too long."

"Sorry."

"No, you're not." She laughs. "You're flushed and have that lightness to your eyes." Waving a hand dismissively, she adds, "Don't mind me. I need to live vicariously through you since my job and school are so crazy and zap any energy I might otherwise have to try and find a guy."

Leaning closer and lowering her voice, she sobers. "Seriously, though. What's going on? Are you and Ry a thing, now?"

My lips part to answer her, but then my ears catch a hint of a familiar ruggedly male voice saying, "It's not serious, then?" There's a pause. "Yeah, Ry, I get it. It's cool. We can still get together later on this week."

Right then, it's as if I can actually feel my face lose all color, like it drips downward, leaving me a pale mess. My heart's racing wildly, and I think I might need a brown paper bag to hyperventilate in. What's worse is that I shouldn't be feeling any of this because Ry and I aren't even together. We aren't a thing. We aren't anything. So what if he's talking to Jack about me, telling him it wasn't serious, and they'll likely get together again this week.

So. What. I don't care.

Crap. I'm a horrible liar even when trying to lie to myself. Talk about pathetic.

"Maggie?" Sarah's staring at me oddly, and I realize I've been sitting here and never answered her.

"Hello, ladies." Jack's voice greets us, standing beside our table with his own iced coffee in hand and wearing a warm smile on his face.

"Hi, Jack." Hurriedly, I rise from my chair and push it

in noisily, frantically needing to escape. "Bye, Jack." Racing over to give Sarah the quickest hug in the history of mankind, I whisper a quick apology in her ear about having to leave right away.

Exiting the coffee shop as though the devil himself were at my heels, I nearly sprint down the sidewalk to the apartment. Because I can't do this. What was I thinking? I wasn't. It had just been too long since I'd been with a guy, and I had a weak moment.

Okay, so a lot of weak moments if you count how many times Ry and I have, um, done … *things*.

Over the past month.

Holy shadoobie. I've been sleeping with Ry that long already? How is that even possible? It's like the guy has cast some sort of creepy spell over me or something.

But that's not the worst part. The worst part of this whole debacle is the fact that I've been starting to … have feelings for him. The more-than-friends kind of feelings. Like I want to hang out, watch movies, and eat popcorn with him just like normal except for the fact that I'd also like to eat the popcorn off his body. And lick off every smidge of salt left behind. And have him return the favor by ensuring no salt remains on my body.

Especially in the area between my legs. Because, you know, things can collect there. He'd have to use his tongue to really get in there.

Whew! I'm getting myself all hot and bothered just thinking about this scenario. There's a problem with this, though. He evidently does not feel the same way. That much was clear from the conversation he just had with Jack.

Which means I have to end it before I get hurt, before I get too attached. *Er*, okay, more attached than I already am. I have to put him back in that box, the one specified as roommate and best friend only, and remove the additional, temporary sticky label of "sex partner."

Yeah, that bums me out just thinking it. Not only because he's phenomenal in bed—he is—but because when we have sex, it's almost like … more. Like there's emotion behind it. More emotion and feelings than just two people's bodies coming together for pleasure; more than two people, who get along really well outside of the bedroom, having sex. More than that.

It was like, maybe—just maybe—hearts were getting involved, too.

CHAPTER FORTY

Ry

The door opens, and I hear Maggie enter the apartment from her coffee date with Sarah. Glancing at the time, I note that she's home far earlier than I expected, especially since I made her late.

There's no way to restrain the smile forming on my face thinking about *how* I made her late. After her disclosure that no guy had managed to make her orgasm more than three times in a row before, I had been determined to surpass that.

And I had. Oh, how I surpassed it. The memory of it has me adjusting my now hardening cock. I'd gone down on her, licking her, devouring her, tasting her when she came that fourth time this morning.

Sitting at the table looking over some spreadsheets for work so I wouldn't miss her being gone—I know, totally pathetic—I had called Jack to see if he'd be able to free up some time to go over some things with me. The last time I'd asked him to look over things, it ended with someone being fired. This time, it wasn't as serious; I merely wanted another set of eyes to check things over, and Jack's one of the best business consultants I know.

Looking up, I know I have a goofy ass grin on my face,

waiting for Mags to walk down the hall to me. My grin drops as soon as I catch sight of her because something is definitely wrong. Abruptly rising from my seat, I walk over to her. Reaching for her, she shrinks back. It's not overly obvious, but I notice it.

"Mags? What's wrong?" My eyes search her expression for any hint as to what might be bothering her.

She lets out a long exhale, moving to set her purse and keys down on one of the chairs before pulling off her fleece and tossing it down beside them. "We need to talk."

My eyes fall closed on a silent curse because everyone who has an IQ of at least ten knows that phrase never bodes well.

Never.

Shoving my hands in the pockets of my pajama pants, I try to maintain some modicum of calm. "Mags, talk to me. Please."

Whirling around, she waves a hand in gesture. "I just think that maybe this was a mistake, you know? We probably shouldn't have veered into this territory, muddying the waters of our friendship, especially since we're roommates, too. Too messy. And I think the right thing to do is to go back to the way things were before." Her words are rushed, as though she's forcing them out in rapid fire. "We need to forget anything happened." She punctuates this last part with a quick nod.

And me? I'm not sure how I'm still standing upright because her words gut me.

Abso-fucking-lutely gut me.

Just as my lips start to form a protest to try to convince her that she's not thinking clearly and to give it some more thought, it all gets tossed out the window with one softly spoken word.

"*Please.*"

My eyes close on a wince, that word piercing my damn heart and soul at once.

Please.

Please forget that I ever made love to her.

Please forget that I had my mouth on nearly every inch of her beautiful body.

Please forget that every time our lips met, I was kissing her with my entire heart.

Somehow, I manage to swallow past the lump in my throat, the blatant rejection washing over me. Blowing out a long breath, I open my eyes to find her watching me with a pleading look on her face. I don't even think—I just blurt out words.

"On one condition."

Her brows furrow. "One condition?"

"One condition." Because no way in hell am I going to bow out quietly.

"What … condition is that?" Her hesitance is evident.

Stepping closer, I reach out, grateful that she doesn't shy away from my touch this time, my hands cradling her face. "My condition is if this is it, then we need to end it right."

Something shifts in her expression. "And how do you suggest we end it?"

Closing the distance between us, I let her feel my arousal, hardening at the thoughts in my mind, at the prospect that she might give me one final time with her. The way her lips part when she notices, when she feels me, urges me on.

"I suggest," I lean in closer, brushing my lips against hers, "we do it right." My hands slide down to cup her ass, pulling her into me as I rock against her. "To have one last time where I make you come all over my cock." Trailing wet kisses across her cheek to her earlobe, I smile at her gasp. "And then over my tongue and fingers." Her breath is coming out in harsh pants now, eyes closed.

"Does that sound all right to you, Mags?" My voice is low, husky as I rock myself against her once more.

"Yes," she breathes, one of her hands moving between us, palming my hard length through my thin, cotton pants. Unable to withhold a groan as she works me with her hand, I nearly lose it the moment she slides beneath the waistband and grasps me, working her hand up and down along my thick shaft.

"You'd better voice any complaints now." I gasp when her thumb grazes my tip, running over the slit and gathering the moisture there. "Because I'm about to take you right here against the wall."

"Do it," she whispers, her eyes watching me, filled with so much heat that it nearly takes my breath away.

Instantly, I lift her, her legs wrap around my waist as I stalk to the wall, caging her against it. Her simple, black pair of yoga pants barely serves as a barrier when I press my cock against her core, eliciting a moan that sends pride running through me. Her fingers dig into the muscles of my shoulders as our lips meet in a feverish, rough kiss with our teeth knocking one minute before our tongues dart and retreat.

It's like a war; a battle. I'm intent on claiming her one final time. There's only one problem. One of us is giving *in* while the other is giving up everything to the other.

The other person is giving up their heart, offering it in silent desperation.

Begging to be loved back.

CHAPTER FORTY-ONE

Maggie

There's a split second when I think to myself, *Why am I saying yes to this?* But then Ry touches me, and well ... all he has to do is touch me. Heck, I'm pretty sure all he actually has to do is lay a finger on me, and I start melting.

The moment he picks me up and pushes me against the wall is the moment everything fades into nothing but Ry and me. The way he feels, the way he moves against me, the way he's kissing me. And, God, the way he's kissing me right now is unlike anything I've ever known. His kisses are more fierce and more passionate than any kiss I've ever experienced. His lips are like the gateway drug for me: once he kisses me, I'm a goner.

My legs wrap around him, my back presses against the wall, and I honestly don't register the firmness of the plaster at my back. I concentrate on the taste of him on my lips, the way his tongue spars with my own, and the way he's pressing his cock into me, nudging me right where I ache for him most.

His hand gliding up along my side has me immediately arching, as if urging him to touch my breasts, to toy with my nipples. I wish, desperately, that we were already naked with no barriers between us.

Using his body weight to hold me in place, one of his hands slides beneath the hem of my shirt, shoving my sports bra up and out of the way. His calloused thumb and forefinger wreak havoc on my hardened nipples, tweaking them until I'm aching for his lips and mouth to do the same. His other hand delves beneath the waistband of my pants, his fingers sliding between us to glide over my core and trace over the folds to gather the wetness there before focusing on my clit. My inner muscles clench, and I silently mourn the fact that he's not already inside me.

"You want me inside you?" he says with a husky growl in my ear.

Okay, so maybe I wasn't so silent in my thinking.

"God, yes."

"Open your eyes." He takes tiny nips along the column of my neck before his tongue darts out soothingly. The moment I open my eyes, he slowly peels my shirt off me with my sports bra following. One hand comes up to cup a breast, thumb grazing over the tip, and I can't withhold the sharp inhalation at the touch. It's like every single nerve ending is in an overly sensitive state, a jolt shooting through me at the feel of the slightly roughened skin of the pad of his thumb over the tip of my nipple.

"You like when I do that?"

How the heck is he sounding so composed right now? When I'm here—against this wall—an aching, wet, aroused mess just waiting for him to put me out of my misery?

I can only manage to whisper a soft, "Yes," before he dips his head to latch on to my nipple. Instantaneously, I feel a rush of arousal flood me, so soaking wet for him in anticipation of him pushing inside me soon.

Please let it be soon.

"I need you, Ry." The words are out before I can think—before I even realize I've said them.

His gaze is so intense that it nearly takes my breath away. "What do you need?"

Rocking myself against him, I can't restrain my whimper. "I need this. You."

His fingers roughly shove down the waistband of my pants, setting me on my feet before he kneels down to remove them from around my ankles, baring me. Still crouched before me, his eyes slowly take me in, moving up, up, up, and stopping right there. At the apex of my thighs, the part of me that yearns for him the most.

Reaching up slowly, he moves to trace the crease of my entrance with his index finger, top to bottom, achingly slow, before suddenly sliding inside me. I gasp loudly, my head falling back against the wall. He works his finger in and out before adding another, and I note how easily they move, gliding through my wetness.

"I need you inside me." I don't care how needy I sound right now. If I don't have him pushing his hard cock inside me, if I don't feel him stretching me with his size, then I'm pretty certain I'll go insane.

His hazel eyes rise, holding my own while he slides his fingers out of me. Bringing them to his mouth, he slides them between his lips. His eyes fall closed at that moment, appearing to savor my taste on his fingers by sucking my essence off them. When his eyes find mine once again, he slowly rises, thumbs slipping beneath the waist of his pajama pants and shoving them down to kick them off to the side. He quickly rids himself of his plain cotton T-shirt, standing there before me in his full, naked glory. His cock is breathtaking, so thick and hard, jutting outward as if waiting for me to—

"Have you always used a condom?" The words are out before I even think it through.

His eyes are watchful. "Always, Mags. I've never been with anyone unprotected."

That's the answer I wanted—needed. Dropping to my knees, I grasp him in my hand before my tongue darts out to lick the tip, tasting the drop of fluid there, reveling in the salty taste before sliding my lips over him. Using my hand, mouth, and tongue, I suck and slide over his length, feeling him grow harder inside my mouth. When his fingers tangle in my hair, I glance up to see him watching me, lids low, eyes hazy with heat, lips parted, breathing ragged. And it's then that I feel pride—an empowering pride—that I made him this way.

Even though it's the last time this will ever happen.

That thought elbows its way into my thoughts, but I try not to let it derail my intent. I feel as though his gaze locks with mine in a way that's compelling me not to look away. The connection we have right now, while I'm pleasuring him with my mouth, is so intense that every part of my body is tingling with awareness.

The moment his fingers tighten their grip on my hair, I know he's close. The instant he pulls away from me, away from my mouth, I feel a sense of loss. Before I can voice this, he scoops me up in his arms, and we hurriedly make our way down the hall to his bedroom. Setting me on the mattress, he joins me, his body hovering over mine, all the curves and sharp indentations of muscles flexing above me.

I'm operating on feeling alone, not necessarily thinking like I normally do but going along a more visceral route. Grasping his firm length in my hand, I brush his tip against my opening, coating him in my wetness. Watching him as I do this, the way he clenches his jaw tight and swallows hard, his eyes maintaining a laser-like focus on mine, encourages me.

The moment I press upward while guiding him to me, he tenses, stopping me.

"Mags."

There's a brief moment of silence as I wait for him to finish, watching him carefully.

"I have to get a c—"

He breaks off the moment I arch upward, pressing him into me. "No. Not this time." My eyes plead with his. "I'm on the Pill. Please. Just this once."

Don't ask me why I'm doing this, why I'm asking this of him when I've never done this before in my entire life. Not even Shane, who'd always insisted on wearing a condom because he'd wanted to "wait to take chances on starting a family." Who knew what a godsend that would be?

I've never been with a guy unprotected—never truly trusted anyone this much. But I trust Ry.

I don't want to admit why or delve into anything pertaining to it. All I know is that I need him inside me without any barriers.

I need to *feel* him.

One last time.

CHAPTER FORTY-TWO

Ry

Five, ten, fifteen, twenty, twenty-*fuuuuuuck*…

My attempt at counting by fives to try to keep myself under control is failing. Miserably. Being with Maggie like this, sliding inside her without a condom, is unbelievable. And it's making it so hard to maintain control and not come inside her wet heat within one and a quarter thrusts like a completely inexperienced prepubescent boy.

Sinking inside her, I hope—hell, I pray—that her request means something. Anything. It has to. As I slowly, gradually work myself deeper inside her, my eyes stay on hers, watching them nearly glow with heat. Finally sliding in as far as I can, I still.

"Mags," I whisper against her lips. With that one word, my thumb grazes the side of her face along her cheekbone, and I will her to see in my eyes what I'm silently professing.

I love you.

You're the one for me.

Please forgive me for lying to you.

Please love me back.

When she shifts beneath me slightly, making us both inhale sharply, it breaks the moment. Her hands glide over my shoulders, my chest, and down my stomach, my muscles contracting at her touch. One soft hand slides over my hip while the other traces lower, closer to where our bodies join. Lifting up to allow her more room to roam, I feel her finger trace down below my belly button, down to the base of my shaft that's slick from her. Carefully, achingly slow, I move out barely an inch before sliding back inside her as we both watch the movement.

My eyes dart up to see her face before returning; my eyes tracking my slow thrusts, noting the shiny slickness of my cock and the knowledge that it's her—it's *my* Maggie who's making my cock that wet—makes me grow even more impossibly hard.

"Faster, Ry," she whispers, her eyes rising to meet mine. At that moment, there's nothing I wouldn't do for her if she asked me.

Bracing myself, my hands on either side of her, I begin to thrust as deep as possible while simultaneously praying I won't come too early in the game because … hell. The intensity of sensations, being inside her like this, feeling *everything*—the heat, tightness, the wetness—is nearly overwhelming. And I have to tell her.

"Mags, I—" My words cut off because, at that moment, she clenches around my cock, so impossibly tight, before the spasms begin and her inner muscles clench and release, clench and release. Her body arches, rosy nipples puckered, eyes closed as her head tips back on the pillow, lips parting.

It's right then and there that I know without a doubt I've never before witnessed anything in my entire life as decadently beautiful as this. As her.

Giving more powerful, deeper thrusts as she rides out her release, I feel the telltale tingling.

"Mags." My breathing is ragged, labored, and in the next second, I pull out of her, coming all over her stomach in strong spurts. I collapse beside her, my chest rising and falling.

"Promise I'll clean you off. As soon as my legs start working again."

She gives a huff of a laugh, turning her head to look at me. Shifting to face her, she's watching me with an odd expression.

"You didn't ..." She trails off before finishing with, "... come inside me."

My eyes flicker to her stomach, and instead of answering, I jump up, quickly heading to my bathroom for a damp washcloth. Returning to my bedroom, I carefully clean her stomach, speaking softly, my eyes focused on the task.

"I've never done this with anyone. And since it's the last time"—I break off with a slight shrug, still avoiding her gaze—"I didn't think it was smart to play with fire even more than we already were."

Tossing the damp cloth into my empty laundry bin, I climb into bed with Maggie, lying on my side and propping my head in my hand. My other hand traces along a random path, circling her breasts, her nipples, and down over her stomach, which she sucks in the moment I veer down over it.

My eyes dart up to hers, looking at her quizzically. She looks away, muttering, "My stomach isn't super awesome. I don't have abs like yours."

I give her a look. "Mags. If you had abs like mine, that would be weird."

"I have a one liter."

A laugh bursts free. "You do not have a one liter." Leaning closer, I press a soft kiss to the smooth skin of her stomach. "It's perfect." Raising my eyes to hers, I press another kiss. "Just like you."

She stares at me. "Well, doesn't Jack have pretty hard core abs?"

Shit. My eyes fall closed on a slight wince because, well, yeah, he does. Not that I've ever touched his abs. That's just disgusting.

Damn it, I need to come clean. This can't go on.

"I need to talk to you about Jack. I—"

She presses an index finger to my lips, stopping me. "No. You don't owe me any explanation, Ry." Her finger traces over my lips. "I know you'll likely get back together with him, and I understand that."

"But Mags—"

"Ry." The tenderness in both her eyes and tone has me faltering. "Please. Let it be just about us."

Knowing I'm unable to deny her anything, when she reaches for me, pressing her lips to mine in what has to be the sweetest kiss, I make it a point to give this my all.

Go big or go home, right? Well, I'm going to go big— go all out—and give this everything I have. Even though I can see it in her eyes; I can tell that this is it. This is all she's going to give me.

I love her throughout the day and into the night until we're both too exhausted to move, curling up beneath the covers. I watch her sleep, knowing this is the last time I'll get to witness her in my bed like this, before finally giving in to the tiredness and falling asleep with her in my arms.

And in the early morning light of dawn, when I feel the quiet, discreet shifting movement, I force myself to keep my eyes closed. I can't bear to see her tiptoe out of my bedroom like I was some sketchy one-night stand she's already regretting. I can't bear to watch her leave me.

Taking my damn heart right along with her.

CHAPTER FORTY-THREE

Maggie

"You're a horrible person. Don't even look in the mirror because it'll crack."

If you think that's an awful thing to say to someone, I'd agree with you … at any other time. Right now? Not so much.

Because *I'm* the person saying it. To *myself*.

Have you ever done something where you're like, *Wow. I actually did that. That was so unlike me.* And then you get this huge smile on your face that feels like it stretches for miles and miles, it's so wide. While at the same time you're like, *Whoa, you dirty girl, you! What the hell were you thinking?*

That's what I'm feeling. Because let's face it. We've all been in that situation where we do something we aren't super proud of. Like the one time in college, I went down on this super-hot guy just because I was feeling insecure and desperately wanted him to like me.

Yeah, I know. Stupid doesn't cover that, let alone degrading. Don't judge. We all do crap that's sketchy at some point in our lives. *Alllll* of us.

Except that right now, I'm fully judging myself. Because I had sex with my roommate—again—and with no protection. I mean, sure, he pulled out and everything—every single time—but …

Okay, so here's the thing. Each time he did that, I felt kind of deflated. Like he was holding back from me. Which is ridiculous since I'm the one who told him it was the last time that it could happen between us.

And now, while I stare at the steamed-up mirror, standing on my plush bathroom mat with my towel wrapped around me, I know the second I move or shift in any way, I'll feel that soreness between my legs. From him. Because last night was …

My forehead thunks against the mirror. "Phenomenal." *Thunk.* "Hot as hell." *Thunk.* "Heartbreaking." *Thunk.*

Wait, what? Heartbreaking? My eyes fly open as I straighten, frantically scrubbing at the steam in the mirror until I can make out my face. The truth is there in my eyes. Heck, it's written all over my face.

It's a good thing I said that last night was it. The last hurrah. Because I know what it would lead to. Me ending up madly in love with Ry. Ry leaving me to be with Jack again. God, it's like some cheesy soap opera.

Staring back at my reflection, I inhale a deep breath, holding it for a second before letting it out slowly in an attempt to calm myself. To assuage the panic pulsing through my veins.

"You will move on from this. Store it in the recesses of your memories. But you *have* to move on and find someone right. Someone who will love you and give you what you need." I say this so confidently to my own reflection that it's almost believable.

Almost.

* * *

You know that acronym *FML*? People toss that around on-line, and I always felt put off by it. I mean, really. Your life can't possibly be *that* bad, right? To the point where you actually say, *Fuck my life*?

All the scoffing I've done at people who have posted that? I take it back. Alllllll of it. I take it all back. Why? Oh, I'll tell you why.

Right now. Right here. That's why.

"So tell me more about how you place your bets, Simon," Ry gushes, leaning closer to the guy I was talking with not but five minutes ago.

And, no, I'm not exaggerating. He's gushing. It's a puke fest. I know, I know. Cue the *My heart bleeds for you* violins, right? But seriously. He's clam jamming me.

Again.

For the third time this week. The third!

First, I met Tucker when I was riding the elevator to work on Monday. He had been dropping off some files to the offices on a different floor. He was a super-cute guy who worked in marketing and had the longest eyelashes I'd ever seen on a guy.

Of course, when we made plans to meet up on Tuesday, Ry miraculously decided to pop in to the same bar after work and began chatting up Tucker. I excused myself to use the restroom, trying to give myself a pep talk, regroup, and figure out how to bring things back my way, but when I came back out, I found the two of them missing. Two seconds later, I got a text message from Ry.

Ry: Hey, Mags. Sorry, but Tucker insisted I see him home. Be careful getting home. I shouldn't be gone too long. Love you.

Seems sweet, right? He had just met Tucker and was helping his new friend home because he'd had too much to drink.

Except for one problem: Tucker hadn't been drinking alcohol. He had told me initially that he wasn't drinking and was doing some sort of cleanse where he abstained from alcohol and caffeine.

Yep. So that could only mean one thing. Tucker was interested in Ry and vice versa.

Sure didn't take long for Ry to jump back in the saddle after our little—

Crap! *Don't go there, Maggie.*

Moving on … Then, there was guy number two. Max. I've always liked that name. There's just something sexy about it. I ran into him—literally—at the coffee shop when I was leaving after one of my and Sarah's coffee dates. I was talking to her over my shoulder, exiting the shop, and totally not looking where I was going and *bam*! into a brick wall.

Of manliness.

Yep. Max was hot. Tall, dark, and handsome. Literally, he was all of those. Dressed impeccably, no less. After apologizing incessantly, he insisted I give him my number and meet him for a drink after work. Slick, right? That's what I thought, too.

It was all super fun until Ry showed up. And seriously, did he plant a homing beacon in my shoe or something? I still don't know how he found me. It wasn't like I told him where I was going—our dry erase calendar was noticeably void of any of our social plans. Then Ry shows up and instantly comes over to introduce himself to Max. Before long, they're chatting and laughing like long, lost friends, resulting in Max inviting Ry back to his place at the end of the night.

The third one was the strangest because I went to the gym—a place I hate and only go because Sarah tells me scary stories about young people dropping dead and ending up in the ER because they don't exercise regularly. And yeah, I know that exercising regularly isn't the same thing as once a week. I thank my birth parents—whoever and wherever they might be—for giving me good genetics and the ability to eat just about anything and not get so large that I end up needing a crane to remove me from my home.

While I'm at the gym, this cute guy's little silicone earbud thingy rolled right over by the toe of my shoe. Of course, I picked it up and handed it to him. He was the one who gave me that megawatt smile and introduced himself. Dean—great name, right?—told me he'd come over to where I was planning to use the elliptical machine once he'd finished his run on the treadmill.

So what happened to that one? Well, I caught sight of Dean making his way over to me just as Jack and Ry were exiting the racquetball courts. Ry caught up with Dean, they exchanged a few words, each of them glancing over at me before Dean's expression paled. Immediately, he swiveled in the opposite direction of where I was and disappeared. Ry and Jack waved at me, both flashing me wide smiles, and exited the gym.

I still haven't managed to get any information out of either of them as to what happened with Dean.

Come back to the present, to right now where Simon hasn't said one word to me in approximately twenty-two minutes.

I know. I've been timing it.

Just when I'm about to give up and head home to take a long, hot shower, curl up on the couch, watch television until I fall asleep, and dream about how I'll likely never manage to meet anyone who actually likes me more than Ry, I hear a male voice to my right.

"This is going to sound like a terribly cheesy line, but you're seriously too beautiful to be here alone. You're with someone, aren't you?"

CHAPTER FORTY-FOUR

Ry

I have to continue to remind myself that this is worth it. Especially while Simon drones on and on about how he places his bets on the horse races during the track season here in Saratoga. I don't give two shits about gambling, the odds, or which horse is favored. Running defense for Maggie is getting to be damn near exhausting. Not to mention the Tucker dude actually tried to kiss me.

Yeah. Really. It's the second damn time that's happened to me. Awkward doesn't cover it.

The gym guy was an easy mark, though. Hell, that one even got me a free smoothie at the coffee shop courtesy of Jack who was still laughing all the way there. I'd seen the guy through the Plexiglas racquetball court, chatting with Maggie. It worked out perfectly that Jack and I finished our game in time to catch the guy on his way back over to Maggie. I appeared concerned, utterly serious, as I informed him that she was my roommate, but that I wanted to give him a heads-up that she was in therapy and working through some issues. And that the last guy she dated had to relocate.

I may have also implied that Maggie veered off into the bunny boiling, *If I can't have you, no one will* kind of personality.

The Max dude was harder to sway my way, though. Shit, he nearly made me feel bad about what I was doing. Almost. Until, after exhausting all of my usual ploys and failing, I finally offered him fifty bucks to leave and never contact her again. The fact that he accepted money to leave a beautiful woman alone says he's a king of douches.

What I didn't plan on was having a dude come up and chat with Maggie while I was attempting to charm the pants off—not literally, of course—Simon. So while I want to break it up, I'm stuck with Simon droning on and on about betting on horses.

Until finally, he has to use the restroom. As if suddenly realizing that Maggie has found someone else's attention, his eyes narrow in an annoyed manner that I'm not a fan of.

Which is when I go in for the kill.

Leaning close to Simon—far closer than is permitted between two heterosexual men—I make my voice husky. "So what do you say, Sim?" I huff out a hot breath against his ear, and he jerks back. "Want to get out of here? You and me?"

The fear in the man's eyes would be hilarious if it were any other situation. Doing my best to maintain eye contact and give him my best "sultry" look—whatever the hell that even is—he moves hastily off his barstool, pulling out his wallet and plucking out some bills before tossing it back on the bar, mumbling something about having to go.

Phew.

After he's gone, I turn to take in the scene to my right. Maggie is talking with a guy, and he actually doesn't scream "douche," which I begrudgingly admit. Very begrudgingly.

"Hey, man," I interrupt them, holding out my hand to him. "Ry James, Maggie's roommate. Nice to meet you."

There's no way I can miss the way Maggie's smile tightens, knowing what's on the verge of happening. What's been happening for a while now. Every single time.

Ever since that night she deemed as our last.

The guy reaches out, shaking my hand firmly. "Hey, Ry. Nice to meet you. Tanner Matthews."

Tanner. I hate him. Don't know him—don't have to. I dislike him and every bit of his perfect, easy, friendly smile, his nice clothes, and kind eyes. It only gets worse.

"I work over at Eastern Sports as tech infrastructure lead." I let it hang out there because surely, this will do it. It'll be the zinger. But all I receive is a polite, "Cool," with a short nod before he turns back to Maggie, resuming their conversation about … laziness?

What the fuck?

"So you've got the good genes, too?" he asks her with a smile. "I avoid the gym like the plague. Except for once a week since my best friend pressures me into going."

"Yes! Exactly," Maggie agrees excitedly. "Same here."

"My weakness is the Cantina's lobster burrito." Tanner pats his flat stomach. "Those are the best."

What. The. Fuck.

Now, *I'm* getting weirded out because that's Maggie's—

"That's my weakness there, too," Maggie says, astonishment lining her tone.

—weakness, too. Did this guy dig up some intel on her somehow?

"Well"—he lowers his voice, like he's going to say something embarrassing—"to be honest, my all-time favorite indulgence is Max Londons' white sangria." He holds up both palms in defense. "I know, it's not the least bit manly, but their sangria is the best."

I think I'm going to puke.

Hopefully, all over Tanner.

The look on Maggie's face is priceless. "That's mine, too." She tosses a glance over at me, her tone full of surprise with a hint of wonder. "Seriously, Tanner. I love the sangria there."

"Well, what do you say we go and have some? I mean," he hesitates, a sheepish grin on his face, "if you want to, that is. No pressure." He turns a friendly smile on me. "You too, Ry."

He can't possibly be this friendly. There's just no fucking way.

Maggie slides off her barstool, and he's the one who reaches out to steady her when her heel slips a bit upon the slick bar floor.

His hand steadies her. Not mine.

The center of my chest pinches at the expression on her face as she looks up at him. "Thanks." She smiles. "Let me use the restroom real quick, and we can head over to Max's."

"Take your time." He winks and watches her make her way through the crowded bar. And begrudgingly, I have to give the guy credit. His eyes follow Maggie—not her ass. They actually follow her, and the way he's watching her is—

Abruptly, he turns to me, flashing an apologetic look. "Sorry, man. I guess I'm a little …" He shrugs, faltering for his words. "… dazzled. She's just great, you know?"

Yeah. I know.

He laughs. "What am I saying? Of course, you know. You live with her, after all, right?" He slides his hands in his pockets, still looking at me with that friendly expression. It makes me want to kick him in the junk while simultaneously feel like shit for thinking that because he just seems … *nice.*

Nice. And exactly the kind of guy Maggie's looking for. He's the kind of guy who would adore her, who wouldn't think of doing her wrong.

One who wouldn't consider lying to her just to find a way to be close to her and get to know her.

CHAPTER FORTY-FIVE

Maggie

November

What is *wrong* with me? There has to be something wrong with me. Maybe I've contracted Ebola? West Nile virus? Yellow fever?

When I call Sarah on my lunch break, she thinks I'm hilarious. And delusional.

"You don't have a contagious disease, Maggie. I've already run down the symptoms, and you have none of them."

I'd like to note that her bored tone is *not* appreciated.

"There has to be something wrong. Because Tanner's perfect. He's smart and funny and has a great job and thinks I'm the greatest thing since sliced bread."

"But," Sarah leads in.

"But I …" I huff out a long breath, disgusted with myself. "I don't know what it is. I just don't …"

"Feel anything for him past friendship." She says it as a statement, knowing me too well.

"Yes." My answer comes out with a whoosh of defeated breath. Leaning my forehead against my desk calendar, I let out a soft groan. "What's wrong with me? I told a perfectly perfect guy I couldn't see him anymore."

My question is greeted with silence. "Sarah?"

"Yes?"

"Ummm, a little help here, please?"

She huffs. "Maggie, what do you want me to tell you, exactly? That what you're looking for is right in front of you? Or that—" She's interrupted, and I hear voices in the background. "Sorry, Maggie. I have to run. They're short-handed today, and I need to cut my break short. Call me later, okay, sweetie? But you're going to be fine. I promise."

We say our hurried goodbyes, and I hang up my desk phone. Only to have it ring a second later.

Wearily, I glance at the caller ID. On a day like today, a call from him barely brings a smile to my lips.

"Mags, Mags, Mags. What's wrong?"

Slumping back in my desk chair, I sigh. "I don't know. I'm just in a funk."

"You can't be in a funk on a Friday. It's illegal."

My lips curve upward just slightly. "Pretty sure that's not even a bit true."

"Ah, but it got you to smile just a tiny bit more."

"Ryland James! Are you spying on me again? Didn't they make you give those binoculars back?"

"I may have forgotten to return them."

My smile widens a notch. "You're such a creeper."

"Only for you, gorgeous." His voice sounds huskier, more intimate, sending shivers down my spine. "Only for you."

Did I say that those shivers went down my spine? Well, those shivers also have an effect on other areas, too. Like downtown. You know what I'm saying?

Panties damp? Oh, yes. Which means I'm in trouble. Because Tanner doesn't make my panties damp. They stay Sahara-dry around him.

Umm, wow. That's just weird sounding, but you get the point. Good God, I'm so screwed up. Sarah has to be wrong. I have to be coming down with something major.

"You feeling all right?" Ry's tone is concerned, and I realize I've been massaging my temples.

"You really need to stop spying on me, Ry." My tone is sharper than I intended, and I am instantly remorseful.

Especially with Ry's quiet response. "Sorry, Mags. I'll leave you be."

With a soft click, the call ends, leaving me to feel like a complete jerk.

* * *

Once I finally drag my weary butt home, I enter the apartment only to find it eerily silent.

"Ry?" I call out hesitantly.

When I don't receive a response, the knot in my stomach tightens. My boss had bombarded me after my lunch break ended; the far side of my desk still piled high with files and paperwork I'll need to tackle bright and early on Monday.

Glancing over at the clock, I cringe at how late it is. Nearly six forty-five. I'm selfish for even expecting Ry to be here after the way our call ended. Not to mention, I was barely keeping my head above water the remainder of the day and hadn't had time to breathe—meetings back-to-back—let alone time to call him back.

"I should have made time," I mutter, tossing my briefcase onto one of the barstools and shrugging off my coat onto the back of the stool. And that's when I see the note on the counter.

Didn't want to bother you, but if you feel up to it come out and join me and Jack at The Parting Glass.

Love,

Ry

Clutching the note like it's a lifeline, I feel the tightness in my chest ease. He can't be that mad at me if he's inviting me out, right?

So then why the heck am I bummed that he's with Jack?

"Geez, Maggie! You just want it all, don't you?" I grumble, hurrying to my room to change. Tearing open my closet doors, I frantically scan for something to wear. Fall is definitely upon us now, and I love the fact that I can fully embrace sweater weather.

Choosing a thin, strappy camisole and a forest green off-the-shoulder sweater, I slide on my favorite pair of dark jeans and my favorite light gold-hued Christian Louboutin peep-toed heels. Retouching my makeup, I choose a darker lipstick, smoothing my curls in an attempt to make them appear less unruly.

Notice I said attempt. I'm not a miracle worker here.

Cleaning up the makeup supplies on my bathroom counter, I place them back in their designated spots. And freeze.

My eyes slowly travel up to my reflection in the mirror as I'm hit with the realization. I'm going to far greater lengths to join a friend out at the bar on a Friday night than I've done for any of my random dates in recent months.

Swallowing hard while I stare at myself in the mirror,

I'm faced with an undeniable fact. I've just gone to all this trouble to try to make myself as pretty as possible for a guy. But not just any guy. For my roommate. For my gay room-mate. The one I'm—

"Say it, Maggie. Just say it," I whisper the words to the mirror's reflection.

Like a total weirdo. But I don't care because facts are facts, regardless of whether you want them to be.

"I'm in love with Ry."

My whispered words seem to echo in my mind the entire walk to the elevator, as I travel down to the lobby, and as I walk the two blocks to The Parting Glass.

While part of me is relieved to voice it—even if it's only to myself—the other part of me is scared to death.

Because seriously. Of course, *I'd* be the one to fall in love with a freaking gay guy. It's just my luck.

And I have no clue what to do about it.

CHAPTER FORTY-SIX

Ry

I hate the way things ended today with Maggie. Which is why I made sure to leave a note. I just hope she sees it and decides to come out.

I shouldn't have hung up so abruptly, but I … I'd gotten my damn feelings hurt like a little kid. And I should've known better. It was clear that Maggie had been having a rough day.

"So you're planning to tell her tonight?" Jack asks, eyeing me as he takes a swig of his beer.

Nodding, I blow out a long breath. My eyes drift over to the main entrance every so often, silently begging her to show. "I have to. I can't do this anymore."

He clinks the neck of his beer bottle against mine. "It's the right thing, man." He smirks. "Plus, you've been a terrible boyfriend. You never put out."

"You're hilarious."

My eyes flicker over to the doors once again, and it's at that moment that I feel my jaw slacken.

"Holy shit." Maggie looks … Hell, I don't even know how to describe her. She looks so fucking gorgeous yet also like … a wet dream come true.

"What?" Jack twists to see what's snagged my attention,

quickly turning back around and letting out a slow whistle. "Is she meeting someone here tonight?"

Fuck. "I hope to hell not."

My hope increases when she stops at our table. "Hey, guys." She smiles down at Jack and me before her eyes fall back to rest on me. "Mind if I join you?"

Wordlessly, I step out of the booth we're sitting in to let her slide in. And that's when it happens.

She begins uncinching the wide belt at the waist of her black, knee-length coat, and the moment the lapels part, my breath stutters as I reach out to help her out of it. Because that sweater, the way the one side slips off her shoulder, baring creamy skin that begs me to touch it, kiss it, and lick it over and ov—

Then I catch sight of her shoes. Fuck-me shoes. *Sweet Jesus.* The images flickering through my mind right now of her bare legs wrapped around me with only those heels on …

She's trying to kill me. That's the only explanation.

Please, God. Let her not be here to meet another guy. Please.

Sliding in beside her, I look over to see her smiling up at me, her lips painted a deep, rich dark pink color, and I have to shift in my seat, adjusting myself.

"Well, I hate to cut out early but"—Jack makes it a point to check the time on his watch—"I've got to call it a night."

"So soon?" Maggie frowns. "But the sign out front says the band's going to start playing in a bit."

Jack flashes her a remorseful look. "Sorry, Maggie. I have meetings tomorrow, too, and I have to prep." When his eyes flicker over to me, I realize what he's doing. He gives me a nearly imperceptible nod, moving out of the booth to stand. I stand again, shake hands, and he pulls me in for a brief hug. Maggie slides out, stepping up to hug him good-bye.

"Take good care of him, Maggie." With a quick wink, he's off, weaving through the growing crowd and making his way to the exit.

Maggie turns to me. "Can we talk for a moment?"

Warily, I try to gauge her expression but come up empty. "Sure." I take Jack's seat as she slides back in on the other side of the booth, facing me.

Leaning her arms on the table, her focus drops to her hands. Taking a deep breath, her eyes rise to meet mine, and I see nervousness shining in the depths. "Can I ask about you and Jack?"

"Of course."

"Well, here's the thing. I—" She breaks off with a nervous laugh, looking away, her eyes drifting over the crowd among us. Turning back to me, her gaze has a unique intensity. "I wanted to know if you and Jack were still … together in any way?"

"No." I shake my head. "Not at all. We're just friends."

Her lips curve upward in a relieved smile. "Okay, good."

"But I wanted to tell you—"

Holding up a hand to stop me, she shakes her head. "I don't need to know anything else." When my lips part to protest, she interrupts. "Please. Not tonight."

I can't argue with her hopeful, pleading expression. Not when she looks at me like that.

Nodding slowly, I say, "Okay." All the while, my mind is screaming, *Tell her! Tell her now!*

The band, which had been setting up, starts playing a song, and Maggie's face lights up. She pops up from her seat, which has her back to the band, and comes around to slide in beside me to watch them perform.

Moving over to make more room, my right arm drapes along the back of the seat behind her. What happens next makes my heart nearly beat out of my chest.

Maggie slides in closer to my side, her scent drifting over me. Here, sitting like this with her, just the two of us, I feel like this is how it could be.

Just me and my Mags.

My eyes take in her profile, the soft curves of her cheekbones, the sharp bridge of her nose and her lips, lush and kissable.

When she turns, catching me watching her, her expression is curious. "Ry?"

Leaning in, I drag my lips against hers, her soft exhale washing against them. Burying my fingers in her hair, I tease her more, taking her bottom lip between my own before leaning back.

Maggie's eyes drift open, and I witness such intense heat in them, but there's more. Something else flickering in the depths. Something that gives me pause.

I want to say a million different things right now. But they're jumbled in my brain because I want to say them *right*. Because I *have* to say them right.

"Maggie, I …"

She presses a finger to my lips, stopping me. "Just … answer this." Her gaze is searching, pressing her lips thin, as if apprehensive. "Do you want to … be with me?"

CHAPTER FORTY-SEVEN

Maggie

I'm holding my breath waiting for Ry's answer, the hope and fear warring inside me. I know I just posed a loaded question, and maybe he won't see through it and see what I'm really asking.

Do you want to be with me the way I want to be with you?

Do you love me?

Wonderful. Now, I'm thinking along the lines of *Do you like me? Check yes or no.* Could I possibly be more lame?

Just when I'm about to rescind my question—to try to laugh it off—his lips curve upward in what has to be classified as one of the sexiest yet sweetest smiles I've seen.

Leaning in, he brushes the tip of his nose against mine, and his eyes remain locked on me. But when he answers, I find myself gasping at the sincerity—and vehement certainty—in his words.

"More than anything in the world."

Both hands delve into my hair, his lips crashing against mine in a hungry kiss, and when his tongue sweeps inside, heady arousal strums through me. When he breaks the kiss, his lust-hazed eyes meet mine, intense heat in the depths.

"Can we …" Trailing off, I worry my bottom lip.

His mouth curves up in a sly smile. "Why, Mags. Are you asking me to come home with you?" Smile widening, he leans in. "You little hussy, you."

Shoving at his chest playfully, I roll my eyes, looking up at the ceiling. "Why me, Lord? Why did I get stuck with the cocky roommate?"

"Not everyone can be so blessed, my child."

"You'd make one hell of a priest."

Ry stares at me in mock horror. "As if I could manage to abstain from sex for eternity."

"Mmm, minor complication."

He looks at his crotch as if it's going to chime in the conversation. "Not minor at all."

Covering my face with my hands, I groan with a little laugh. "Ryyyyy."

Snagging my wrist, he presses a kiss to the inside, over where my pulse is beating wildly. "Let's go home." Pulling out some cash, he tosses it onto the table.

"Wait." Laying my hand on his arm, his eyes meet mine, a mixture of disappointment and apprehension in them. "Before we go." I smile, sliding one of the napkins in front of me before reaching in my small purse for a pen.

His features relax, and he watches me as I write.

I want to be someone's everything.

Sliding the napkin closer to him, I hand him the pen. His expression is unreadable as he stares down at my words. Appearing to ponder what to write for a moment, he glances over at me before focusing on the napkin, using an arm to shield my view of what he's writing.

"Hey!" I protest, trying fruitlessly to make his arm budge so I can see.

He drops his arm, handing my pen back. One large

palm splays over the writing, a cryptic smile playing on his lips.

"Let's go." Giving up, I slide out of the booth with him behind me. Helping me back into my coat, Ry fastens the belt, and tightening his fingers over the lapels, he tugs me close to press a swift kiss to my lips. He tucks something in my right hand, closing my fingers around it.

The napkin.

The entire walk to the exit doors, I feel the heat from Ry's palm at the base of my back, the possessive gesture fueling my anticipation. But that isn't what makes me stumble. It's the moment I look down at what he'd written on the napkin in my hand.

You already are.

* * *

We're walking hand in hand along the sidewalk, crossing over Division Street on our way back to the apartment when I see him.

"Wait." I tug on Ry's hand, cocking my head in the direction of a man sitting on the lone bench beneath the streetlight a mere three feet away from the Adirondack Bank building.

No one knows his name, but he's evidently homeless. He always has a shopping cart full of things—bags of cans and bottles that he's planning to exchange for the redeemable deposit fees and bags containing who knows what else. Whenever I run errands for work, and I see him on what most of the locals deem "his bench," I'll stop in the local bakery and grab a bottle of water, a hot cocoa, and a few muffins for him. On days he's not there, I worry about him but always end up seeing him pushing that cart down another street.

He's not clean and usually smells pretty ripe, but I've never seen him with any liquor or anything else, so I don't think he's on the streets due to addiction. The man always avoids meeting anyone's eyes, and the times I offer him food and drink, he'll shy away from me, leaving me to set the items I bring him in his cart or on the other end of the bench where he sits.

"I don't have anything to give him except maybe money." The bakery has long since closed for the day. Pursing my lips in thought, I peer up at Ry.

"Let me check on something real quick." Steering me to stand beneath the streetlight at the corner of the sidewalk as numerous couples and groups of people walk past, enjoying the cool, crisp Friday evening, he steps away, walking over to approach the man on the bench. Ry nears him, stopping just a few feet away, speaking quietly in a hushed tone. A moment later, Ry returns to me, grasping my hand and leading me back in the direction from which we started.

"Where—"

"He's in the mood for wings. Apparently, people give him pizza all the time." I notice Ry's lips are curved up slightly. "So I told him we'd get him some wings real quick."

Stopping at the nearby pub, we slip inside and weave through the crowded establishment until we're at the end of the bar. Ry's hand is at my back, leaning in to place a to-go order with the bartender, and I find myself glancing around taking in the others on dates or together as couples or friends.

My eyes focus on one couple in particular who appear so at ease with one another, the affection they feel toward one another so obvious.

"Hey." Ry's husky voice in my ear makes me turn, and he's watching me expectantly, one eyebrow cocked.

"Twice in one night? Wouldn't we be jinxing things?" I tease, eyeing the napkin he has beneath one hand.

"Nope. You'll see." He extends his palm, waiting for me to hand him a pen. Once I do so, he hurriedly writes:

I want a beautiful woman who trusts me to please her ... and to maybe take her against the door because I might not be able to wait to have her.

I roll my lips inward to try to hide my smile at his words. Accepting the pen, I slide the napkin closer to me.

I want a handsome man to make it so that I <u>can't wait</u> to be taken against that door.

With a wide, satisfied grin, I slide the napkin over for Ry to see and can tell the moment he reads it, his eyes instantly darkening with intent. Dipping his head, he places his lips to my ear, and the hand at my back drifts down ever so slightly, his palm grazing my ass.

"I can't wait either, Mags." His teeth discreetly nip at my earlobe, sending shivers down my spine. "I can't wait to feel how wet you are." His fingers tighten on my ass before releasing me once the bartender sets a plastic bag on the lacquered wooden bar top, and Ry whips out his card to pay. Within a moment, we're exiting with a large order of wings, napkins, and two bottles of water in hand.

Bringing it back to the homeless man, we carefully

approach. Ry stops me a few feet away from the bench, asking me to wait. He then walks over and sets the bag on the far end of the bench where the man's still sitting. They have a brief, quiet exchange, and within a moment, Ry returns to me, fingers linking through mine as we resume our walk home.

"Thank you for that." I gaze up at his profile.

I see and feel his shrug. "No big deal."

"But it is. It's huge. For that man, especially." I focus on the crowded sidewalk ahead of us.

"No more than you do."

His response makes me falter. "What do you mean?"

He glances at me before refocusing ahead. "I know that you bring him hot cocoa and baked goods. Michelle at Sweets N Treats always talks about how you do that when you spot him on that bench. How you never mention anything about it, but she watches through the storefront window. Says it always makes her day when you do that for him."

If it were possible to be a human firestarter, that would be me right now; my cheeks are flaming with such intense heat because I don't do any of that for attention. I do it because it's the right thing to do.

Because if, by some random chance, that man were me, with a gesture like that—setting all pride aside—I would feel somewhat human, somewhat more worthy.

"I don't do it bec—"

Ry stops, steering me out of the way of oncoming pedestrians to beneath an awning of a boutique that's now closed. Skimming a thumb across my cheekbone, his gaze is watchful, intense.

"I know, Mags." His eyes briefly flicker down to my lips. "It's one of the many things I love about you."

So what you're saying is you love me? But do you love me-love me?

Seriously, people. Could I be more juvenile? Maybe I should just start crimping my hair and obnoxiously chew a massive wad of bubble gum, too? And insert a bunch of *likes* into my speech? Cue the eye rolling.

Hello, my name is Maggie Finegan, and I'm mega lame.

Do they even have support groups for that? People who are mega lame? Because they should. I could be the leader. *Obviously.*

"So you love that about me, huh?"

His eyes lighten. "Are you fishing for compliments?"

With an expression of faux dismay, I gasp. "Me? Never. But really. What else do you love about me?"

He throws his head back on a laugh; the cords of his neck become more visible, and I swear I get the urge to sink my teeth into it. Weird, right? Like maybe I've watched those *Twilight* movies one too many times or something. Not that I'd take it that far. No way. I'm not a fan of blood.

At all.

But still. Something about his neck makes me want to nip at it.

"Whatever you're thinking, yes. Let's do that at home." My eyes dart up to meet his, which are dark and hazy with intent.

Oh, yeah. It's go-time, people.

CHAPTER FORTY-EIGHT

Ry

When Maggie grabs my hand and tugs me, starting to walk—rush, really—down the sidewalk, I can't help my laughter.

"In a hurry?"

"Yes." That's her answer. Simple. To the point. Her steps are hurried as if she doesn't want to waste any time getting back home.

"It's go-time, people."

I turn my head at her mumbled words, amused. "Go-time? Really, Mags?"

Her face takes on a sheepish expression as if she didn't mean to say that aloud. But then she decides to own it.

"Yep." We're a foot away from the doors to our building. "I'm going to rock your world, buddy." She turns, grinning cockily, but her smile slips when she notices the way I'm watching her. I wonder if she can see the combination of love and heated lust in my gaze. Wonder which of those gives her pause.

"Ry?"

Shaking it off, I wink, reaching out to grab the door and open it for her. "After you." Turning to head inside, I give her a swift smack on the ass just as she crosses the threshold.

"Ryland James!" Her tone is admonishing but also laced with amusement.

Slinging an arm around her shoulders and tugging her close to my side, I lower my voice. "I love it when you go into full name mode on me."

"Good evening, you two." Startled, I had forgotten about Mr. Charlie at the desk.

"Hey, Mr. Charlie."

His gaze is assessing, but kind, as it darts back and forth between us. "You two kids have fun." There's a brief pause. "Be safe."

Be safe? My head cocks to the side at his words. His eyes are trained on me, and it takes me a moment to understand where he's going with this.

Ah. *Safe.* Got it.

"Always," I say with a firm nod. We bid him good night and walk over to the bank of elevators.

Leading Maggie into one, she slides over against the back wall, and I can feel her eyes tracking my movements as I press the button for our floor.

"God, even your hands are sexy."

Surprise etching my features, I turn to face her, and she's now covering her face with her hands as if embarrassed, continuing to mutter under her breath.

"Look at me. I'm lusting over a guy's hands now. I've got it bad." Dropping her hands from her face, she looks up at me. "But seriously. Some guys have chubby fingers or knuckles that appear swollen, like they've cracked them too many times or something. Your fingers are just … manly and long, and heck, they even look muscular."

Grateful it's only the two of us alone in the elevator, my thoughts turn naughty. Thoughts of those movies where the guy shoves the woman against the elevator wall, their kiss one of those that's basically two people making love with their mouths. And then, he lifts her up to have her wrap her legs around his waist, and they practically fuck with their clothes on.

Closing the distance between us, I flatten my hands on either side of her against the wall and lean in. "When you look at me like that," I brush my lips against her cheek, "it makes it difficult not to tear off those sexy jeans and shove deep inside you."

I jerk when she palms the front of my pants over my hardening cock, and I can't resist rocking against her hand. Fuck. She's the one woman who can push me to the edge with just one touch.

"Mags." I speak her name through gritted teeth, eyes closed in a near wince as I attempt some vestige of control.

She glides her hand up and down over where I'm tenting my pants, and I feel the combination of disgust and relief when the elevator dings to announce we've arrived on our floor.

"Ry." Her voice is husky, and when my eyes open, she's gazing up at me, her tongue darting out to wet her bottom lip.

Swiftly turning, my hand grasps hers, and I practically drag her out of the elevator, stalking to our door. Reaching into my pocket, I gingerly attempt to remove my keys from my pocket without unmanning myself, and then I shove the key into the lock with no finesse whatsoever.

When Maggie gives a light tug on our joined hands as soon as I twist the knob, I pause, turning to rest my eyes on her in question.

"Are you still planning to," she pauses, her lips curving into a sly grin, "shove me against the door?"

Without answering, I push open the door, tugging her inside with me. Removing my key from the door, I toss them toward the kitchen counter, not caring when they miss their target and, instead, hit the hardwood floor.

Kicking the door closed and hurriedly locking it, I walk her body back against the door, my mouth finding hers in a hungry, hot kiss. My fingers make quick work of her coat, tugging it off her before pulling up the hem of her sweater. I lift it over her head before carelessly tossing it to the floor. My palms glide down from her shoulders to cup her breasts through the thin fabric of her camisole, her hardening nipples visible through her bra.

"Ry." My name slips from her lips on a breath, and that combined with a flash in her eyes slows my movements. That flash of something—a part of me wants so badly for it to be more than just lust—sends a sliver of insecurity through me.

This is the moment where I wrestle with being Ry, a hot-blooded guy about to have what I already know will be mind-blowing sex, and Ry, the guy who's head over heels in love with a woman whom he's lied to and made believe that he's gay.

"What's wrong?" Maggie asks when I stop, gently dropping my forehead to her shoulder to hide my face. I hear the uncertainty in her tone. With a tinge of rejection.

She thinks I'm rejecting her. I can't have her thinking that. Not for a single minute.

Lifting my head, I meet her eyes, and the wariness in her gaze unsettles me. "Mags, I have something to tell you." Inhaling a deep breath, I prepare to disclose everything. But her finger pressed to my lips stops me.

"The only thing I want you to tell me right now is," she pauses, as if attempting to remain confident, and rises to her tiptoes to press an open-mouthed kiss against the side of my neck, "that you can't wait to be inside me, making me cry out your name." Her whispered words are punctuated with the tip of her tongue darting out to taste me before gently nipping at my flesh with her teeth.

"But Mags—"

"Shh." Her thumb brushes against my bottom lip, and I can't resist wrapping my lips around it. Sucking it deeper into my mouth, I watch her eyes darken with heat as I taste her. Even if that's not the part of her I want to taste.

When her other hand slides down over the ridge of my cock, stroking me through my pants, I lose all train of conscious thought about coming clean—of confessing. Instead, all that's going through my head are thoughts of how fast I can push inside her, how wet she'll be, and how badly I want to taste her and make her come undone with my tongue, my fingers, and my cock.

My hands fly to grip her hips, lifting her, her legs wrapping around my waist so that I'm nestled between her thighs. Rocking into her, I hear her breath catch. Our lips meet, our mouths frantic as if we're both unable to get enough, to taste deep enough, our tongues sliding against one another. Her fingers grip my shoulders as her tiny moans urge me on.

My arms secure around her, I walk us back to my bedroom. She dusts kisses along my jawline before her teeth tug gently on my earlobe. My words come out guttural with lust.

"Just so we're clear, you're not leaving my bed anytime soon."

Leaning back slightly to meet my eyes, I see a smile tugs at the corners of her mouth. "Is that so?"

"Yes, ma'am." I slowly lower her to her feet. She kicks

off her heels, and my fingers are hard at work, unfastening her jeans. Working them down over her hips, my movement draws to a sudden stop.

"Mags?" My eyes dart up to find her watching me. "Are these ..." *For me?* I silently finish, but I'm too chicken-shit to ask outright. Because if they're not, then ...

"I wore them for you." Her gaze lowers briefly before raising back up to mine. "Only you."

"Holy shit," I breathe out, my thumbs grazing the fabric of her panties with reverence. The front is an artwork of lace with a smattering of tiny, delicate bows. The moment my hands glide around to see if the back consists of the same is when all breath leaves my lungs.

The back is bare, with only a thin strip of fabric separating the globes of her luscious ass. My eyes fall closed at the feel of her silky soft skin, and I lean forward, pressing my lips against her core, her scent emanating. Hearing her sharp inhale is music to my ears as my fingers wrap around the thin, flimsy sides of her panties and tug them down until they pool at her ankles.

My eyes rise. "Take off everything else." Watching as she removes her thin camisole before unfastening her bra, dropping both to the floor, I nudge her legs apart, widening her stance for me.

"I want you to touch your breasts for me. Play with those gorgeous nipples." Slipping one long finger inside her, I find it impossible to stifle my groan at the feel of her wetness coating my finger. Our gazes are locked as I work my finger in and out of her with aching slowness while her fingers toy with her nipples. Witnessing them pucker, I admire her beautiful dusty pink areolas; her nipples are like ripe raspberries, making my mouth water while imagining wrapping my lips around them.

Licking my lips, I add another finger and watch as her lips part, her eyes heavy-lidded, chest rising and falling, breathing becoming more labored. "I can't wait to wrap my lips around those nipples. To suck on them." I feel a gush of warmth on my fingers, my eyes closing on a wince as I try to maintain control. "Jesus, Mags. You liked that, didn't you?"

My fingers have a mind of their own, it seems, as they thrust a little faster, so slick with her arousal. Maggie never answered, her eyes closed, head tipped back, breathing labored as she works her nipples.

"You want to come on my fin—"

I don't get to finish my question when her fingers wrap around my wrist, stopping my movements. Her words are spoken in a ragged breath. "I want to come on your tongue."

CHAPTER FORTY-NINE

Maggie

Oh, holy crap. Did I just say that?

Yep. I totally said that out loud. Dirty Maggie. *Dirty, dirty, naughty Maggie.*

Slowly rising to stand, Ry guides me to lie back on the bed. "Why don't you get started for me?"

Stripping himself of his sweater before tackling the buttons of the shirt he wore beneath it, his fingers fumble in his frantic attempt to hurry and rid himself of his clothing. And I hope that maybe it's because I'm lying on his bed, my finger rubbing my clit in slow circles, that it's pushing him close to the edge.

Shoving down his pants and boxer-briefs in one move, he forgets that he hasn't removed his shoes and nearly trips himself trying to get untangled.

Chuckling softly, I feel my face light up with heat and humor. "In a bit of a hurry, are you?"

Grinning, Ry toes off his loafers, kicking off his pants and underwear before shucking his socks, as they join the rest of his clothing on the floor. "Kind of. It's kind of an urgent matter, here."

Climbing onto the bed, he braces himself above me, and I bite back a hiss at the feel of his naked body. Dipping his head, he brushes his lips against mine. "In fact, it's pretty damn urgent."

"Is it, now?" I whisper back, playfully. My thighs cradle him, wrapping my legs around him, my core radiating heat against where his cock is nestled against me.

"I didn't tell you to stop playing with yourself." He attempts a stern tone.

I cock an eyebrow at him. "Well, it makes it awfully hard when you're in the way."

"So what are you saying? I should move out of the way?"

"Maybe." A mischievous smile tugs at the corners of my lips.

Shifting abruptly, he slides down over me until his face is directly between my thighs. His hot breath washes against my core when he asks, "Maybe I should do this?" Leaning in, he presses an open-mouthed kiss to me, running his tongue along my opening.

"Maybe," I breathe.

He devours me with his tongue and lips, and I slide my legs up, bending them, placing my feet flat against the mattress as I rock against his mouth. When he hums against me in approval, I feel myself flood his tongue with wetness. My fingers move to grip his hair, as I whisper-moan his name.

"Ry …" Another soft moan slips from my lips. "Don't stop."

Shoving his tongue deeper inside me, I rock against his mouth as his hand moves up to roll my clit between his fingers, causing my inner muscles to clench tightly.

"Ry, I'm—" I can't finish as my body takes over, arching, my inner muscles spasm through my release. And he's there, with every single pulse of my body, with every single clench of my inner muscles, lapping it up, urging me on with his tongue and fingers.

Once my muscles begin to relax, he presses a gentle kiss to my mound before moving back up my body to where I lie sated, eyes closed, chest still heaving.

With his lips near my ear, he whispers, "I'm not pleased with you, young lady." My eyes fly open in alarm. "You didn't moan my name loud enough for my liking."

I cock an eyebrow. "Oh, really?"

"Really. You know what that means, right?"

"No, what?"

Shifting so that the tip of his cock presses against my entrance, he answers. "It means I'm not going to go so easy on you next time." Pushing forward barely an inch, we both gasp at the touch. "I'm going to have to go hard on you."

Rocking my hips, it causes him to sink another delicious inch deeper. "I think I can handle it."

I don't care that my breathless words belie my statement. All that matters right now is the fact that he's inside me. My hands are gripping his ass, tugging him forward and causing him to slowly—so achingly slow—sink in deeper until he's buried to the hilt.

Swallowing hard, I watch him, knowing that he's attempting to restrain from thrusting like crazy. He blows out a long breath against my neck.

"You'd better not be trying to slow things down." My husky words cause him to lift his head, regarding me curiously. "Because, if that's the case, there's going to be hell to pay."

The grin that spreads across his face at my playful words is slightly boyish and just … so cute.

God, I love him.

"So what you're saying is if I did something like this"— he slides nearly all the way out of me slowly, only to give one strong, quick, deep thrust back inside—"you wouldn't like it?"

My neck arches, my head back against the pillow, lips parted, eyes closed. "I'm … not sure. You might need to do that again to check."

And he does. Again and again. Throughout the entire night, we love one another, exploring and learning each other's bodies. Until, finally, we're so exhausted that we fall asleep, with his arms wrapped around me, my head on his shoulder and palm on his chest. Right over his heart.

Where I hope—pray—that it beats for me. Pray that it might somehow begin to love me the way that I love him.

* * *

"Sometimes, I feel like your kisses are the kind where I'll end up like, 'Holy shadoobie. I think I just got impregnated.'"

Ry stares at me in the bathroom mirror, rinsing his mouth after brushing his teeth while I twist up my messy morning hair in a clip.

Flashing me an amused look, he cocks one eyebrow. "You do know how babies are made, don't you, Mags?"

"Why, yes, Ry, I *do* know how a baby is made. But you get my meaning. My ovaries practically cry out your name when you kiss me a certain way."

"You mean between your legs?"

Playfully shoving his arm, I let out a huff of laughter. "You're terrible."

He tugs me closer. "You love it."

I love you. "Mmm, maybe." My expression is thoughtful as if I'm considering it.

"Bet if I made you some of my famous bagels, you'd feel better."

Giving him a look, I say slowly, "You put bagels in the toaster and butter them."

He gasps in mock dismay. "You dare to scoff at my bagels? Don't you know I live in a—"

"Glass case of emotion?" I prompt.

Grinning, he gives me a perfunctory kiss on my lips and releases his hold on me, turning to exit the bathroom. "I'm kidding. I'm going to run down to Sweets N Treats and see Michelle about some croissants and good stuff. I'll be back in a few."

"And then what?" I ask curiously, following him out and down the hallway as he scoops up his keys, heading for the door.

His head whips around, his hand on the doorknob. "Then"—his eyes have that spark of something naughty in them—"we feast." Just the way he says the word "feast," I know he doesn't just mean actual food.

He means me.

If I were wearing any panties beneath Ry's large T-shirt he pulled over my head this morning, they'd be soaked.

Scratch that. Those suckers would be gone—up in flames, that is.

CHAPTER FIFTY

Ry

"I'll be right back." Turning, I twist the door handle.

"Wait!" Maggie's tone is urgent, and my head whips around. When I see her start forward, rushing to me, I turn, catching her as she flings herself into my arms. Her palms frame my face before she presses a soft kiss to my lips.

"I know you're only going to the bakery, and I'm being clingy, but," she whispers against my lips, "I'm going to miss you."

I'm not usually one who turns mushy at much of anything but this moment, right here with Maggie, gets me. She's the only woman who can make me melt.

Hell, she's the only woman who has *ever* made me melt.

Grinning down at her, I tease. "I think I like clingy Maggie."

She blushes, ducking her head briefly. "Hurry back." She dusts her lips against mine and when our lips part, her eyes have a different lightness to them. Like happiness with a touch of something else.

I'm so damn afraid to hope for that something else to be love.

"If that's what happens every time I have to leave, you'd

better believe I'll do everything in my power to get back here in record time." Releasing her slowly, I set her on her feet.

Once I leave and close the door behind me, I end up staring at the closed door far longer than I'd like to admit.

Because when I walk back through that door, I'll be walking inside not just as Ry, her roommate, but as Ry, her lover.

Maybe even her boyfriend.

But first, I'll have to come clean. Which is why I'm heading out to get the necessary items. To ensure that our talk goes as smoothly as possible.

* * *

"You having a breakfast get-together this morning, Ry?" Michelle asks as she places the pastries in the large box for me.

I might be going a bit overboard in getting so many, but I want it to be perfect. Last night was fucking perfection in itself, and I don't want to do anything to break that trend.

"Nope." There's no way I can tamp down the dopey grin I know is spreading across my face. "Just me and Mags."

"Ah." That's all she says. Her tone is knowing and not at all surprised, flashing me a kind smile. "I wondered when she'd realize what was right under her nose."

Me, too, I think. *Me, too.*

Carefully holding the large box of baked goods, I exit the bakery. Stopping by the small florist's shop, I choose a purple and white orchid—Maggie's favorite flower—and wait for them to gently place it in packaging for me.

Then when I'm satisfied I have the necessary items to ensure this morning with Maggie will be perfect, I head along the sidewalk to make my way back home. Home to Maggie.

So lost in my thoughts, it takes a moment for me to realize my cell phone is vibrating in my back pocket with an incoming call. Pulling it out, I furrow my brows when I see the caller ID.

Cara. My ex.

We had ended things a while back—before she relocated to Boston upon receiving her promotion. While we'd been serious for a while, after some time, it became apparent things weren't headed in the right direction, and we'd parted amicably.

"Hey, Cara."

"Ry! Hey, I'm in town for a bit, doing some visiting, and have something of yours that got mixed up in my stuff somehow." She laughs. "I've finally finished unpacking after all this time and found one of your hockey jerseys."

I'd been wondering where that jersey had gone. "Cool. How long are you going to be in town? Maybe we can set up a—"

"I'm actually about to get to your floor. I ran into Jack at the coffee shop, and he told me—"

I don't hear the rest of her words. I've already shoved the phone in my pocket, trying desperately to sprint while juggling the boxes in my grasp, dodging early morning risers and dog walkers along the sidewalk.

My stomach is in knots, throat tight, and I'm basically scared shitless. Because if Cara says anything to Maggie before I get the chance to talk to her—before I get a chance to come clean—I'm not sure Maggie'll be able to forgive me.

Hell, I'm not sure I'll be able to forgive myself.

CHAPTER FIFTY-ONE

Maggie

I'm pouring myself a mimosa because how else can one plan to try to convince a gay man—who, after all that's happened, has to also be bisexual, too, right?—that he should be my boyfriend?

By plying him with alcohol, of course. Duh.

I know, I know. I'm terrible. But can you really blame me? Don't even try to tell me you wouldn't be doing this if you were in my position.

There's a knock on the door. Startling me, it causes some champagne to spill over the rim of the glass, splashing onto my thumb. Setting down the bottle, I raise my other hand to suck off the champagne and walk toward the door.

Why would Ry be knocking? Is he being funny?

Hand on my hip, I lay on the sass, flinging open the door. "You get in for free as long as you're putting out—"

Oops. Not Ry.

There's a tall, blond woman standing there, staring back at me curiously. "Hi, I'm Cara." She holds out her hand with a smile.

"Maggie." I shake her hand wondering why she's knocking on my door at eight o'clock on a Saturday morning. And holy crap, I'm still dressed only in Ry's shirt.

"I was looking for Ry, but our call got disconnected or something."

Her words cause me to go still. She's looking for Ry? *My* Ry?

"He should be back in a moment," I say slowly.

Pulling something from her large handbag that looks like a man's jersey, she hands it to me. "This is Ry's." With a little lilt of a laugh, she adds, "I told him I'd finally unpacked, and that somehow ended up with my things."

Suddenly realizing how rude I'm being, I snap out of my daze. "Oh, come on in. Please." She's clearly a friend of Ry's, especially if she has his jersey, right? Closing the door behind her, she follows me inside.

"I'm making some mimosas if you'd like one. Let me just throw on some shorts real quick. Help yourself." I gesture toward the kitchen as I head back toward the hallway.

"Thanks, Maggie. I'd love one."

Hurriedly, I tear into my room, tossing Ry's shirt onto the bed. Luckily, I find a pair of decent shorts, deciding to add a sports bra to the mix to try to be a little more hospitable and less jiggly before pulling Ry's shirt back on. Because God knows there's not much worse than being greeted by another woman's unencumbered breasts. Much less a woman you don't really *know*.

Returning to find Cara with a mimosa in hand and glancing around the living room at all of the framed photographs adorning both the wall and end tables, I watch as she glances over at me. "How long have you and Ry been together?"

With a nervous laugh, I slide my hands into the front pockets of the soft material of my shorts. "We're not really … together."

Shrugging, I add, "I mean, he and Jack had been

together for such a long time and then…" I trail off awkwardly, unsure of how to even begin to explain the situation. Then I realize Cara's staring at me. In a way that sends prickles of unease through me.

Her eyebrows furrow in what appears to be confusion. "What do you mean he and Jack had been together?"

"I mean together-together." My words are drawn out slowly.

After a beat of silence, she throws her head back in a laugh that's … Heck, the only way to describe it is a full-on belly laugh. Cara's laughing so hard, she actually has to wipe away tears from her eyes.

While I just stand there, watching it all happen, wondering what the hell this chick is smoking.

"I'm sorry," she says breathlessly between some more, less hearty laughs. "It's just hilarious to hear that. I mean there's no way Ry and Jack have ever been anything more than friends, let alone gay." Another peal of laughter escapes, and I'm standing here wondering what she's on. Because maybe she shouldn't be drinking that mimosa, after all. Everyone knows you shouldn't mix alcohol with pills …

"I mean I should know, right?" she continues while I eye her mimosa glass, wondering if I should just be ballsy and rip it from her grasp. "I dated Ry for about eight months. I know that was two years ago but still …"

That's the moment it happens. When everything stops.

"I'm sorry, what?"

Surely, I didn't hear her correctly. Because there's no way she dated Ry for eight months, let alone two years ago. Because that just doesn't make sense.

Ry's gay.

Isn't he?

The room feels like it's closing in, air thinning as my mind races. Memories flash through my mind—through all of the encounters I've had with Ry since meeting, since moving in together. The times when he ended up with my dates, the times when the guys ended up seeming to like him more.

Something's not adding up.

"Ry's not … gay?" I ask Cara cautiously, tentatively.

She must notice something in my expression because her features sober, eyes growing wide, her lips parting to answer me.

But before she can speak, another voice answers for her.

"No, I'm not."

CHAPTER FIFTY-TWO

Ry

I'm out of breath from sprinting the remaining blocks to get back here, in hopes that I might be able to get here before anything happened—before any serious talking occurred.

When I hear Cara's uninhibited laughter through the door, I get the worst feeling in the pit of my stomach. Shoving my key in the door, Maggie and Cara must not hear me enter over the sound of Cara's laughter.

"Ry's not … gay?" I hear the confusion in Maggie's voice.

Before Cara can answer her, the words spill out of my mouth.

"No, I'm not."

Startled, Maggie whips her head around; she's staring at me with a combination of hurt and what is now coming to the forefront of her expression—anger.

Then another emotion joins in the mix. Betrayal.

"You lied to me." She doesn't yell, the eerily quiet statement hanging there in the silence of the room as Cara suddenly looks uncomfortable, an unexpected bystander in all of this.

Stepping forward, I start, "Mags, please—"

"Don't." She stops me with a hand. "Don't call me that." The pain etching her features makes me feel gutted. "You lied to me. How could you?" Her voice rises gradually.

"I'm sorry, Mag—"

"You're sorry?" Her tone is rising, incredulous. "You're sorry?" She tosses her hands in the air. "You apologize for breaking a dish or spilling something on the couch. You can't just apologize for lying to me *for over a year*!"

Walking over to the large windows of the living room, she lets out a harsh, humorless laugh before spinning to face me again. "You must think I'm the biggest idiot."

"No, I—"

"Were you ever gay?" Her words lash out at me, dripping with accusation and pain.

"No, but—"

"So you weren't ever in a relationship with Jack?"

Damn it. My throat tightens, and I have to force my answer past my lips, so ripe with regret. "No."

Pain etches her features. "I let you in my life. In my bed! And it was all a lie?!"

Fuck. My entire body is rigid with a mixture of anger, disappointment, and regret, but it's the anger that floods my tone. "I tried to tell you so many damn times, Mags! But you cut me off and wouldn't let me!"

Shaking my head, I take in harsh, ragged breaths. Defeated. "I love you. I just never knew how to tell—"

Her head rears back as if I've slapped her before her expression completely closes off. "You need to leave. Now. I don't want to hear your voice or see your face." Her lips press thin; eyes sparkling with unshed tears before speaking through clenched teeth. "I don't want to see you. Ever again."

Maggie darts over to grab her coat from the chair, along

with her purse and keys, rushing out the door and closing it behind her with a loud *thunk*.

With finality.

Fuck. I've lost her.

Hell, I don't know that I ever had her to begin with.

Cara clears her throat, making me realize I'd forgotten her presence. Her smile is filled with pity. Stepping toward me, she sets her glass of what looks to be a mimosa on the counter.

"Guess you're going to need help packing, huh?"

* * *

I'm living on Jack's couch in his small one bedroom loft. Just living the dream.

The first night, I got stinking, sloppy-ass drunk. And continued throughout the weekend. Because not only am I heartbroken, but I'm royally pissed off at myself for screwing things up.

I've single-handedly managed to make the woman of my dreams hate me.

"You do realize it's Sunday night, right?" Jack plops down next to me on the oversized leather couch.

"Yep."

"You plan to nurse your broken heart forever or what?"

"What are my other options?" I snarl.

He stares at me as if I'm dense. "Uh, getting your shit together and winning her back?" There's a beat of silence. "You can't really be this clueless, can you?"

Flipping him the bird, I refuse to look away from ESPN. Not that I care who's playing or which team's winning. "She told me she never wants to see me again. Ever. Pretty sure that's as clear as it gets."

"And you're just going to let it go? Dude," he shakes his head, "I thought that a chick who's supposedly 'the one' was worth the fight."

Pulling a throw pillow—yeah, Jack actually has fucking throw pillows—from beside me on the couch, I press it over my face, muffling my groan of frustration.

"Whenever you're done trying to suffocate yourself, buddy, I'll be sitting here. Still."

Abruptly dropping the pillow on my lap, it bounces off and onto the floor as I cut him a look. "Can't you leave me the hell alone?"

Leaning down to pick up the pillow, he replaces it on the couch. "Why? So you can wallow in self-pity? In the mess of your own doing?"

"Wow. Keep it up. You're making me feel much better already."

He shakes his head at me. "Dude. Seriously. You're giving up without a fight. That's it?" He makes a scoffing sound. "That's not the Ryland James I know—knew. He's never been a quitter."

"She hates me," I mutter. "*I* hate me. What more is there?"

"Do you love her?"

My head snaps to face him, and I'm wearing an incredulous look on my face. He merely stares back and calmly asks again, "Do you love her?"

"Yeah, I love her," I answer with a sigh, looking away.

"She loves you, too, you know."

That piercing ache in my chest flares up, becoming more painful at Jack's words.

"She just needs to work through everything. Needs to miss you. Then," he nudges me with his arm, "you'll need to remind her how much you love her. Not as a roommate, who's supposedly gay, but as a man who loves her inside and out."

I remain sitting there, still as a statue. Staring sightlessly at the television, I'm silent for a long moment.

"That was pretty deep. You sure you're not the one who's gay?" I quip, the corner of my mouth tipping up slightly.

"Don't make me kick your sorry ass." He rises from the couch. "Now, get the hell off my couch and shower. We've got some brainstorming to do."

CHAPTER FIFTY-THREE

Maggie

"You have to eat something, Maggie." Sarah's exasperated with me and with good reason. I've been living on dry cereal for days now.

Or has it been weeks? Who knows? More importantly, who cares? At least, I'm hauling my butt to work, right? That's the important part. I'm being an adult where it counts.

"I'm eating this because I no longer have a roommate. Which means I'm responsible for the entire rent." Shoving a handful of O's in my mouth, I crunch loudly. "A-gain."

Grabbing the box of cereal from its perch beside me on the couch, Sarah shakes her head.

"Seriously, Maggie."

Oh, no. The hand's on the hip. I repeat, Sarah has her hand on her hip. The sass is evident in her next words. "How did you *not* figure out Ry wasn't gay?"

I stare at her incredulously. "You mean you knew the entire time?" Deflating, I slump my shoulders as I mutter, "Was I the only one who didn't know?"

"Probably." My head snaps up at Sarah's quick response. "I was finally going to say something that day in the coffee shop, but you ran out so fast, like you were trying to beat a

Kenyan in the next Olympics."

There's a pause, and then her voice is softer, gentler. "Look, Maggie. The only reason I didn't tell you earlier is because, after Jack had confirmed things for me, I knew Ry wasn't doing any of this to hurt you. I could tell he loved you, and I figured I'd let it play out."

I can't do this. Can't hear this. It just hurts too much. Standing abruptly, I blurt out, "I'm going to watch the tearful homecomings with all the military members surprising their families."

Reaching for my laptop, Sarah grabs it, tugging it from my grip. "That's totally not a cry for help," she mutters. "No. I can't let you sink to that level."

"But is it even a level? Could rock bottom even be considered a level?" I tip my head to the side in thought.

"That's it," Sarah abruptly announces. "Get up. We're going out."

"No." No way do I want to go out. I get that it's Friday night but no. Just no. I'm off work and want to wallow with my O's cereal. We're happy together. Just the two of us. Maggie and O's. M and O. MO.

Hey, that's kind of cute.

Sarah snaps her fingers in front of my face, drawing me from my weird inner conversation. "If I have to shove you in the shower, I will. Now, go." She points her index finger in the direction of the hallway, eyes narrowed dangerously.

We stare at each other before I finally give in with a loud huff of breath. "Fine. But it doesn't mean I have to like it," I announce petulantly, storming off down the hall for my bedroom and adjoining bathroom.

After I've scrubbed myself clean—and attempted to figuratively scrub myself clean, yet again, of he-who-shall-not-be-named—I emerge from my steam-filled bathroom to find Sarah sprawled on my bed, scrolling through her Facebook newsfeed on her cell phone.

"About time," she announces on an exhale. "If I had to read another person's annoying post about them taking time off from Facebook only to post something two hours later, I was going to scream." Sliding to her feet, she pulls something from my closet and hands it to me.

"Put this on."

I push her hand back. "I'm not wearing that." She's chosen a pair of black stretchy tights and a form-fitting red sweater that falls to mid-thigh.

I do not want to wear that. That's something I'd wear if I felt sexy *or* wanted to look sexy for someone else. And clearly, neither applies right now.

She shoves it back at me. "You are." With the expression she currently has, lips pursed and eyes narrowed, I imagine this is exactly how she has to be with difficult patients at the hospital.

Our standoff slash stare down lasts barely thirty seconds because I realize a losing battle when I see one.

"Ugh, fine." I grab the clothing from her and return to the bathroom to dress, drying my hair and attempting to use the magical thing called makeup to make me look more lively than I feel.

Once I pass muster with Sarah and she "signs off" on my beautification attempts, we head down the hall to leave. As I walk past the closed door to Ry's old room, I get that suffocating feeling. I haven't been able to go in there since that day I kicked him out. Jack had come over for a bunch of things, but I haven't been able to set foot in there to see what he's left behind—if anything.

I still haven't cashed his rent check. He'd sent it with Jack with a message, saying since he'd moved out with three weeks of the month remaining, he'd wanted to pay me in full "for all the inconvenience."

I think I quite honestly saw red when Jack quoted Ry that morning. You know how people always use that expression, but most of us are like, *huh*? Well, I actually understood that saying that particular morning. I'm also pretty certain I had steam coming out of my ears, as well.

As Sarah and I walk along South Broadway to make our way to the Tavern, she links her arm through mine in that way women often do. It's pretty chilly, yes, but more than that, she does it because she loves me and knows I'm having a ridiculously tough time with everything.

"Things are going to be all right, Maggie." My head whips around to peer at her. "I just know it."

I return my attention to the busy sidewalk. "I wish I was as sure."

Slipping inside the Tavern, we immediately loosen the buttons on our coats, and I follow Sarah's lead as she steers us toward the bar for a drink. We manage to find a small spot to slide into, and Sarah snags the attention of one of the bartenders just as I feel the weight of someone's eyes on me.

Tense, my eyes dart around the bar area, and that's when I see him. My vision clouds at the sight of Jack giving me a brief nod; he's still talking to Ry who's sitting beside him at the bar, staring morosely into his beer glass.

I can't do this. I can't be here. I just … can't.

Turning to tell Sarah I have to leave, she grabs my arms. "Just because you both happen to be at the same bar doesn't mean anything." Her gaze is hopeful. "You and I can still have fun."

"Fun," I mutter with zero enthusiasm before attempting more inflection in my tone. "Yay." And I promptly receive a shove in return.

Drinks in hand, she leads me over to a small table against the wall nearby where an obviously competitive game of darts is taking place, and I know we'll be waiting a bit for our turn. I find myself hoping Ry doesn't notice I'm here, yet simultaneously wanting him to notice my presence.

If that's not screwy, then I don't know what is.

Sliding onto the seats at our table, I've just scooted my chair in closer to the table when a shadow falls over us.

Jack.

"Hello, there, lovely ladies. Fancy meeting you here." He blasts us with his pearly white smile.

"Yeah, super fancy meeting us here." Sarah's dry response has me peering over at her. Because that sounded an awful lot like …

"You planned this," I accuse, tossing up my hands. "What the heck?" Turning a sharp glare on Jack, I ask, "Did he put you up to this?"

He holds up both hands in defense. "It was all me, I swear. He's been so damn depressed for the past few weeks." Letting his hands drop to his sides, he shrugs. "I wanted to see if maybe we could get the two of you together to talk it out."

"We?" My eyes volley back and forth between Sarah and Jack. Since when were the two of them a "we"?

She tries to shrug it off, eyes not meeting mine. "Figured it couldn't hurt if you two could meet and resolve your differences."

"Differences?" I stare at her in disbelief. "He lied about being gay!" A few heads turn as my voice gains strength and volume.

Scooping up my purse, I stand. "I'll walk back home."

"But Mag—" Sarah's protest is lost as I rush out of the bar, stopping only once I step onto the sidewalk. Luckily, my apartment is only a few blocks away, and all of it is through areas with high foot traffic, so it's safe, well-lit, and well-traveled.

Trying to regain some composure, I take a deep breath and let it out slowly. Before I can turn and head up the sidewalk, I hear a voice behind me.

"I'm sorry."

My entire body stiffens at the sound of his voice, the deep timbre. My eyes fall closed because it hurts—it physically *hurts*—to hear his voice. God, I miss him so much, it's killing me. But he lied to me. I've already experienced what it's like to be in a relationship with one liar and look where that got me. I can't do it again.

"Are you sorry you got caught? Or sorry you lied to me?" I pose my questions without turning around because I can't bear to look at him, knowing I'm too weak and would end up hurling myself into his arms. Just because I miss how he holds me.

"Both." I jerk at his admission before he continues. "I'm sorry I lied to you. I am. I just thought, at the time, that it was the only way to be near you. And I'm sorry I got caught the way I did. That was shitty, and I was planning to tell you—really, I was. I'd wanted to tell you for a while. I just …" He trails off for a moment. "I'm sorry you had to learn it from someone else."

Giving a curt nod, I blow out a breath in a long whoosh. "Well. Thanks. Have a good ni—"

"I didn't lie about loving you."

My sharp intake of breath is loud, even amidst the usual downtown Friday evening noise. My hand flies to the center of my chest, so certain that I'll find an open wound there; it hurts that bad.

"I have for a while now. I just … I just never knew how to tell you."

"I have to go." My words come out rushed, and I find myself nearly sprinting in my heels in my haste to get away from him.

It isn't until I'm inside the elevator on the ride up to my floor that I finally breathe easier.

But that pain in my chest—in my heart—feels like it hurts more now than ever.

CHAPTER FIFTY-FOUR

Ry

When a woman almost breaks the speed of light trying to get away from you, it's a good sign that things didn't go well. Which is what could be said of the talk Maggie and I just had.

Hell, I don't even know if it could even be classified as a talk.

The door to the bar opens, and someone walks up to stand beside me as I continue staring off in the direction Maggie ran off.

"It went well, huh?" Sarah asks.

"Totally."

"Yeah, I sense that from the fact that I can barely make her out in the distance." Sarah reaches an arm out, using her thumb and forefinger, squinting. "She's about the size of a small beetle now."

I let out a short laugh. "You're crazy; you know that, right?"

She smiles. "Yep." Turning her gaze back to the sidewalk where we're no longer able to see Maggie in the distance, she lets out a long, sad sigh. "You have your work cut out for you, buddy."

"Yeah."

I feel the weight of her eyes on me. "But you're not giving up?"

I take a moment to answer. "No."

She links her arm through mine, giving it a light tug. "Then we need to get back in there with your boyfriend and hash out a grand plan."

My lips curve up slightly at her insistence. It's then that it hits me.

Maggie never said she didn't love me back. And that can only mean one thing.

I still have a chance.

CHAPTER FIFTY-FIVE

Maggie

The first delivery arrives barely five minutes after I sit down at my desk at work on Monday morning.

"Maggie?" One of the new interns, Jess, stands at my door with an envelope in her hand. "This just arrived for you."

Accepting it from her with thanks, she leaves, and I'm left sitting with a mysterious envelope in my possession. It only has my first and last name typed on the outside. Cautiously, I use my letter opener to slide it open. When I pull out the contents, I freeze, my entire body rigid with shock.

He'd kept it.

Staring down at the small, wrinkled napkin in my hand, I recall immediately when this took place. We had gone out for our first outing as roommates to have a drink and bond. Our conversation had turned to what quality we wanted in the other person we were in a relationship with. I had written it on the bar napkin, and he had proclaimed loudly, "If it is written, then so it should be!" in a bellowing voice. I had laughed then, as the other bar patrons had shaken their heads, clearly thinking Ry had been overserved.

I want a guy who will love me even when I have no makeup on and still tell me—and believe—that I'm beautiful.

Ry's response from that night was written right beneath mine. But it seems he'd added something to it; drawing an arrow from my response, he pointed it at something he'd added at the bottom.

I want someone who will be cool with hanging out and watching movies we've seen a million times. Just to be with me.

I know a guy who does. Who always has. From day one.

My boss comes out of his office, rushing into mine and catching me staring down at an old wrinkled bar napkin before I quickly tuck it away. He gives me an update on his upcoming appointments and what materials he'll need before he retreats to his office to make a few calls.

Pulling the napkin back out, I find myself staring at it in wonder. He had kept it? After all this time?

Glancing over at my office window a few feet away, I wonder if he's in his office across the street, and if he's watching me with those creepy binoculars. If he's even in his office today.

A call comes in from one of our more demanding clients, forcing me to push aside the note from Ry.

* * *

I'm reluctantly readying myself to have lunch at my desk yet again, since it's already started out as one of *those* Mondays.

One of our architects submitted his resignation notice—completely unexpectedly, I might add. Now, my boss has that vein on the side of his temple that looks like it will burst at any given moment. Which means it's going to be a *loooooooong* day.

The knocking on my door startles me just as I'm about to pull out my peanut butter sandwich—yes, I'm already imposing my cheapness now that I'm roommate-less—and glance up to see Jess at my door again.

She's holding an envelope similar to the one I received earlier this morning.

This goes on three times a day—morning, lunchtime, and before the workday ends—for the remainder of the week. And I ... I just don't know what to think.

I don't want to admit that I crept into his room the other night. I'd curled up on his bed and cried because I miss him so much. Heck, even his sheets are still on the bed—guess he doesn't need or want them—or his bed—back.

I lay there and cried after I'd come home from work to find an envelope taped to the apartment door. Inside was another bar napkin, and I swear I can recall the conversation we'd had that night as if it were yesterday.

"Is it wrong that I want the whole shebang? I want a guy who will not only love me for me, but someone who's my best friend," I'd told him.

Looking back on that memory, I wonder if there had actually been yearning in his eyes, even then.

"I want the exact same thing," he'd said. And so I'd written:

I want a guy who is not only the love of my life but my best friend, too.

Beneath it, Ry had written:

I want the same. Always.

Now, though, beneath our writing was an addition.

I love a woman who also happens to be my best friend. Except now, she doesn't want to be that anymore since I messed up and broke her trust. I still love her, though. More than anything in the world. Always will.

* * *

It's Saturday, and Sarah and I are having a rainy day TV-watching marathon. We've ordered takeout and have just started the next episode of *Kimmy Schmidt*—no eighties movies permitted since that had been more of a Maggie-Ry tradition—when there's a knock on the door.

I pause the show, get up, and grab my cash to pay the takeout guy. Except when I open the apartment door, no one is there. Glancing around and finding nothing and no one, I frown, stepping back to close the door when something catches my eye.

There's an envelope taped to the door.

Another envelope.

Darting another glance around the hallway, yet still finding no one around, I remove the envelope from the door and close it behind me. Walking back to the couch, Sarah looks over and notices the envelope, recognition lighting her face.

"Another one?" she says with more excitement than I expect.

"Yes," I murmur as I sink back down on the couch, carefully opening and removing another napkin from the envelope.

I want a guy who will be a goofball with me. One who will dance in the rain and kiss me. Just like in the movies.

Ry's response from that long ago night was:

I want to kiss and dance in the rain and actually embrace being a dork with the one I love.

There's an arrow drawn from mine pointing to what he has recently added at the bottom.

Come outside and dance in the rain with me. No kissing necessary. Please. Give me another chance?

"What does it say?" Sarah asks quietly.

Dazed, I hand it to her, watching as she reads it. Her eyes dart up to mine. "Are you going to go?"

"What do you think I should do?"

She offers a tender smile. "I know I wouldn't be able to come up with any guys' names who've gone to this much trouble to show how much they care and love you. That they're sorry." She pauses for a beat. "I think you'll regret it if you don't go down there."

She's right. I know she's right the moment she says it, but something still holds me back...

"He loves you, Maggie." Her tone is gentle. "I doubt he'd go to all this trouble"—she lifts up the napkin—"if he didn't." Tucking her blond hair behind her ear, her fingertips briefly touch her earlobe, triggering something in my memory.

Wait a minute...

Suddenly, my mind flashes back to that first meeting with Ry. When he'd talked about being in a relationship with Jack, he'd tugged on his left earlobe.

Lie.

He'd done the same thing when I'd asked him if he disapproved of me starting to date again.

Lie.

When I'd asked him where Matt had gone that one night in the bar, Ry had tugged on his earlobe when he'd come up with some excuse.

Lie.

Not once had his little "tell" shown up when he'd told me how he felt ... When he'd told me he loved me, he never once tugged on his earlobe.

He'd been telling the truth.

"He really loves me," I murmur, turning to stare at the stack of napkins on the counter that had been delivered over the past week.

Sliding off the couch, Sarah flashes a smile, tugging me from the couch and steering me into the bathroom. "Of course, he does! Now, we have to get you looking a little more presentable for this." Hastily, she applies some blush and a bit of gloss to my lips as I attempt to twist my hair up into a clip.

Grabbing an umbrella and my raincoat from the closet, I slip it on along with my flats and give Sarah a quick hug.

"If I don't hear from you, I'll assume everything worked out well." She winks and slips out the door with a quick good-bye as I grab my keys. Two steps toward the door, I stop, thinking of something I should do first. Once I've done it, I lock up after myself.

Taking a deep breath, I decide to take the stairs instead of the elevator, and the moment I burst through the door to the lobby, I feel like breaking into a full-on run to get to Ry. I rush out onto the sidewalk; I look both ways, trying to figure out where he'll be and hoping he didn't give up on me. But I don't see him anywhere.

Walking down the sidewalk, I try to use another store-front awning to help shield myself and my umbrella from the onslaught of rain, and I still don't see him.

"Darn it," I grumble aloud.

"I wasn't sure you were going to come." His deep, husky voice rolls over me, and I take a deep breath before turning to find Ry behind me.

CHAPTER FIFTY-SIX

Ry

Ducking into one of the small alcoves of a nearby store in order to prevent being washed away by the crazy amount of rainfall, I really don't think she's going to show. Hell, no one with any sense is out here in these conditions, so I can't really blame Maggie for not wanting to show up—among the other more obvious reasons. Gazing down at the raindrops splashing heavily against the sidewalk, I physically jerk at the sound of her voice.

"Darn it," she grumbles loudly, her back to me a few feet away.

Maggie. She came.

Stepping from my spot, my hands are still deep in the pockets of my raincoat. "I wasn't sure you were going to come."

Spinning around to face me, the wariness in her eyes guts me.

"I really didn't think you'd actually come," I say, like a broken fucking record. I think I'm in shock that she's actually here. In front of me.

"Well, I figured I should thank you for all of the napkin notes." She glances down at her shoes before raising her eyes to meet mine. Her gaze is less guarded, and she offers a hesitant smile. "I can't believe you kept them all."

"I kept them because they matter to me." Swallowing hard, I press on. "Because *you* matter to me."

Her lips part to speak, but I rush on. "I don't think I can ever manage to apologize enough for lying to you, but I honestly just wanted to be with you—to be near you in any capacity. And, wow," I break off with a chuckle, "that actually sounds far more disturbingly creepy than I expected.

"I wanted to get a chance to know you without you feeling like you were getting hit on constantly. And I can't say I regret that part of it. Because you were comfortable with me, and you didn't have your guard up. You allowed me to see you—the real you. And that's the Maggie I love.

"I understand if you never want to see me again, but I wanted to apologize one final time—face to face. If you want me to leave you alone," I pause, inhaling sharply at the pain the words cause me, "I will. You have my word on—"

"Did you know that originally, *Pretty in Pink* was filmed with Andie and Duckie ending up together?"

Caught off-guard and unsure of where she's going with this, I hesitate. "Really?"

She nods. Watching me, her expression is guarded, and she falls silent.

"You once told me you wished she would've ended up with Duckie, her best friend." I swallow hard past the lump in my throat. "Do you still feel the same way?"

The silence drags long enough that my chest feels heavy, dreading her answer. Finally, she takes a small step toward me. Yet she's still so far away.

"I've always wanted to be the one who ends up with you," she whispers.

"I love you, Mags"—the words pour out of me—"so

much."

Tipping her head to the side, she remarks softly, "Enough to keep all of the napkins, huh?"

I flash her a sheepish smile. "I'm just relieved it wasn't something a lot bulkier, or I would've had trouble storing those suckers."

"No napkin, now?"

Her words throw me off. "What?"

"You don't have a final napkin?" Her eyes are lit with something that appears almost like mischief.

"No," I draw out the word slowly, uncertainly. "It's raining cats and dogs out here so I just—"

"What about this?" She holds out her hand, fisted, fingers uncurling around something, and I see that it's a napkin with writing on it. Pinching it between her thumb and forefinger, she holds it so that I can read it.

How long will you love me?

I nearly laugh out loud with relief, a smile forming as I raise my own hand to show her what I wrote on my own palm. What I had written, the message I'd been prepared to show her regardless of the way this conversation had gone.

I'll love you forever.

The moment she reads it, her eyes glisten with tears, and she tosses her umbrella to the side, launching herself into my arms.

And I give her what I promised her.

I kiss her in the rain, just like they do in the movies.

EPILOGUE

Ry

Seven months later

I'm waiting on her, sipping my drink at Irish Times while keeping an eye on the entrance. The moment she walks through the door, I wait for her eyes to find me. The moment they do—the moment our eyes meet—is just like that cheesy shit in the movies.

And I get an equally as cheesy grin on my face because of it.

Maggie slides onto the barstool with a long sigh. "Man, am I glad it's Friday." Leaning toward me, she meets me halfway for a soft kiss only for the bartender, Mike, to interrupt us when he sets down a napkin before placing her drink in front of her.

Turning to her drink, Maggie raises the glass halfway to her lips when she notices it.

There's something written on her napkin. Picking it up, she reads what I wrote on it.

I want to ask the woman I'm in love with—my best friend—to marry me. I hope she says yes.

Maggie's eyes dart up to meet mine, finding me watching her expectantly. The smile that spreads across her face is full of mischief.

Taking a sip of her drink, she carefully sets her glass down on the bar, napkin still held in her other hand. Raising an eyebrow expectantly, she says, "Why don't you check your napkin?"

Drawing back in confusion, I turn, noticing our bartender has just placed a fresh napkin beneath my drink. Lifting the glass from it, I slide the napkin closer and see one word written on it.

Yes.

My head whips around to stare at her. "How did you—"

"I didn't." She smiles, leaning in to kiss my lips as I sit, stunned. "I was just hoping. So I asked Mike to keep one stashed, just in case." Maggie gives a little laugh and whispers, "There was another one, too."

"Oh?" I whisper back. "And what did that one say?"

The way she smiles at me, the way her eyes light up, the corners crinkling … There's not a more beautiful sight than this.

"It said, 'I love you. Now are you going to marry me or what?'"

I barely get out a short laugh before she presses her lips to mine. I kiss the hell out of her right there in that bar before proudly sliding the diamond ring on her finger. And I can't help but think …

Who knew this much happiness could come from a little clam jamming?

THE END

Dear Reader,

Thank you so much for taking the time to read this book! I'd love to hear what you thought about Maggie and Ry's story. If you would be so kind as to leave a review on the site where you purchased the book, it would be appreciated beyond words. And if you send me an email at rcboldtbooks@gmail.com with the link to your review, I'll send you a personal 'thank you'!

Please know that I truly appreciate you taking time from your busy schedule to read this book! If you'd like to stay up to date on my future releases, you can sign up for my mailing list via this link: http://eepurl.com/cgftw5

Also by RC Boldt

The Teach Me Series:
Wildest Dream (Book One)
Hard To Handle (Book Two)
Remember When (Book Three)
Laws of Attraction (Book Four)
Out of Love

Stay Connected to RC Boldt:
Facebook: https://goo.gl/iy2YzG
Website: www.rcboldtbooks.com
Twitter: https://goo.gl/cOs4hK
Instagram: https://goo.gl/TdDrBb

ACKNOWLEDGMENTS

This book would have never been possible if it weren't for the following individuals (in no particular order):

My readers! The fact that I actually have readers is just … incredible!! Thank you for choosing to read these books. Without your support, your sweet emails and reviews, none of this would be possible. I am forever grateful.

My husband, for being my *everything*.

Sarah, my Australian BFF. Seriously. I don't think I could've made it this far without you … or our WhatsApp texting, voice messages or phone dates. Thanks for letting me vent and brainstorm ideas with you. You've become such a treasured friend and I am incredibly grateful for you. I love you. Long time. ;)

My incredible 'pimpers' galore and my street team—thank you for <u>everything</u> you do!!! You ladies are the best!!

Amber G., I adore you and your gracious generosity! I'm so incredibly grateful for all of your help!!

Boldt's Beach Babes—you ladies are the most stellar individuals! I am beyond grateful for your support, excitement, and feedback when I share my ideas with you. I'm clearly biased but I think I have the best readers group!! Love you all!!

All the book bloggers out there who have been so wonderful to me! I could never manage to truly show my gratitude for all of your support. Please know that the time you take to read and review my books and/or do promo posts is appreciated beyond words.

My beta readers who spent their own time to comb through my book and help me refine it! You all are freaking stellar and I'm so grateful for your help!!

Kata C., for being gracious beyond words to offer to do a third proofreading of this book. I love you, mi playa.

Leddy H.—I'm convinced it was fate that led you to my signing table (and not Teresa, lol!) that day. To say I'm grateful for you and all of you help/insight would be a vast understatement. Love you!

Ms. Jenny at Editing4Indies for helping to polish my writing and for catching things like how they went from sitting at a table one second to sitting at a bar the next … when the book includes zero magic or teleporting. LOL. Thank you!!!

Ms. Marla at Proofing with Style for ensuring this book is as perfect as possible. Your eagle eyes are much appreciated!

Ms. Letitia at RBA Designs for creating this gorgeous cover!!

Ms. Stacey at Champagne Formats for being so patient, professional, having such a quick turnaround and, most of all, for putting up with me!

My parents for making me. Now, you can go ahead and admit I'm your favorite. I won't tell my brother. Promise. ☺

ABOUT THE AUTHOR

RC Boldt is the wife of Mr. Boldt, a retired Navy Chief, mother of Little Miss Boldt, and former teacher of many students. She currently lives on the southeastern coast of North Carolina, enjoys long walks on the beach, running, reading, people watching, and singing karaoke. If you're in the mood for some killer homemade mojitos, can't recall the lyrics to a particular 80's song, or just need to hang around a nonconformist who will do almost anything for a laugh, she's your girl.

RC loves hearing from her readers at rcboldtbooks@ gmail.com. You can also check out her website at www. rcboldtbooks.com or her Facebook page www.facebook. com/rcboldtauthor for the latest updates on upcoming book releases.